Wild Tropics

CHRISTMAS KEY, BOOK TWO

STEPHANIE TAYLOR

For Kelcey and the years we spent learning to love Florida and all of its quirks. (And for all the years you've loved me and all of MY quirks...)

"The world is before you and you need not take it or leave it as it was when you came in."

—*James Baldwin*

Chapter One

The triplets have replaced the usual Christmas door swag on the front of Tinsel & Tidings Gifts with a garland of glittery black spiders and miniature light-up pumpkins for Halloween. They've unscrewed the lights on the ever-present holiday decor, and carefully switched the clear bulbs for orange ones. A scarecrow is parked on a hay bale near the front door of the shop, arms outstretched, face frozen in a blank, cheerful grin.

Gwen, Gen, and Glen sit on a bench in front of their store with matching cans of Diet Coke in hand as they watch the golf carts crawl down Main Street in the middle of a smothering heatwave. All morning long, islanders have driven past them slowly, fanning themselves and sipping water as they try to stir up a breeze by putting the gas pedals of their carts to the floor. Some have stopped to buy ice cream or cold drinks at Tinsel & Tidings, but most have kept moving, fearing that a trip into the air-conditioned shop will make it impossible to head back out into the hot weather and get back to their own cool houses.

"No costumes, ladies?" Holly Baxter calls out as she comes to a stop in front of the store. She sets the park brake on her hot pink golf cart and peels the backs of her sweaty thighs off the seat.

"We have witch hats and little capes, but honey, it's way too hot to wear black right now," Gen says, tipping back her can of soda as she takes a long drink.

"This heat obviously hasn't ruined your festive mood, Mayor!" Glen says, shielding her light blue eyes with one hand as she takes in Holly's costume from head to toe. "You look adorable," Glen proclaims, smiling at the younger woman. "If I had legs like yours, I'd be gallivanting around in a tiny piece of fabric myself."

Holly glances down at the purposely-torn leopard print fabric she's wrapped and pinned around her torso. The hem is frayed and split like fringe, and beneath the fabric that ends at the tops of her thighs is a pair of stretchy black shorts. She has a choker made of shells tied at her throat, and a pink and yellow frangipani flower from her own yard tucked behind one ear. Her light brown hair is loose around her shoulders, and her freckles are uncovered by make-up.

"Well, if I'm going to be Jane of the Jungle, then I'd better dress the part, right?" Holly smiles at the women. "Hey, anyone want to sell me a Diet Coke?"

"Help yourself," Gwen pipes up, waving a hand lazily at the door of their general store. "It's too hot to get up."

"Should I leave a dollar on the front counter?" Holly's been sweating profusely all morning as she makes last minute arrangements for the arrival of the crew from *Wild Tropics,* a reality show that's about to start filming on Christmas Key, and a Diet Coke sounds amazing.

"Consider it a trick-or-treat prize for wearing the best costume we've seen today." Gwen winks at her.

"You've seen others?" Holly looks out at Main Street, but all of the golf carts are parked and unattended. When she turns back to the triplets, all three women have busied themselves with their cans of soda, identical eyebrows raised innocently. "What?" Holly frowns.

Glen clears her throat. "Officer Zavaroni is wearing a costume."

"Kind of," Gen adds.

Holly looks at her watch. "I'm curious to find out exactly what that means, but I really need to grab my Diet Coke and get over to the B&B."

A blast of arctic air engulfs Holly as she pulls open the front door of Tinsel & Tidings. The air-conditioned store is empty. She walks down a deserted aisle toward the glowing refrigerated case at the back. Holly slides open the glass doors and reaches for the familiar silver can of soda and a visible cloud of cold air puffs out from the tall refrigerated unit. She cracks open the can and chugs the carbonated drink thirstily.

As she walks back outside, a wall of heat hits Holly in the face like the open palm of a hand. She inhales sharply. "You're right: it *is* too hot to move today," she says to the triplets, the Diet Coke in her hand already half-empty.

Glen picks up a folded section of the *Miami Herald* and fans herself. "You got your bathing suit on under that costume? If you can get away from the B&B for a while, a nice dip in the ocean might do you some good."

"Yep. Always." Holly plucks the strap of her swimsuit from under the fabric of her costume and stretches it like a rubber band as proof.

"This wouldn't be Christmas Key if the mayor didn't wear her swim-suit to work!" Glen says with a laugh.

"You know, that's not a bad tagline," Holly says. "Mind if I use it?"

"It's all yours, love," Glen assures her. "I've got plenty more where that came from. After forty years of marriage to an ad man, I can come up with a slogan for pretty much anything."

"Remember that time little Benny had lice when your boys were kids?" Gwen asks her sister, slapping her bare thigh playfully.

"If it looks like rice, it might be lice!" the three of them sing-song in unison.

"I'm not sure I actually made that one up…" Glen chuckles, remembering. She holds out a hand, the gold bracelets on her arm clinking together. "But if you need a good jingle, you know where to find me, Mayor."

"You three are the best," Holly says. "Thanks for the soda, ladies. Happy Halloween!"

The women smile and wave as she hops back into the golf cart and releases the park brake.

Gwen turns to her sisters. "Do you think Jane of the Jungle will find her Tarzan?"

"Hard to say." Gen tips her head to one side, watching as Holly zips down Main Street toward the dock, where she'll do a walk-through to see that everything looks sharp for the reality show crew's arrival that night. "It's a jungle out there."

Glen reaches over and swats her sister on the knee with her folded-up newspaper, rolling her eyes good-naturedly.

* * *

"Oooooh, sugar, I think someone is messing with you!" Bonnie Lane says, waving a manicured hand at her boss as she enters the back office of the B&B. She looks Holly up and down, admiring her costume.

"I'm scared to ask," Holly says, pulling the sweaty hair from the back of her neck and twisting it into a low bun. She grabs a rubber band from the drawer of her desk and wraps it around her hair.

"Haven't you seen Jake yet?"

Holly sighs and falls into her chair, grateful for the air-conditioning. "Not yet. Wait, who are you supposed to be?" She pushes back from the desk and eyeballs her assistant. Bonnie's red hair is in perfect sausage curls, pinned close to her scalp on the sides and teased into what looks like a nosegay above her forehead. She's drawn on her lips in a sharp, glossy-red Cupid's bow, and her brows are perfectly filled in.

"You like?" Bonnie touches one palm gently to her heavily sprayed coif. "I'm Lucille Ball."

"Wow, you look *amazing*!" Holly says, admiring the way Bonnie has perfectly captured the comedienne at the height of her 1950s glamour. "You just put my shredded leopard-print bed sheet to shame."

"Nah, you look like a million bucks, girl," Bonnie says, waving a hand at Holly to dismiss her self-criticism. "Oh! Sugar! Look out the window!" she cries excitedly, shifting gears in the blink of an eye. "Look who's out there trying to hunt you down, Jane of the Jungle."

Holly stands and walks to the window: there's Jake, standing at the curb, one foot propped up on the edge of his police golf cart. His profile is turned to Holly as he makes conversation with Cap Duncan.

"Yeah, it's Jake. So?" She rests both hands on her hips, watching as his strong shoulders ripple beneath the thin white fabric of his t-shirt.

"You oughtta go out and say hi, hon," Bonnie urges. "I'll grab the phones."

Despite the fact that she's only just come in from the unbearable heat, Holly makes a beeline for the front door of the B&B. She reaches Jake as Cap waves and crosses the street to open up his cigar shop.

"Happy Halloween, stranger," Holly says. Her tone is light, but she's guarded; things with Jake are still very much touch and go after their tumultuous summer.

"Right back at you," Jake says, turning to face her. There's a wicked grin on his handsome face, and his cheekbones are sharp beneath dancing eyes.

It's then that Holly sees the front of his t-shirt: he's taken a pair of scissors to the sleeves and cut the hem off the bottom of the shirt raggedly. On the front are block letters that he's clearly drawn on with a Sharpie.

"'Me Tarzan?'" Holly reads, folding her arms across her chest and nodding at his shirt. "Seriously?"

Jake shrugs helplessly. "How was I supposed to know you'd turn my old sheet into a…what is that? A dress?"

"*That* is a ridiculous costume," Holly declares, ignoring him. "It's not even really a costume at all." A flood of stubborn defiance washes over her and she takes a deep breath, mentally putting the brakes on before she lets Jake get the best of her.

"Hey," he says conspiratorially, taking a step toward her. "Remember that one time—before you slashed my sheets to pieces—when they were still on your bed and we—"

She knows exactly the one time he's talking about, and her face burns at the memory.

"Well, aren't you two adorable," Iris Cafferkey coos in her Irish accent as she walks up the sidewalk, pausing behind Jake. She's got an iced coffee from Mistletoe Morning Brew in one hand. "I saw your t-shirt earlier, Jake, but now it makes sense. Did you two kids plan this?"

"Yes," Jake says firmly at the same time that Holly gives an emphatic "NO."

Iris looks back and forth between them, trying to gauge their responses. "Anyway, cute idea. Hey, do you like my costume?" Iris steps back and holds her iced coffee out to the side so they can admire the white lab coat and stethoscope she's wearing. "I borrowed them from the good doctor, but she made me promise not to operate on anyone or give out any prescriptions."

"You look great, Iris," Holly says. "I'd trust you to shoot a little Botox into my forehead, or to put my baby toe in a cast."

"I don't think we put baby toes in casts, love. But I'd surely tape it up for you. And you aren't in need of the Botox yet, lass."

"Well, I'd still trust you. And 'Dr. Cafferkey' has a nice ring to it," Holly says.

"Thanks for that. I'll see you both tonight, right? Are we still meeting at the Ho Ho at eight?"

"That's the word on the streets," Jake says.

"Then that's where I'll be." Iris winks at them and heads west on Main Street, white doctor's coat flapping behind her.

A bead of sweat runs down Holly's temple and into her right ear. She puts one foot out in front, resting her weight on the heel of her flip flop as she examines the bright orange polish on her toes. "So, anyway…" she says, glancing around to make sure they're really alone. "Let's not talk anymore about the mileage we put on your sheets, huh?"

Jake gives her a lopsided grin, both dimples showing, and slides onto the seat of his golf cart. "Tarzan is going to get out of here now so you can get back to prepping for the reality show." He twists the key on the dash of his cart to turn it on, his innocent smile turning into a joking leer. "But you know where to find me if you feel like taking a swing on my vine later."

Holly rolls her eyes as he drives away.

Back inside, Bonnie is standing at the dry erase board that covers most of one wall in the B&B's office, a marker in hand as she consults the list of things to do in November. "So, what did Officer Cutie-pants have to say?"

"He played dumb," Holly says, flopping down in the chair again and holding her arms out to her sides so the air conditioning can dry the perspiration that's making her costume stick to her body. "He's been weird lately," she confesses, putting her arms down.

"Men are always weird, sugar." Bonnie reaches up to add a few items to the list in her neat handwriting.

"I mean weirder than usual. For the past week or two he's been flirting with me like he has amnesia. Or like he wants to pretend we never broke up and River never came to Christmas Key."

"He's probably feeling a little frisky. You let him follow you home that one time at the beginning of the summer, but that was ages ago. And unless you think he's used his handcuffs on some other woman since then, I'd guess he's just got an itch that needs some scratchin', doll."

"But *who*? What are his options around here?" Holly's face is incredulous.

"Exactly my point, sugar. There aren't many options for *companionship* on this island when it comes to people your age." Bonnie wiggles her eyebrows suggestively. "You and Jake really only have each other."

"We *did* only have each other…until River showed up."

Bonnie sets the dry erase marker on the metal ledge under the white board and rushes to Holly's side. "Holly Jean, are you having second thoughts?" she asks, her voice breathy and disbelieving.

"About River?"

"I don't know how you could have second thoughts about a hunk like River. No, I mean about Jake—are you re-thinking the whole breakup?"

Holly shrugs and examines her cuticles. "I don't know. Not the whole breakup, but maybe the us-sleeping-together-whenever-we-want part."

"Okay, well, I see two options here. Not that you're asking, but I think you either let the Tarzan and Jane thing happen, or you get River on the phone and let him know you're ready for a visit. Immediately."

"Oh, Bon. It's not that urgent. I don't know…it's probably stress. And this weather." Holly glances at the watch on her wrist. "It's almost eleven. I'm supposed to meet the supply boat to make sure we have all the food we need for this week. Do you have that list we made up?"

"I've got it—just give me two shakes of a tail feather, and it'll be in your hot little hands," Bonnie promises, sitting down in front of her laptop and punching a few buttons. The printer's electronic innards click and clack on the table near the door as she runs off a copy of the list of supplies they're expecting to arrive at the dock in ten minutes.

Holly takes a minute to log into her own computer and scan her emails. *Last minute details from Wayne Coates at NBC: boat delivering everyone at the dock around five or six. Eight crew members. Lots of equipment.* Got it. *An email from a college friend of Holly's who wants to book a room in January.* Mark as unread; respond later. *Message from Coco regarding the reality show she heard about through their lawyer: does Holly have a ballpark figure for how much the network is shelling out for room and board, and an idea of how long they'll be staying?* Holly frowns at the screen. She hasn't heard from her mother directly in the past couple of months, and this email is a reminder that the friction between them has ratcheted up a notch from merely sour and unpleasant to blistering and hostile.

Without Holly even noticing, Bonnie gets up from her chair and fetches the list from the tray of the printer. "Here you go, boss," she says, handing over the paper. "Whoa, that face!" Bonnie points at her, laughing. "You look like Coco just walked into the room." Holly levels a serious gaze at Bonnie, waiting until the laughter stops. "Oh," Bonnie says, sobering. The giggles trail off. "You got an email from her, didn't you?"

Holly nods and consults the list of supplies.

"Well, it's hotter than the hinges on the gates of hell today, innit?" Bonnie asks, fanning herself with a manicured hand as she tries to change the subject. "Honey?"

"Yeah, it's a scorcher," Holly says, but she's still distracted by the paper in her hands. "Looks like we forgot to add toilet paper to this list."

Bonnie grabs a pencil from the cup on her desk and picks up her own copy of the supply list. "I'll check the toiletries closet, and if we're running low, I'll put a call out and see if we can scrounge up a few rolls from around the island to hold us over until the boat comes again on Monday."

"Right. Okay, that should work." Holly pushes her mother, the oppressive heat, and Jake's ridiculous Halloween costume from her mind so she can refocus on the task at hand. "And I'll get everything sorted out and delivered to where it belongs. We've got food going in our fridge here, some going over to the Jingle Bell Bistro for extra storage, and the wine and spirits we pitched in on for Jack Frosty's are going into Buckhunter's storage."

Bonnie follows along on her paper. "Sounds good, sugar. I'll hold down the fort around here while you try not to melt out there."

Holly is up and on her feet again, hair still held in place with a rubber band. It's too hot to even think about letting it down, and she's forgotten about it anyway. "Be back as soon as I get things sorted out for the Halloween party at the Ho Ho," she promises. "But I may need to shower and change my costume before then, because this old bed sheet can only handle being wrapped around a sweaty body for so long."

Bonnie's eyebrows shoot up. "Oh? *Do* tell."

"Scratch that," Holly says immediately. She slides her sunglasses on as she heads out the door. "I'll be back."

"All right. You let 'er rip, tater chip."

Chapter Two

"You changed," Jake shouts at Holly, jogging to catch up with her on the sidewalk outside of Jack Frosty's later that afternoon.

Holly stops in front of the open-air bar, hands in the pockets of her white cutoffs. "So did you," she says. "And I'm about to start wondering whether you're pulling a Peeping Tom on me when I get dressed." Holly nods at the Miami Dolphins jersey he's wearing and tugs at the sides of her own shirt for emphasis; his jersey is identical to the one she put on after her shower that afternoon.

"Hey, how was I supposed to know what you were going to wear? We're fifty miles from civilization. It's not like we can run over to Target and grab Darth Vader masks or cat ears for a night on the town."

"Good point." Holly takes a few steps toward the bar.

"You look like a real football player in that jersey," Jake says from behind her. "And the pigtails and eye black are too cute to ignore." He smiles at her hair and at the smear of grease she's streaked under each eye.

"Jake." She stops at the entrance to Jack Frosty's, a sigh in her voice. "The NBC crew is going to be here in less than an hour and I've got stuff to do. I'll see you tonight at the Ho Ho, okay?"

"Joe made a batch of pumpkin-flavored rum for tonight," Jake says as Holly walks up the steps to Jack Frosty's. "The first round is on me," he calls. "And if you promise to get up on stage and sing 'Genie in a Bottle' like you did last Halloween, the second and third rounds are on me, too."

"Sorry. I only do my Christina Aguilera impression when Halloween falls on a Friday," she shoots back. "I'll see you tonight."

Holly raises a hand in the air and waves over her shoulder.

"Someone's got a shadow." Leo Buckhunter says, wiping the counter of his bar with a damp rag. He's been observing the whole interaction with an amused smile on his lips.

"Come on, Buckhunter. It's just Jake." Holly leans against the jukebox, scanning the song list; she punches a button and Bruce Springsteen's 'Glory Days' comes on.

Buckhunter pulls out a glass from behind the bar and fills it halfway with iced tea, then tops it off with lemonade. He jabs a neon green straw into the clump of ice cubes at the bottom of the glass and slides it across the bar to Holly. "You two looked like you wanted to tackle each other."

"It's just the football jerseys. Trust me." Holly takes a long, grateful drink of the Arnold Palmer.

"Awww, come on. Tell Uncle Buck what's bugging you," Buckhunter teases, rearranging the bottles on his shelf.

"It's bugging me that you promised not to make me call you Uncle Buck, and you're now referring to yourself as *Uncle Buck*."

"Jeez, woman, give me a break. It's my first time being an uncle. I'm still getting used to it."

In a bizarre twist of fate, Holly had discovered over the summer that Leo Buckhunter—her next-door neighbor and frequent antagonizer—was actually the illegitimate son of her late, beloved grandfather. It was a shock to Holly to find out that her grandparents had kept something so important from her, but the realization that she had family living on the island softened the blow. The real added bonus was the fact that Buckhunter shares ownership of Christmas Key with Holly and her mother; his vote alongside Holly's is currently the only thing standing between them and some corporate resort moving in, taking over, and turning the island into a giant lazy river, with signature cocktails and fake tiki huts on the beach.

"All right, I'll cut you some slack. But we need to talk business for a sec. Are you fine with the *Wild Tropics* crew running tabs here at the bar while they're on the island?"

"Sure. If they try to stiff me, I'll send a bill directly to NBC."

"Perfect." Holly sucks down the rest of her Arnold Palmer through the straw until she's slurping at the dregs in the bottom of the glass like an eight-year-old. "Thanks for the drink, Buckhunter. I'm going to head down to the dock and see if they're getting close."

"Find some shade, kid, or that eye black is gonna melt and leave you looking like you got caught in the rain wearing a gallon of mascara. You'll look like Tammy Faye Bakker."

"Solid advice. But I am curious how you know so much about mascara..." Holly stands and tightens her pigtails one at a time.

"I know you see me as nothing but a grubby hermit with an attitude problem," Buckhunter says, palms flat on the bar. "But there's been a lady or two in my life who've been able to see through the surly layers and find the tender, loving man beneath. These angels taught me everything I know about the fascinating world of eye makeup."

Holly snorts. "Okay. That's odd. Odd, but sweet. See you tonight?"

"Wouldn't miss it."

"Will you be wearing a Halloween costume?"

Buckhunter pretends to ponder this. "I *was* thinking of dressing like Matthew McConaughey," he says, looking into the distance and holding his chin theatrically.

"Messy blonde hair, wiry body, smelly cigar habit…you already *are* him. That's too easy."

"You didn't ask me *which* Matthew McConaughey."

"Okay, which one? Not the *Magic Mike* McConaughey, I hope…"

"Nah, I was thinking more of the *Dazed and Confused* Matthew McConaughey. You know, like: 'I love those redheads!'" he says in a convincingly McConaughey-like drawl.

"Right, 'redheads' because of Fiona—I see what you did there." Holly points at him, narrowing her eyes and nodding. Dr. Fiona Potts is Buckhunter's girlfriend, but she's also the island's only doctor, and Holly's best friend. "Okay, I'm outta here. Catch you later."

Buckhunter chuckles to himself and sets Holly's dirty glass in the sink as she hits Main Street, her pigtails bouncing as she strides down the sidewalk with purpose.

Chapter Three

Eight golf carts wait in a row near the dock, each loaded with scratched, heavy, black cases stamped with the "NBC" logo on all sides.

"We've got a boom mic, a few cameras, some editing equipment, and lights," Wayne Coates explains, ticking off each item on his fingers. "But of course we'll have a lot more coming with the next load of crew members—we're starting with a skeleton crew now just to get things off the ground."

Holly nods in response, eyes wide above her streaks of eye black. It had felt perfectly natural to celebrate Halloween on Christmas Key as she always did: fully costumed and ready for an evening of music and dancing with her neighbors, but now she can only imagine how the ponytails and cutoff shorts must make her look to this cosmopolitan television crew. She runs her sweaty hands down the front of her white denim shorts self-consciously.

"Cute costume, by the way." Wayne nods at her Dolphins jersey.

"Oh, thanks." Holly looks down at the turquoise and orange jersey. "We're kind of holiday junkies around here."

"Hey, Holly. Good to see you again." Leanna Poudry steps off the boat and extends a hand in Holly's direction. Leanna had come with Wayne when they'd first flown in by helicopter to check out the island in

August, and Holly had been impressed by her big city fashion and her commanding attitude.

"Hi, Leanna. It's good to see you, too." Holly shakes Leanna's hand, taking in her olive green linen overalls and black tank top. The pants are cropped at the ankles, and Leanna is wearing black wedge sandals. Her toes are done in a bright fuchsia polish.

"So, we'll stay in the B&B for now," Leanna says, hoisting a leather duffel bag onto one shoulder. "But when more of us start to arrive, they'll set up the crew's camp and quite a few of our staff will stay over there."

"Okay," Holly says, nodding again. It's not that she doesn't know how to make conversation, but the excitement around *Wild Tropics* has been building for so long that having the crew there feels almost surreal. "Sounds good. When do the contestants arrive again?"

Wayne and Leanna exchange a look.

"Here, let me take your bag," Wayne says to Leanna, reaching for her leather duffel. "That looks heavy." He busies himself with loading luggage and equipment onto the back of the nearest cart. Leanna puts her hands into the deep pockets of her overalls, assessing Holly carefully with a studied smile on her face.

"We've got everyone arriving on November eleventh at this point, which gives us less than two weeks to get everything set up." Leanna starts walking alongside the golf carts, and Holly follows along obediently—almost as though she's forgotten that it's *her* island, and that these people are the visitors, not her. "By the time the contestants get to Christmas Key, we need it to be camera-ready. The goal is for them to see nothing but what we *want* them to see."

"What do we want them—I mean, you—what exactly do *you* want them to see?"

"Well, we want them to see wild tropics, of course," Leanna says, wrinkling her nose like Holly's just made an intentional joke. "We'll have them delivered to the undeveloped side of the island where they'll find a campsite that looks like it's somewhere in the South Pacific." Leanna uses her hands to point out imaginary details in the air as she talks. "Rustic tents, torch-lights, a fire pit, lots of greenery—it's going to be perfect," she says.

"You're going to build all of that on our beach?"

"Of course we are," Wayne Coates says, falling into step with them as they stroll alongside the golf carts. "We're in the business of making magic, and we've got great stuff to work with here." He holds his hands out expansively, indicating all of Main Street. "Really. This is a dream lo-cation."

"But if all you want is a remote island to pitch tents on, you could have gone almost anywhere—why Christmas Key?" Holly's face flushes deeply the second the words are out of her mouth; she doesn't want Wayne and Leanna to think she's ungrateful for the chance to have her island featured on their reality show, but she has been wondering what made Christmas Key stand out above the other islands they'd considered.

"True," Wayne says, nodding as he folds his arms across his chest. "True. But the real surprise is when the last competitors standing find out they've been living on a Christmas-themed island all along. A place filled with middle-aged people in Hawaiian shirts, iced coffee and fresh scones, and a beautiful B&B with hot showers and comfy beds. It's going to be great."

"And hopefully there'll be some sort of romance brewing between the final contestants. It would make for great TV if their stay in the B&B was a little steamy. It might even lead to a spin-off show of some sort." Leanna's eyes glint calculatingly.

"*Wild Tropics, Wild Hearts,*" Wayne proposes, spreading his hands across the sky like he's imagining the words emblazoned across a huge billboard.

"*They started out eating rice on a tropical island to survive, and they ended up catching rice on their wedding day,*" Leanna intones. It sounds like she's doing a voiceover for a television show.

"Oooh, I like that," Wayne says, slapping her bare upper arm with the back of his hand. "Write that down."

Holly laughs, but from the serious look on his face, Wayne is clearly not kidding. Leanna pulls out her iPhone and opens a voice app, repeating their exchange word-for-word into the mouthpiece of the phone as they wait. She clicks off the recorder and drops the phone back into the pocket of her overalls.

"I can't wait to get to the B&B and unpack," Leanna says, raising both arms in the air as she stretches her spine. "We haven't slept much these past few days, and I think it's catching up to me."

"Of course. Let me get you guys settled in and you can rest. If you're up for it, we've got dinner in the dining room at seven, and then we're all headed over to the Ho Ho Hideaway for a little Halloween gathering—costumes are optional, obviously," she adds, "but taking a shot or two of Christmas Key's special pumpkin rum is probably not optional."

"That sounds great," Wayne says, pointing at Holly's pink golf cart. "Isn't this you?"

"You remembered." Holly smiles. She'd ferried the crew around on their initial visit in her hard-to-miss hibiscus pink golf cart, showing them the holiday decorations and all of the best spots on the island.

"Let's get checked in, and then we can sort out the luggage and stuff later. I'm eager to get a fix on our home base for the next couple of months." Leanna slides into the cart next to Holly. With her green overalls and toned biceps, she looks like she's about to go on a safari rather than take a ten mile per hour ride up a roughly-paved road.

"You got it," Holly says, pulling the cart onto Main Street.

Within twenty minutes, she's got the crew checked in and pointed toward their rooms. The lobby is filled with boxes, bags, and equipment from the golf carts. The mad rush of adrenaline to meet, greet, sort, and appease the newcomers has abated, and Holly is left standing behind the counter in her Dolphins jersey and smudges of eyeblack, staring out at Main Street.

She exhales and tilts her head to one side, watching Cap Duncan struggle with a giant poster on the opposite side of the street. He's standing on a three-step ladder outside of North Star Cigars, taping what looks like a piece of butcher paper to the outside of his window, but the unwieldy poster keeps slipping from his grasp as he tries to affix it to the building.

Holly comes out from behind the front desk and walks over to her own large window to watch, arms folded. Her first instinct is to race across the street and offer him a hand, but something holds her back. Cap has a fat cigar clamped between his lips and he appears to be swearing and muttering as the tape grips the glass for a minute, then gives way on both sides of the sign. The paper flutters to the ground three or four times and Holly frowns, more concerned with whether or not he'll get the sign hung than with what the paper actually says.

It's only when he finally steps down from the ladder and stands on the sidewalk to check out his work that Holly reads the carefully painted words spelled out in thick block letters:

CAP DUNCAN FOR MAYOR—VOTE FOR THE MAN WHO <u>HAS</u> NO PLAN!

Chapter Four

"Did you hear? I can't believe it…"

"I know—the nerve of that man!"

"It's like he fell headfirst into a bottle of scotch and can't figure out which way is up."

Holly elbows her way through the small crowd that's already gathered at the Ho Ho Hideaway, a hesitant smile on her lips. The bar is decorated with strings of blinking orange twinkle lights that Joe has roped through the railing all around the dance floor, and electric jack o'lanterns leer at everyone from the tops of the bistro tables. Holly tries to meet the eye of each person she passes, but she can't help but overhear snippets of their conversations, which are—without fail—all about Cap's newly announced bid for mayor.

"Isn't it too late, sugar?" Bonnie asks, grabbing Holly's elbow and yanking her over to Joe Sacamano's bar. "Tomorrow is November first…"

Holly reaches for the shot that Joe sets on the counter, downing it in one gulp before she answers. She grimaces, feeling the burn of alcohol in her chest. "This isn't a presidential election, Bon. We aren't limited to the first Tuesday in November."

"But you've been doing this for a couple of years now—"

"And doing a fine job of it, I might add," Joe Sacamano interrupts, patting the top of his bar as an apology for butting into the conversation.

"Thanks, Joe," Holly says. She turns back to Bonnie. "Yeah, I've been mayor for almost three years, and I had no idea Cap was this unhappy with anything I've done."

"Until recently," Bonnie reminds her, wagging a red-tipped finger. She's referring to Cap's uncharacteristic turn as the village drunk over the past couple of months. His outburst at their August village council meeting had both embarrassed Holly and potentially jeopardized their chances with the *Wild Tropics* crew, as they'd been visiting the island and were present at the meeting when Cap had stumbled in, loud and blustery and opinionated as all get out.

"Right—until recently." Holly wipes at the sweat on her brow with the back of her wrist. "Listen, the crew is right behind me." She grabs Bonnie's hand and glances back over her shoulder to see if they've followed her into the bar. "I need to put this on the back burner for the time being and focus on the show."

"You're right, sugar. We've got our hands full here." Bonnie gives her a concerned look. "You go and glad-hand these guys, and I'll field questions from the locals."

"Thanks, Bonnie. I mean it." Holly squeezes Bonnie's hand and scans the bar for their guests.

"Oh—wait, sugar?" Bonnie calls to her as she's walking away. "What exactly *should* I tell people when they ask?"

Holly pauses for a second, thinking. "I guess we should tell them the truth: our island's charter says that if an elected official runs uncontested, they can be challenged at any point by any person who wants to run for the position."

Bonnie clucks sympathetically, touching her Lucille Ball curls to make sure they're still in place. "Damn. That Cap Duncan sure caught us with our pants down, didn't he?" She shakes her head, resignation written all over her smooth, carefully made-up face. "Okay," she sighs. "I'll just go about my business like things ain't all catawampus around here. If anyone can challenge your position, then I guess anyone *can*. But it doesn't mean they'll win." Bonnie is getting warmed up, the resignation replaced by determination. "I just don't see how someone who sits around here like a bump on a pickle all the livelong day thinks he's got a chance in he—"

"Bon," Holly grabs both of her friend's hands and gives them a tug like she's shaking out a bed sheet. "Focus. Breathe. One thing at a time."

Bonnie looks into Holly's eyes for a beat and takes a deep breath. "Got it. Go take care of business. I've got this handled, honey."

Wayne Coates and Leanna Poudry are waving at Holly from the entrance to the bar. The five young crew members who arrived with them are checking out the scene from behind Wayne and Leanna, hands in their pockets as they take in the older crowd.

"Hey, welcome to the Ho Ho!" Holly says with a grin. Like Bonnie, she's already decided to act like nothing out of the ordinary is happening on the island. "We've got Jimmy Buffet manning the bar over there," she says, pointing at Joe Sacamano in his Hawaiian shirt. "And Lucille Ball on the dance floor next to Thing One and Thing Two," she adds, nodding first at Bonnie, then at Emily Cafferkey and her dad, Jimmy, in their matching *Cat in the Hat* t-shirts.

"We came as ourselves…I hope that's not too much of a disappointment," Wayne says, his eyes skimming the islanders' rudimentary costumes.

"Of course! I mean, we're not really dressed to the nines ourselves. The pickings are pretty slim around here for costumes—but we like to have fun."

"Yet another reason why we chose Christmas Key, Mayor." Wayne claps her on the shoulder, a look of wry amusement on his unshaven face. "Now, I was told there'd be pumpkin rum. Can you point us in that direction?"

Holly walks the crew over to Joe, where he lines up seven shot glasses on the bar and starts regaling their guests with the details of how he made this particular batch of rum. This distracts their guests long enough for Holly to slip away.

Frank Sinatra is singing 'Witchcraft' over the speakers, and Millie Bradford sashays around her husband, Ray, on the dance floor, a tall, sweaty Screwdriver clutched in her right hand. Ray and Millie are known around the island for their enviable, decades-long love affair, and it's easy to see when they look at one another that they are still each other's biggest fans.

"Hi, Millie," Holly says, turning sideways as she passes them to avoid bumping into the dancing pair.

"Hi, sweets," Millie says, puckering her lips and blowing a kiss. She's wearing a handmade lei that's heavy with tropical flowers, and a long, sleeveless shift dress. It looks like she's dressed for a luau.

Ray raises a meaty hand in Holly's direction. "Hello there, Mayor Baxter!" he calls to her, eyes twinkling.

She blows a kiss back and leaves them to their dancing.

"…he has the right to challenge her, but the man really doesn't have a leg to stand on," Bonnie is saying to Wyatt Bender. Wyatt, who spent his career sizing up opponents and opportunities in the oil field, is now sizing up Bonnie as a potential opportunity on Christmas Key. His eyes graze her ample bust as she talks.

"For all we know, the man might have a head for business. We haven't heard a word from him yet about his intentions," Wyatt drawls, his Texas roots oozing from every pore.

"Like hell we haven't!" Bonnie says, her face flaming with indignation. "The man's intentions are to find a drink and run his damn mouth!" In all the years Wyatt Bender has been spending his winters on the island, Bonnie's taken the bait from him every time he throws it out.

Holly is usually entertained by their exchanges and by seeing the un-flappable Bonnie get flustered by a man, but this time it's about her, and she's less than tickled. "If you'll pardon my interruption," Holly says deli-cately, stepping into their conversation. "Mr. Duncan has clearly stated his intentions on his hand-painted sign: he says he has *no* plans, and I believe he means it. If Cap had his way, we'd all sit around smoking cigars—"

"And knocking back the scotch," Jimmy Cafferkey adds, nudging Wyatt with his elbow as he joins the small group. He clutches his chest, still out of breath from his turn on the dance floor with his daughter.

"—and we'd let the jungle reclaim the island. He's made it clear that he isn't a huge fan of my expansion plans," Holly continues. "And if we don't figure out a way to corral him, he's going to make us look like id-iots on national television." Holly gives a discreet nod in the direction of the *Wild Tropics* crew.

"Of course, the television production," Wyatt Bender says, dragging out the syllables of the words 'television production' until it feels like he's trying to turn them into the Preamble to the Declaration of Indepen-dence.

"The crew—well, the first part of it, anyway—arrived today," Holly says, smiling at Wayne Coates as he holds up a shot glass in her direction from across the bar. "They're all checked-in to the B&B, and tonight is their first night mingling with the islanders."

"This TV show is a real doozy, young lady. Mighty impressive the way you're taking the bull by the horns and getting us some major exposure." Wyatt nods at her. He's not much taller than Holly, but he's lean and

muscled under his crisp Western shirt and Wranglers. His only conces-
sion to the overly-warm evening has been to leave his cowboy hat at
home, and without it, he looks like a slightly older, more weathered version of the original Marlboro Man.

"I'd like to take credit for it, Wyatt, but it was actually Fiona who
tipped me off about the network looking for a location to do the show."

"Well, I'll be monkey's uncle if the smartest and prettiest women
aren't living right here on Christmas Key," Wyatt says, shaking his head
over the mug of beer he's about to put to his lips.

Holly glances over at Bonnie; she's watching Wyatt's mouth hungrily
as he speaks. 'Witchcraft' is still playing in the background, and the
timbre and tone of the music rise and fall in time with Bonnie's quick-
ened breaths.

"Speak of the devil," Holly says. "Fiona and Buckhunter just got here.
Excuse me." She waves at Fiona and leaves Bonnie to her flirtatious,
never-ending game of tug-of-war with Wyatt Bender.

"What in the world is going on around here?" Fiona shouts.

"This is ludicrous." Buckhunter's voice is gruff as he looks around the
bar. It's obvious he's looking for Cap Duncan so that he can have a word
with him in private.

"It's okay, guys. He has every right to run against me and to call for an
election. But I wish he hadn't done it while we have guests on the island."

The opening notes of 'Thriller'—with its creaky coffin door and omi-
nous footsteps—fills the bar.

"I'll catch him when he's sober and we'll hash this out," Buckhunter
says over the music.

"Shhh, it's 'Thriller'—we need to dance!" Fiona grabs Holly's hand
and pulls her onto the nearly empty dance floor. Holly follows helplessly,

her pigtails swaying in the slight breeze that's coming in off the water beyond the open-air bar.

"Are you two seriously going to moonwalk right now?" Buckhunter calls to them.

"There's no moonwalking in 'Thriller'!" Fiona yells back, getting into position.

Before Holly can protest, Fiona has her following along and doing the stiff-legged zombie dance from the music video. At first, Holly moves half-heartedly, watching from the corner of her eye to see if the television crew is laughing and pointing. But they aren't, and before she knows it, the music and Fiona's unabashed joy win her over. Without even a glance in Wayne and Leanna's direction, Holly throws her curled, clawed hands in the air to the beat of the song, baring her teeth like fangs at her best friend and then laughing hysterically.

Holly is about to beg off while Fiona finishes out the song, but as she's pulling away, Wayne, Leanna, the other crew members, Jake, and Buckhunter join them on the dance floor. Holly is stunned as they all fall into a loose formation and start moving to the music. It takes a few tries for everyone to get in sync, but (fueled by several shots of pumpkin rum and driven a little crazy by the heat of the long day) the 'Thriller' dance quickly comes back to the group—at least enough that they can do a reasonable impersonation of the zombies in the music video.

The older islanders have gathered around the edges of the small dance floor to watch them dance, and when the song ends they break into applause and a round of appreciative hoots and hollers.

"Good dance!" Fiona says, wrapping Holly in a sweaty hug. "I knew you had it in you."

"I didn't," Buckhunter says, throwing an arm around his niece's neck. "She's kind of young to remember 'Thriller,' isn't she? Maybe even too young to remember when MTV actually played music videos."

"That's what YouTube is for," Holly shoots back. She bumps Buckhunter with her hip and he lets her go.

"You damn kids," Buckhunter growls, teasing her. He's only a year older than Holly's mother, but sometimes the seventeen years between Holly and her uncle feel more like forty.

"Speaking of the younger set," Wayne Coates says, rubbing his hands together as he approaches, "I was hoping I could talk to you for a second, Holly. Can I buy you a drink?"

Holly pulls her Dolphins jersey away from her body and blows air from her lower lip up to her forehead to dry the sheen of perspiration. "Of course. I'm all ears."

Buckhunter grabs Fiona and pulls her in for a slow dance as Holly follows Wayne to the bar.

"What's up?"

"It's about the show." Wayne slides onto a bar stool and taps the counter with two fingers like a player at a card table. Joe raises an eyebrow in their direction. "Two of whatever you recommend for someone who just sweated away half of his body weight in the past eight hours," Wayne says, making an exaggerated face like a panting dog.

"Two gin rickeys coming your way." Joe tosses a lime into the air with his left hand and catches it behind his back with his right.

"Ladies and gentlemen," Holly jokes, "Tom Cruise in *Cocktail: The Golden Years.*"

Joe smirks as he makes their drinks.

"So," Wayne turns to face her, his clean, square hands folded on the bar top. "We've run into a bit of a snafu, I'm afraid."

"Oh?"

Wayne presses his lips together. "One of our competitors bailed at the last minute." He tips his head toward Holly's and puts one hand next to his mouth like he's letting her in on a big secret. "He got another acting job. Most reality shows are stocked with moderately attractive wannabe actors, you know. So if they get a bigger gig, then they jump ship faster than a passenger on the Titanic."

"No, I didn't know that."

"Yeah, it's sort of a rite of passage in Hollywood to make the reality show circuit." Wayne shrugs, like *whaddya gonna do?* "Anyhow, this kid got a job as a stunt double on the new Bruce Willis movie."

"Bruce Willis is still acting?"

Wayne gives a hearty laugh. "Believe it or not. And now we're down a competitor for our show. It'd be fairly easy to grab one of our eager-beaver alternates and slide him into that slot, but…Leanna and I had a different thought."

Joe lays down two square napkins and places the gin rickeys on them with a flourish. "Bottoms up," he says with a wink.

"Okay, I'm listening." Holly squeezes her wedge of lime into the drink and takes a sip; the carbonation from the club soda tickles her nostrils.

"We need someone young—someone fit and competitive," Wayne explains, stirring his cocktail with the spear that Joe's stuck through his slice of lime. "It's a very physical competition, and we need someone who can keep up."

Holly's heart starts to race. She has a fleeting vision of herself racing down the beach to be the first competitor to get her hand-hewn raft into the water and prove that it's seaworthy. Her tanned, toned limbs race across the television screen in her mind, and she flashes on an image of River sitting in front of his TV in Oregon, watching her swallow live minnows in order to win an extra cup of raw oats for dinner. She's ready to say yes before Wayne even starts talking again.

"I want you to hear me out," he says, interrupting her thoughts. "I know you're the mayor around here, and this show is only happening because of you, so I need to acknowledge how important you've been to this production already."

Holly picks up her drink and swirls it around in the glass, smiling. One of her light brown ponytails fall over the cheek that's closest to Wayne while she tries to imagine his next words.

"I think this show is going to be great simply because we've got a killer location and a solid premise, but I think it will be even more appealing if we mix in a local and toss them into the competition. What do you think?"

From the corner of her eye, Holly sees Jake talking to Fiona and Buckhunter. Jake is a good seven or eight inches taller than Fee, and he's bending down politely to catch whatever she's saying. Buckhunter is looking on with a smirk, so Holly knows Fiona must be telling them something entertaining or off-color. She drags her eyes back to Wayne.

"I think it sounds really interesting," she says, trying to keep her excitement in check. "It's a different angle, and you're definitely getting raw talent here—there are no actors on this island!"

Wayne slaps the bar for emphasis. "Perfect. We thought so, too. As soon as we saw Jake we knew he'd be an amazing competitor."

The hand Holly's holding her drink in is suspended above the bar, halfway to her mouth. *Jake?* She couldn't have heard that right. Did he say *Jake?*

Wayne lifts a hand and gives a confident wave to beckon Jake over to the bar. With a nod, Jake finishes what he's saying to Fiona and heads over.

"Hey," Jake says. He signals Joe to let him know he's ready for a beer. It's a cocky, self-assured move that tells Holly he's been waiting for this moment—waiting for her to hear his good news. "What's up?" Jake asks innocently.

"I've been filling the mayor in on the good news."

Jake smiles back-and-forth between Holly and Wayne. "Pretty cool, huh? I'm excited."

"Yeah, pretty cool," Holly says. She's trying to muster even a tiny drop of enthusiasm. It's not that she isn't happy for Jake, but…it's hard to let go of the image of herself gracing small screens in living rooms all across America.

"I guess you'll be able to say that you knew me when, huh?" Jake takes the beer that Joe sets on the bar. "Thanks, Joe."

"I guess I will."

"I'll need to work out how to cover my position while we're filming, but I'm due for some vacation time, so don't worry about that."

"I'm not," Holly assures him. The fact that the island's only police officer will be spending the next month or two sleeping in a tent on the beach and trying to spear fish with a pole instead of doing his job hasn't even crossed her mind. "I'm sure it will work out, even if we don't get someone to cover for you."

"Besides," Jake says, clinking his beer against Wayne's gin rickey, "you won't even notice that I'm not patrolling the mean streets of Christmas Key."

"How do you figure?"

"I hear you've got your hands full," he says, tipping his bottle of beer toward the steps that lead up to the bar. Holly's eyes follow his motion, and there—shoulder-length, wispy, white hair flowing, thin Hawaiian shirt almost totally unbuttoned—is Cap Duncan. The dark night is like a backdrop behind him, and the twinkling orange lights around the bar cast a warm, autumnal glow on his smiling face.

Holly sighs. "Yeah, I think I do."

Chapter Five

"I need you here now." Holly is using her speaker phone as she washes her face in the bathroom sink, hair pulled back with a clip and a headband. She's attacking the black grease under her eyes from her Miami Dolphins costume with a cotton pad and a bottle of witch hazel while her golden retriever, Pucci, watches from the doorway.

"Well, it's nice to be needed so fervently," River says from three thousand miles away. A fairly constant stream of texts, phone calls, and emails have flown back and forth between them since his first visit to the island three months ago.

"Things are way more stressful than I thought they'd be," Holly says, wiping roughly at the skin under her eyes. "Ouch."

"What happened?"

"Oh, nothing." She leans into the mirror. "I almost rubbed the skin off of my face—no big deal."

"Stop doing that. I like you with skin."

"Haha." She tosses the blackened cotton pad into her wastebasket and digs out a new one from the glass jar on her countertop.

"What happened to make things so stressful? I thought you were totally prepared for the show to start filming."

"I was, but then they got here to set up, and tonight at the bar I found out they lost a contestant."

"They lost someone on the boat ride over? Didn't they have life vests?"

"No, the guy dropped out—he got another acting gig."

"Wait, are you trying to tell me that reality shows aren't *real*?" River asks, his voice laced with mock surprise.

"I guess they want it to be at least partially real, because they asked Jake to fill the guy's spot." Holly wipes at her face with a clean washcloth. "Which means we don't have a cop on the island during filming."

"And are you expecting a band of merry pirates to invade anytime soon?"

"Probably not," Holly admits, taking her hair down and shutting off the bathroom light. She's wearing nothing but an oversized t-shirt and a pair of underwear as she carries her phone out to the lanai and sits down in the dark.

"Okay, I don't want to downplay your distress, Mayor, but what's the big deal here?" She can hear River's doorbell in the background. "Sorry, it's only eight o'clock here, so I've still got trick-or-treaters," he says.

"Awww, I used to trick-or-treat when I was a kid," Holly remembers fondly. "Emily and I would dress up together, and my grandpa would drive us from house to house to collect cookies and cupcakes and stuff from everyone on the island. One year we dressed up like princesses, which was basically just us in oversized ball gowns and as much costume jewelry as we could wear on our wrists and around our necks. Emily's mom put lipstick and mascara on us, and we thought we were movie stars."

"I bet you two were adorable," River says, his words slightly muffled as he opens the door and hands out candy. Holly can hear small voices shouting "thank you!" before he shuts the door.

"Any cute costumes there?" She puts her feet up on the table, listening to the sounds of the night in the thick trees around her house.

"Let's see: fireman, a bumblebee, and some sort of superhero."

"Batman? Wonder Woman?"

"Nah, someone with yellow face paint, goggles and a blue cape. I lose track of what's cool."

"Are you sure it was a cape? It sounds like a Minion."

"Huh. I guess I'm a little behind on this stuff, because I have no idea what a Minion is." He pauses and they sit in silence for a few seconds. "So what else is happening on Gilligan's Island? All of this anxiety can't be just because of the show."

Holly chews on the inside of her cheek. "Today I was checking everyone in at the B&B, and when I looked out the window, I saw Cap hanging a sign on the cigar shop."

"I'm listening," River promises. "I'm just handing out candy again while you talk. Go."

"It said: CAP DUNCAN FOR MAYOR—VOTE FOR THE MAN WHO HAS NO PLAN," she says flatly.

"What does that mean? Is it time for you to run again?"

"I ran uncontested the first time, and no one has challenged me in the three years I've held office. But Cap's made no secret of the fact that he hates having the reality show filming here, so I'm guessing his disapproval is what's behind this."

"But 'the man who has no plan'? How is that supposed to entice voters?"

"I'm not even sure he really wants to win. I think he wants to stir things up while the crew is on the island. Or maybe my mother talked him into it. I don't know."

"Your mother?"

"She still wants to sell the island, and I wouldn't put it past her to cook up some plan to make me look bad in front of the TV crew and the rest of the islanders."

"Hmmm, maybe. But how would her getting Cap to run against you work in her favor?"

"She's a master manipulator—the grand poobah of the mind game. She probably thinks that if I feel like people are against me, it'll ruffle my feathers and I'll give up. Trust me on this one—it's a real possibility."

"That seems like a long shot, but…I guess you know her better than I do."

"Don't kid yourself. I've probably spent less than an eighth of my life living under the same roof as Coco—her *mailman* knows her as well as I do. I just know how she operates."

"Huh."

"Huh, what?" Holly stands up and walks into her kitchen from the lanai.

"It's just foreign to me, but I'm not judging."

"My relationship with my mother?" The light from the open fridge is the only light in the room. Holly peers at the paltry display of contents on the shelves before closing the door again. "I'd judge the hell out of it if I were anyone but me, so don't worry about it." Holly opens and shuts the cupboards in quick succession, making a face at the lack of anything edible in her cabinets. "Listen, I didn't eat lunch or dinner today, and I'm starving. But I have exactly zero morsels of food in my kitchen right now, so I might need to drive over to the B&B in my pajamas and raid the fridge."

"How do you have no food?"

"Things have been crazy this week and I forgot to order groceries."

"Maybe the triplets will open the store for you and let you grab a few things," River offers. There's the rustle of paper on the other end of the line, followed by chewing.

"I'm sorry, are you *eating* right now? My cupboards are bare, my stomach is growling, and my boyfriend is *eating* in my ear. Unbelievable." Holly stands in the laundry room, sifting through the clothes in the dryer that she hasn't had time to fold in the past three days.

"I'm eating a mini Snickers bar so I can turn off my porch light and put an end to these goblins ringing my bell for the night."

"You're eating the Halloween candy so you don't have to give it to children?" Holly's words come out choppy as she bends over to dig through the dryer for a pair of shorts.

"I am. And I'm also wondering if I heard you right. Did you call me your *boyfriend*?" he asks around a mouth full of candy.

Holly is holding a pair of faded yellow running shorts. She slams the dryer door with her bare foot, realization dawning over her. "I think I did."

There's a pause on the other end of the line. "I think I like it."

She smiles, clutching the shorts to her chest as she resists the impulse to do a happy dance in her t-shirt and underwear. "Okay. I mean... okay."

"Okay. Then I guess we have that settled." There's another awkward pause. "So let me check my schedule and see when I can get down there again. I've got a fishing competition in Montana in November, and my kids are playing a baseball tourney in Seattle right after that, but I'm sure I can squeeze something in." River is a former minor league ball player for the Mets, but since a career-ending shoulder injury a decade ago, he's made his living in fishing competitions around the country. In his spare time he volunteers for a non-profit organization that sponsors and coaches sports teams for foster kids, an endeavor that warms Holly's heart.

"I'm ready for you to get here right now," she says, pulling her shorts on over her hips and tying the waistband while she holds the phone between her shoulder and ear.

"You got it, girlfriend."

"Wait," Holly holds the phone with her hand again while she searches the living room for her flip-flops. "Is that 'girlfriend' as in girl-who-is-a-friend? Or 'girlfriend' as in, you know…"

"I think I hear the doorbell again. Call you tomorrow?" There's amusement in River's voice as he dodges her question.

"Oh, fine. Go give them the rest of what's in your candy bowl and then turn off your light. I'll be down at the dock camping out until your boat arrives."

"Sounds good. Talk to you later."

Holly is still holding the phone in her hand when she hears a knock at the door, and she opens it without even looking through the window.

"Hey," Fiona says. She's standing on Holly's porch in a tank top and a skirt, face washed clean of make-up, hair pulled back from her forehead. "You're still up. Good."

"Of course I am. It's Halloween and I'm waiting for trick-or-treaters."

Fiona barges through the front door and pulls her best friend into a concerned hug. "We didn't really get to talk at the bar. Are you okay?"

"I'm starving, but other than that, I'll probably live." Holly gives Fiona a squeeze and lets her go.

"Don't you have anything to eat?"

"No, I'm headed to the B&B on a food extraction mission. Wanna come?"

"You're going to rob your own business?"

"I like to think of it as borrowing against future revenues. Or like I'm being paid in dinner rolls and Perrier. Kind of reimbursing myself for unpaid time and labor, you know?"

"Hey, you had me at dinner rolls. Let's go."

The pink paint of Holly's golf cart is so bright and shiny that even in the dark it gleams hotly under the moonlight. She unplugs the cart from its electronic docking station and they climb in.

"Were you at Buckhunter's?" Holly clicks the accelerator pedal and releases the park brake.

"I just came back with him so that I could see you. I wasn't going to stay over there." Fiona places the bottoms of her flip-flops against the dashboard.

The warm night air blows through their hair as they pull onto Cinnamon Lane, and the sound of cicadas singing in the thick trees and bushes surrounds them. Holly's headlamp cuts through the dense black night, casting a soft glow for a few feet in front of the cart. The island feels so much more desolate and remote when the sun goes down, in spite of the major infrastructure work that Frank and Jeanie Baxter accomplished in the twenty-five years they owned the island. When they'd moved Holly there as a toddler, Christmas Key had been no more than a mound of dirt with palm trees and a mosquito problem. But with love and perseverance, they'd managed to pave and gravel several roads, run electricity, schedule phone service, a mail boat, and bi-weekly supply deliveries for the island. It had been a massive undertaking for two middle-aged people—and even more work as they'd aged and their health had failed—but Frank and Jeanie Baxter had done it, and in the process, they'd created a home and a paradise for their young granddaughter.

Holly snaps her fingers. "I know, let's make pancakes!" she says, her body arched forward over the steering wheel as she squints into the darkness.

"Ooooh, breakfast! Do you have bacon?"

"I think we have sausage. And we need to scramble some eggs." Holly swerves around a pothole she can't see but that she knows from memory is there.

"I didn't even realize I was hungry," Fiona says. "Maybe all that rum masked my hunger."

"Or it's after midnight and we're already craving hangover food." Holly slows down as she crosses over from the sand and gravel of Cinnamon Lane onto the paved road of Main Street. The B&B is on her left, and she turns into the lot carefully, driving under the street lamps whose posts are wrapped in orange and black tinsel for Halloween. Soon the fall decorations will come down, and the usual Christmas ones will go back up.

"Do you think the crew is asleep?" Fiona whispers as they park.

"Maybe. Let's sneak in through the side door just in case." The gate to the pool deck opens with a metallic squeak, and both women wince like cartoon burglars trying to break into a bank vault.

"Shhhh!" Fiona hisses, slipping off her flip-flops and holding them in one hand. "Don't wake them up—I'm not sharing my pancakes with anyone."

Holly holds one finger to her lips as they tiptoe down the short hallway that leads past the B&B's back office. The darkened lobby is lit from the outside where the street lamps from Main Street spill in through the huge picture window, bathing the wood floor and the bamboo of the front counter in light.

The wide hallway that leads to the kitchen is dark, save for the dim wattage coming from the conch-shaped wall sconces. Holly and Fiona eke their way through the swinging door to the kitchen, letting it settle on its hinges before Holly finally turns on an overhead light. They stand there in silence for a beat, watching one another as they wait to see if anyone stirs.

"I think we did it," Holly whispers gleefully. "Let's pillage and plunder."

"You are a true pirate, my friend. A rebel. A rogue," Fiona says. "I admire you."

They work quietly and in sync, moving around one another with ease as they pull metal mixing bowls from shelves. Fiona grabs a carton of organic eggs, a vacuum-sealed package of spicy breakfast sausage, and a quart of milk from the industrial-sized refrigerator.

"Will you turn on the griddle?" Holly calls across the kitchen in a stage whisper, pointing at the flat plate nestled beside the gas range on the stovetop. "The cooking spray is in the cabinet." She flings her hand to point at the cabinet while she's still holding a spatula dripping with batter. "Oops."

"You can't leave a trail of batter, Hansel," Fiona laughs quietly. "They'll know we were here!"

"Okay, Gretel," Holly says. "But we might never find our way home."

"Or it might not matter, because we'll eat until we can't breathe and then pass out on the dining room floor anyway."

"Good point. How are the eggs coming?" Holly asks, nodding at the bowl Fiona's been cracking eggs into.

"Fine and dandy. I can handle the eggs, Baxter. You focus on the pancake batter."

They work together in companionable silence, piecing together their midnight breakfast.

"Should we eat in the dining room?" Fiona asks, holding her plate and a bottle of maple syrup.

"It echoes when it's empty," Holly whispers. "We could eat in the office, I guess. It's far enough away from the guest rooms."

"Do you think Bonnie would take kindly to finding dried syrup on her desk in the morning?" Fiona points out.

"I think she would not."

They look around the kitchen, hands full of food and silverware. "We could hit the lights and sit over there by the window?" Fiona nods at a giant rectangle of moonlight covering a section of the tile floor. She walks across the room and uses her elbow to turn off the light. "See? That's a good spot."

Holly looks at the hard floor, unconvinced. Finally, she shrugs. "I'm too hungry to care. And I'm exhausted. Let's eat."

They sit on the clean floor and make an imaginary table between them by setting up the syrup, salt and pepper shakers, and a bottle of Tabasco sauce on top of a red-and-white gingham kitchen towel. The light from the bright, full moon is broken only by the palm trees swaying beyond the window pane.

"So how did today go—other than the Cap thing?" Fiona spears a three-layer bite of pancake that's dripping with syrup.

"It was pretty good. They crew is here. They're settled. We'll see."

"You don't sound overly confident, friend." Fiona looks down at her plate as she holds a sausage in place with her fork, using the other hand to cut it with her knife.

"I'm just worn out, Fee. Cap caught me off guard, and Jake joining the cast of this reality show is messing with my head."

"But why? Cap will get *maybe* two votes if he goes through with this, and we'll survive without a police officer for a while. I mean, let's be honest: it's not like Jake has a full schedule of cop duties to attend to everyday. He mostly drives around and drinks coffee with everyone on Main Street."

"True. But I'm nervous anyway."

"What's to be nervous about?"

Holly jabs at her eggs so hard that the tines of her fork scrape across the plate. "All of it. Strangers on the island. The filming process. How they'll make us look on national television. Whether or not it will actually help us in the long run."

"Oh, is that all?" Fiona picks up the syrup, unscrews the cap, and pours it over the remnants of pancakes and sausage on her plate.

"And the Cap stuff is annoying, too. He made a crack a couple of months ago about me being a kid—something about me running off and playing Barbies instead of being mayor. It was dumb, but it stuck with me."

"Oh, honey, he's totally gas-lighting you. He's making you doubt yourself. Trust me—I've been through this."

"When?"

"Remember the ex-boyfriend I never want to talk about?"

"Yeah."

"He used to buy me drugstore perfume when he could have easily afforded to spend a few more dollars. He'd tell me that *if* I finally became a doctor someday, the lab coat would cover up all of my best assets. And one time I asked for a subscription to a medical journal for my birthday, and he got me a subscription to *Us Weekly* instead."

Holly drags her fork around in the puddle of syrup on her plate, listening.

"Do you see my point? He was telling me I wasn't classy enough for Chanel No. 5. He wanted to make it clear that my brain wasn't my best asset, my boobs were, and I was a woman and therefore should have been more interested in gossip than medical journals. But he was very stealth about it—sometimes I didn't even realize he was beating me down. Classic gas-lighting." Fiona puts a huge bite of pancake and sausage into her mouth.

"I see what you mean," Holly says, thinking back to the things Cap has said to her recently. "Remember the time Cap came to the village council meeting and reamed me in front of everyone? That kind of shook me, too."

"Exactly my point. You're letting him rent space in your head for free, so knock it off." She puts a forkful of eggs into her mouth and chews. "Hey, are you gonna eat that sausage?"

Holly holds out her plate; she isn't as hungry as she thought she was.

Fiona eats the sausage and then takes the plate and stacks it on top of her own empty one, setting both aside on the tile floor. "I think we need to kick back and enjoy the moon."

"Right here?" Holly glances around. The floor is shiny and smells like lemons and soap, but…it's still the kitchen floor.

"Sure." Fiona stretches out her short, muscular legs. She's about five inches shorter than Holly, and her small frame is compact and toned. Freckles cover all of her extremities, and her strawberry-blonde hair falls in waves around her shoulders as she leans back on the cold tile. "Oooh, chilly." She smiles at Holly. "Come on. We need to let this food settle for a minute anyway."

Holly hesitates before putting her legs in front of her and rolling her spine out slowly on the cold floor. She takes a deep breath and gazes out the windows at the huge, glowing moon.

"You miss him, huh?"

"Who?"

"Silly girl—River."

"Oh, yeah. Him." Holly turns her head so she can see Fiona's face. "I called him tonight and asked him to come for a visit soon."

"That might take your mind off everything else."

Holly looks back to the ceiling and slides an arm under her head for support. She stares at the sturdy beam of light from the moon.

"Fee?" she says tiredly. "Do you think I'm going to pull this off?"

"Girl, you are made of sturdy, adventurous stuff. Plus you have me," Fiona reminds her, reaching out a hand and lacing her fingers through Holly's. "So consider it pulled off."

"Thanks, doc."

"You're welcome," Fiona whispers.

Chapter Six

"Ooooh, that man gets me all fired up like the fourth of July," Bonnie says, her back to Holly in the office of the B&B. Bonnie is standing at the giant picture window that looks out onto Main Street, arms folded across her chest. With her thick, southern accent, 'July' comes out sounding like *Jooo-lahhh.* "Do you know when he saw me standing here, he took off that damn cowboy hat of his and tipped it at me like we're in some sort of cowboy movie?" She presses her lips together and shakes her head slowly.

Holly slips a file into the tall metal cabinet against the wall and shuts the drawer with a shove. "You still watching Wyatt out there?"

Pucci is resting on his dog bed next to the filing cabinet, and he looks up at his mistress questioningly, big, brown eyes following her around the office as she works.

"*Watching Wyatt,*" Bonnie mutters, her dimples showing as her face twists into a mask of disapproval. "I'd like to watch him get right back onto the horse he rode in on and disappear into the sunset."

"That'd be interesting, given that he'd have to cross about fifty miles of water just to get to Key West." Holly inhales and exhales calmly, trying not to look out the window and catch a glimpse of the scene on Main Street.

"You know what I mean, sugar," Bonnie says with mild irritation. "I'm trying to stick with the cowboy theme here. Keep up, will you?"

Holly chuckles as she uncaps a marker and crosses an item off the to-do list on the dry erase board. "So what's going on out there?" she asks, giving in to her curiosity.

Bonnie frowns at the glass. "Looks like Cap is walking around with a clipboard asking people to sign it, and Wyatt is holding up a giant sign on a stick that says 'Don't be a sap, vote for Cap.' They look like a couple of bloomin' idiots if you ask me."

"Catchy slogan," Holly says through gritted teeth. "I didn't know he'd enlisted Wyatt as a campaign manager."

"Oh, honey. Don't you pay them any mind. I heard from Gen and Gwen—or maybe it was Glen and Gen—dammit, now I'm not sure..." Bonnie's brow furrows. Telling the triplets apart is nearly impossible without knowing the color schemes each woman wears as a clue to her identity. "Anyhow, two of the triplets were behind me in line at Mistletoe Morning Brew this morning, and *they* told me Wyatt's only helping Cap to get my goat."

"To get *your* goat?"

"Mmmhmm. Men." Bonnie rolls her eyes. "They think they have flirting figured out the first time they chase a girl around the playground with an earthworm and make her scream. Most of 'em never develop their technique much beyond that."

"Wow. You and Wyatt. Didn't see that one coming." There's a layer of sarcasm in Holly's voice that's as thick as buttercream frosting.

"You didn't see it coming because it *ain't* coming." Bonnie shakes her head vigorously. Bonnie's normal m.o. is to ogle and appreciate anyone of the male persuasion, but something about Wyatt agitates her like nothing Holly's ever seen.

"Okay. Whatever you say, Bon." Holly takes her big straw purse off the hook by the door, fishing around inside for her baseball cap. When she finds it, she sets the hat on her head and puts her purse over one shoulder. "I'm going to run over to the beach and meet the crew. You good here?"

"I'm fine." Bonnie gives her a distracted wave. "Nice hat, hon. Mets today, huh?"

"Yeah." Holly readjusts the bill of her cap. "I'll be back in a while."

River had sent the hat to her after his visit in August. Their initial meeting had been filled with friendly banter and attraction, but Holly— a die-hard Yankees fan with a much-loved and well-worn baseball cap to prove it—had been thrown for a loop when River's fellow fishermen outed him as a former pitcher for the Mets' farm team. Now that the hat is in her possession, she switches out her Mets and Yankees caps whenever the mood strikes.

There aren't many places to hide on Main Street, so Holly drives slowly out of the sandy lot behind the B&B, pulling into the street so she can make eye contact with Cap Duncan and Wyatt Bender. If she can't duck and run from the humiliation of Cap's cheesy slogans and his petition-on-a-clipboard, then she can at least face them head-on with a hard stare.

"Gentlemen," she calls out, giving a salute from behind the wheel of her golf cart. It takes all the fortitude in her bones to smile at them con- fidently. Holly's had a few days to think about the situation with Cap since Halloween night in the B&B's kitchen with Fiona, and she's pretty sure Fiona is right: he won't get the votes. More importantly, she won't let him shake her.

"How do, Mayor?" Wyatt yells out gruffly, lifting his hat. Cap is talking to Maria Agnelli on the sidewalk, and he doesn't even bother to look up and greet Holly. She's pleased to note the way eighty-six year old

Mrs. Agnelli—with her little brocaded purse hanging off her elbow and her slightly-stooped shoulders—is lecturing Cap with an outstretched finger that's dangerously close to poking him in the chest. Mrs. Agnelli is the fierce Italian widow of the island—a grandmother with a sharp tongue and a colorful vocabulary—and she adores Holly. There's no way Cap will be getting *her* vote.

Holly presses on the gas pedal as she turns onto Pine Cone Boulevard and cruises toward December Drive. A sand dune buffers the beach along December Drive and she parks behind it, leaving her cart out of view. On the beach, the crew has started erecting their tents, and people are dragging things to and fro, shouting at one another as they set up camp. Leanna Poudry is wearing a sunhat and a summer dress, pointing and directing the crew.

"Holly!" Leanna waves, holding her hat down with one hand as she jogs across the sand. "This weather is so much better today than it was when we got here."

"A heatwave like that on Halloween is a fluke—you should be good now," Holly assures her.

"It's still warmer than I'm used to, but you won't hear me complain about getting a tan in November!" Leanna pulls her phone out of the black leather fanny pack that hangs loosely over her narrow hips. She taps on the screen of her phone. "Wayne is still at the B&B and I need to check with him on something."

"I just came from the B&B. I could have given him a ride over if I'd known you needed him."

"It's fine," Leanna says, holding up a finger to silence Holly as she puts the phone to her ear. "Hey, I'm at the site right now," she says into the receiver. "Yep. Got it. No, I was hoping you had some idea of how you wanted that to work." Leanna turns her back on Holly and starts wandering away as she talks.

There are eight large canvas tents set up on the sand, and a fire pit is in progress away from the water and the sleeping area. Two crew members are carrying rocks to and from the fire pit, stacking them in a ring around the hole in the ground. Tiki-style torches on long stakes jut out from the ground around the makeshift camp, and each tent has a string of clear lights hanging around its perimeter.

One of the tents is flapping open in the midmorning breeze, practically inviting Holly to take a peek inside. In it, there are two low cots. Rolled-up bedding lays at the foot of each cot, and a metal beam overhead runs the length of the large tent. From the beam hangs a gas lantern. Holly has no idea where it came from (or where *any* of this stuff came from) but a rustic nightstand sits between the two cots. She runs her hand across the smooth wood, admiring the drawer pull made of rope. Did the crew ship eight nautical-looking nightstands to the island along with their equipment? Did they build them from driftwood while the rest of the island slept? And what about the lanterns—have the triplets been selling them at Tinsel & Tidings unbeknownst to her? It's amazing how good it all looks after only a few days of prep and set-up. Holly closes the flap and walks back to Leanna.

"So, what do you think?" Leanna steps over a tangle of black and orange electrical cords. "It's coming together, isn't it?"

"Yeah, it looks great."

"Here, Leanna—catch." One of the crew members tosses Leanna a roll of duct tape. She catches it easily and pulls a Sharpie from her fanny pack.

"I need to label some of the items in the tents so that the right contestant ends up with the right stuff."

"Isn't it all the same?"

Leanna pulls a piece of tape off the roll and bites it with her teeth so she can tear it. "Yeah, essentially. But there are slight—and important—

variations to the items." She tucks a wavy strand of hair behind her ear. Even with the drop in temperature, Leanna still has the overheated sheen of someone who isn't used to working in the Florida sun all day. She opens the flap of a tent and walks inside, sticking the piece of tape to the top of a first-aid kit on the nightstand. The tent Holly examined had no first-aid kit.

"Oh. So some of them have a slight advantage over the others or something?" Holly asks.

Leanna is writing on the tape with a firm stroke of the pen. The tip of the Sharpie squeaks across the surface as she writes a number and two letters. "Ummm…unofficially, but yeah. That's how it works," Leanna recaps the pen. "But this is top secret reality show info, *capiche*?"

"Of course. Got it." Holly follows her into the next tent where Leanna opens the drawer of the nightstand. It's stocked with energy bars and Advil. "So, what about Jake?"

"What about him?" Leanna tears off smaller pieces of tape and sticks them to the backs of the energy bars. She divides the pile in half, writing a different number and different letters on each pile.

"I mean, don't you think he has an unfair advantage? He knows the island really well. Jake knows the tides and the types of fish that come near shore, he knows how to crack a coconut and get all of the meat and water out of it, and he's really good with his hands."

"Oh, is he?" Leanna looks up at her from her perch on the end of the cot.

Holly blushes and ignores the innuendo. "Won't the other contestants think it's unfair to play against a local?"

"I've been meaning to get with you on that." Leanna puts the energy bars back into the drawer. "Jake's on board with the plan, and I wanted to let you know so you could spread the word."

There is a noticeable shift in the energy between them, and Holly knows she's going to be asked to do something she doesn't necessarily agree with.

"Jake's not going to let on that he's a local; none of the other contestants will know." From the seemingly bottomless fanny pack comes a pack of matches inside a plastic sandwich bag. Leanna pulls another, longer piece of tape, writes on it, and then gets on her knees next to the cot. She fixes the bag of matches to the bottom of the cot with the tape, her back to Holly. "More importantly," she says, getting to her feet, "we're going to offset that advantage by giving some of the other contestants a few tools that Jake won't have."

Holly narrows her eyes at Leanna. In her gut, she'd been feeling that something like this was about to come along. "So you're setting him up to fail?"

"Not *fail*, Holly. He's not going to lose every competition. And yes, there are some behind-the-scenes...*machinations* that are necessary, but they're strictly to raise the interest level on the show."

"Huh." Holly folds her arms, shifting her weight from one foot to the other. "So this is the kind of stuff that happens on *The Bachelor?*" She wants to understand—to believe—that Jake isn't going to be put at a disadvantage solely for ratings and entertainment.

"Oh, of course! Tweaking and pulling strings to make magic is what it's all about. Everyone knows that Hollywood is made up of fairy dust and glitter with a whole lot of superglue to hold it all together." Leanna smiles knowingly. She zips her fanny pack and pushes it onto one bony hip. "So I need you to A, let everyone on the island know that Jake being a local is a secret, and B, not tell Jake that the other contestants are getting a book of matches or a PowerBar when he isn't, okay?"

Holly shrugs. It's probably okay. Television and movies aren't exactly her area of expertise, but she enjoys the end result of their production as much as the next person. "Sure. I understand."

"Great." Leanna rests a hand on Holly's arm as her cell phone buzzes on her hip. "No rest for the wicked, huh? I'm sure that's Wayne," she says, stepping outside the tent to dig her ringing phone out of her pack.

Everyone is still hard at work, fastening strings of lights to tents, filling the now-complete fire pit with camera-ready, perfectly chopped logs, and setting up scaffolding and ladders from which to shoot the scene with their videocameras. Production is in full swing as Holly walks back across the beach to her golf cart. She turns and gives the campsite one last look: the torch lights, canvas tents, turquoise waters, and the tall, green palm trees swaying over the site give the scene a remote, Polynesian feel, and it'll look amazing as the show unfolds on television screens around the world.

Even though Holly knows she probably shouldn't—she has no permission, and would most likely get reprimanded for doing so—she pulls her cell phone out of her purse on the seat of the cart, turns it sideways, and opens the camera app. Looking out from under the brim of her Mets cap, she takes it all in on the screen of her phone and snaps a quick picture. One fast photo for posterity. After all, her little island home is on the cusp of becoming a household name—a famous, exotic travel destination that everyone's heard of…hopefully for all the right reasons.

Chapter Seven

"Morning, Carrie-Anne," Holly says as she walks into Mistletoe Morning Brew. The sleigh bells tied to the doorknob jingle festively. The coffee shop is the first storefront on Main Street after the dock, and like every other business on the street, its large windows look out onto the sidewalks and right at the hustle and bustle of the main drag.

"Morning, young lady," Carrie-Anne says cheerfully. The shop's owners, Carrie-Anne Martinez and Ellen Jankowitz, are partners in life and in business. They manage a tight schedule in order to keep the coffee shop open and running seven days a week, and neither has taken a vacation off the island in several years.

"You know, sometimes it takes me weeks to pick up on the theme, but November is already feeling very Edgar Allan Poe." Holly glances around at the recent changes to the store.

"Right you are, chickadee." Carrie-Anne pulls down the lever of the shiny espresso machine behind the counter. Carrie-Anne and Ellen are movie and literature buffs whose interests are reflected in the constantly evolving interior of the coffee shop, and they usually change things up so that each month has its own theme. "What gave it away?"

"The giant raven painted on the front window was a pretty good clue, but the bookmark Ellen gave me yesterday with my coffee had a quote from *The Telltale Heart* and a drawing of a creepy-looking blue eyeball."

"You should see the coasters she spent the last month making. She used cork board, copies of *The Cask of Amontillado,* and a bottle of Mod Podge. They're over there on the shelf."

"She cut up books? Isn't that blasphemous or something?" Holly searches her purse for the change she knows is floating around the bottom of the bag.

"Oh, she would never do that," Carrie-Anne scoffs. "Her daughter made hundreds of photocopies at her office in Philly and mailed them down. It's been quite a project." Carrie-Anne snaps a lid on the espresso she's been making and calls out to Heddie Lang-Mueller, who is sitting with her spine straight and shoulders back in a wooden chair at a bistro table. Heddie slips off the chair and leaves her novel facedown on the table while she retrieves her coffee.

"Good morning, Holly," Heddie says in her thick German accent, pulling a paper napkin from the dispenser on the counter. "How is everything coming with the television people?"

"Not bad. I went out to the beach yesterday to see their set-up. They've got tents and a fire pit and all of their cameras and equipment. It's really something."

"I heard Jake is participating in their game," Heddie says formally, wrapping the napkin around the base of her paper coffee cup.

Holly braces herself. She hasn't given a lot of thought yet as to how she'll deal with Jake's absence from his police duties, or whether it'll even be an issue at all. "That's the rumor," she says noncommittally.

"I hope he's prepared for the scrutinizing, unforgiving eye of the public," Heddie warns. She adjusts the silky scarf around her throat as she holds her coffee in the other hand. Even in her seventies, Heddie looks every inch the film star she'd been in her youth. No one is quite sure why she gave up the spotlight in Germany and washed up on the shores of an American island that's barely more than a speck on a map, but Heddie is a much-loved member of their community, and everyone loves to speculate about her glamorous past, though she'll confirm nothing.

"I hope he's ready, too, but we haven't talked much lately, so...I really don't know."

"Speaking of ready, what can I get you, Mayor?" Carrie-Anne nods at the fistful of change Holly's managed to cobble together from the bottom of her bag. "You know I could run you a tab if you didn't want to give me your sweaty coins and pocket lint."

"I'd just as soon get rid of this change. It's been jangling around in my bag like pirate's booty, and I think I might have enough for a salted caramel mocha."

Carrie-Anne holds out both hands like she's cupping them beneath a waterfall, and Holly pours the money into her palms. "Iced?" Carrie-Anne asks.

"As always." Holly smiles. "Oh, hey—what's Ellen raising money for this month?" Ellen is famous not only for her themed decorating, but for championing as yet unheard of causes. Each month the proceeds of her projects and crafts benefit important efforts like the protection of the Hawksbill turtle nests around the Keys; The Naked Clowns Foundation ("Because who doesn't love a naked clown?"); and funding educational retreats on metaphysics in Santa Fe.

"There's a donkey shelter in Colorado she's hoping to adopt from. We're in the process of getting screened to make sure we're suitable donkey parents." Carrie-Anne spreads Holly's change out on the counter and pushes it into piles of like coins: nickels, quarters, dimes, and pennies. She sorts and counts, dumping the piles into the separated drawer of the till. "One salted caramel iced mocha, comin' up."

"Wait—a donkey? And it's coming here?"

The sleigh bells on the door jingle as Maria Agnelli totters in. "Did someone say we were getting a donkey?" she asks with delight.

"A *donkey*?" Holly turns to Mrs. Agnelli with a frantic look on her face. "Mrs. Agnelli, have you ever heard of such a thing?"

"I've never heard of such a thing as a parrot who roams around an island and does whatever he damn well pleases, but that hasn't stopped Cap Duncan from taking on a stupid bird as a pet. The old fool," she mutters, setting her large purse on the counter. She's referring to Marco, the parrot who considers Cap his master and treats the island like his own personal playground. "I've also never heard of a single woman in her thirties letting a hunky cop get away so that she can carry on with a man who lives all the way across the country, but what do I know?"

Holly takes the salted caramel iced mocha from Carrie-Anne, who shoots her a meaningful look. "Mrs. Agnelli, I *just* turned thirty," Holly counters, pulling the wrapper off a straw and poking it through the hole in the lid.

"Let the girl have her fun, Maria," Carrie-Anne admonishes. "We've already been young, and I'm sure the choices we all made seemed strange to everyone around us."

"Says the woman who let a hunky architect slip through her fingers so she could carry on with another divorced woman."

Holly's eyes go wide as sips the coffee through her straw. The ice-cold caffeine shoots through her body, sharpening her senses. Maria Agnelli is as widely known for her ability to speak her mind colorfully as she is for her penchant to ruin any dish she cooks by tossing in a disgustingly inappropriate ingredient or two.

"Hey, love is love, Maria," Carrie-Anne says, unapologetic. She gives Mrs. Agnelli the wry smile of a woman who's used to putting up with unsolicited commentary about her lifestyle.

"Eh," Mrs. Agnelli admits, "you're right. I'll probably die without ever waking up next to another naked person in my bed, so maybe I'm the one who needs romantic advice." Holly chokes on her cold coffee. "You got any single lady friends you can fix me up with?"

Carrie-Anne throws her head back and howls with laughter. The crow's feet around her eyes deepen, and the silver fillings in her back teeth are visible as she laughs. Holly sputters and coughs.

"Well, well, well, if it isn't my feisty opponent," comes a voice from the doorway. Cap steps over the threshold and into the coffee shop, his large presence nearly blocking the sun behind him. "You mingling with the voters, Mayor?"

Holly pats herself on the chest and gives a final cough. "Morning, Cap."

"I'm glad you're here," Cap says. "We need to talk details." He closes the door and ambles up to the counter. "Hey, Carrie-Anne. Cup of the strong stuff, please." Cap pulls a wrinkled dollar from the wad of bills he takes from his breast pocket. As always, his shirt is undone just a button or two beyond where it should be, and his white chest hair is curled against his tanned skin.

"What details?" Holly holds her coffee in front of her body subconsciously—like a barrier between them—and squares her shoulders.

"You're acting like a damn fool, Cap Duncan," Mrs. Agnelli pipes up. "Nobody wants an old fart who doesn't know his ass from a cannoli running this island." She narrows her eyes at him. "And I'm helping myself to this, Carrie-Anne." Mrs. Agnelli takes a bookmark from the pile of Poe items on the counter and holds it in the air as she walks toward the door. "I'll see you all later."

Carrie-Anne waves at Mrs. Agnelli, but returns her attention to Cap and Holly as the bells on the door jingle.

"When is the next village council meeting? I think we should run our separate campaigns and promote our individual platforms until the meeting, and then we should talk to our constituents from the stage."

The words *stage, platforms,* and *constituents* ring in Holly's ears. It's a little early for her to be having a face-off with Cap, and she hasn't had enough caffeine yet to talk politics. "The next meeting is November sixteenth," she says, jiggling the melting ice in her plastic coffee cup. "And what platforms are you referring to?"

"Well, mine is 'Just Say No to Progress,' and I'd assume yours is simply the opposite."

"Right. Yes." Holly hadn't really declared a platform when she'd taken office initially, but her focus has always been on progress, so she figures this isn't the time to change tracks and start talking about something totally different. "Progress is my middle name," she says, her tone taking on an edge of defiance.

"Pardon me for butting in here," Carrie-Anne says, passing Cap a steaming paper cup of black coffee. "But what's your objection to progress, Cap? Holly isn't doing anything that won't benefit us in the long run, so what dog do you have in this fight?"

Cap lowers his head, looking at the women from under his thick, wiry eyebrows. "That's my personal business, Ms. Martinez. I don't like things the way they're going, so I have a right to step up to the podium and try to change them."

Carrie-Anne shrugs, lips pursed. "Doesn't sound like much of an argument to me, Mr. Duncan." She turns her back on them and starts taking apart the espresso machine to rinse out the metal filter. "But you got a right, so I suppose we'll be hearing you out on the sixteenth."

"Suppose you will." Cap holds up his cup of coffee in a parting toast. "Can we call a vote at that meeting, or will we have to wait for the next one?"

Holly inhales through her nose, trying to summon a measure of calmness and patience that she isn't really feeling. "I looked at the island's by-laws, and it clearly states that candidates need to campaign for a full thirty days after declaring their intent. Since the third Wednesday of December isn't until the twenty-first, we'll have to do it then. We can call a vote at that meeting."

Cap grunts and takes a drink of his coffee. "Waiting that long won't help me get this damn television show off the island, but it's a start. Fine —December twenty-first it is. And put me on the schedule for the meeting this month so I can say my piece, will you?"

Holly gives him a curt nod. Cap lumbers out the door and back onto Main Street, coffee in hand. The sleigh bells hit the wood frame of the entrance with a distorted jingle as he shuts the door with a bit more gusto than is necessary.

"Is he gone?" Ellen Jankowitz says from the small back room of the coffee shop. She pokes her dark, curly head out and looks around. "That man is a menace when he's drinking. He keeps offering to take me to the Ho Ho and show me what kind of fun I'm missing by swearing off men."

Carrie-Anne gags as she slides the clean filter back onto the espresso machine. "Let's make that Exhibit A in the case for swearing off men," she says, shaking her head in disbelief.

Ellen comes out of the back room and straightens the coffee cups and lids behind the counter. "How come we never saw this side of Cap before?"

"Because he was never drinking before," Holly says. "At least not like this."

"It's weird," Ellen says. "He's got a real Jekyll-and-Hyde thing going on. Remember all his ranting and raving at the meeting this summer? I'm dying to know what deep, dark secret he's so desperate to keep."

"Who knows." Holly sips her coffee. Now that Cap is gone, the adrenaline rush that comes from a good confrontation is pumping through her body on overdrive and making her hands and legs shake. She takes a deep breath and tries to steady herself.

"Hon, you don't look so good." Ellen comes out from behind the counter and holds out a sun-freckled hand covered in delicate gold rings; a tangle of gold chain bracelets is wrapped around her wrist. "Wanna sit?"

"I should get to the B&B," she says. "Bonnie'll be waiting for me."

"Sure, sure," Ellen says soothingly. "You get on over to work."

At the door, Holly pauses. "Hey, Heddie?" she calls.

Heddie is still sitting at the bistro table, sipping coffee, holding her book open. "Yes?"

"Did you hear what Cap said? About the meeting on the sixteenth?" As the village council secretary, Heddie is in charge of both the meeting schedule and the meeting minutes.

"I heard," she says, giving an icy German stare that Holly knows is meant for Cap.

"Can you put him on the agenda? Both of us, actually."

"Of course. Consider it done." Heddie turns back to her book.

"I guess I need to go and work on my platform now. Bye, ladies," Holly says, walking out the door in a daze.

"Poor girl." Carrie-Anne watches her go. "She's got her hands full with this reality show business—she doesn't need this."

"And then there's Coco," Ellen adds. "Don't forget that uppity mother of hers."

Carrie-Anne *tsk-tsks*, shaking her head. "She should really take Jake back. No one should have to go through all of this alone."

"Not our business," Ellen says, holding up both hands in surrender. "I've made the mistake of meddling in my own kids' love lives, and I'm not doing it here."

"True," Carrie-Anne acquiesces. A golf cart with Christmas ornaments dangling around the perimeter of the roof drives down Main Street slowly and Glen waves at them as she passes by the huge picture window at the front of the shop. Carrie-Anne waves back. "I guess all's fair in love and war."

"And politics," Heddie adds, not looking up from her book. "All's fair in love, war, and politics."

Chapter Eight

It's been a full week since the Mistletoe Morning Brew face-off with Cap. Holly is resolutely refusing to openly campaign for herself, but Cap hasn't missed an opportunity to stump and to make declarations on every street corner and during every happy hour where there are voters in attendance. It's been maddening for Holly to re-route her trips around the island and to skip evening gatherings at the Ho Ho and Jack Frosty's just to avoid him, but for her own sanity, it's worth it.

"Thanks for driving me," Jake says, looking around at the scenery as Holly shuttles him over to the *Wild Tropics* campsite. Rather than delivering the contestants to the dock the way every other boat that visits the island does, the NBC crew has insisted on a boat that can anchor on the north side of the island, far from any sign of civilization. Wayne and Leanna have invited Holly to join the crew as the contestants wade through the shallow waters and up to shore, and she's agreed to park her hot pink golf cart well out of view in order to keep up the illusion that they're landing on an uninhabited island.

"Good, you're early," Leanna says, clipboard in hand. She buzzes around, pointing people this way and that, shouting instructions through a megaphone so that she can be heard over the roar of the ocean. "Did you leave everything at home?" Leanna asks Jake, letting the megaphone fall to her side. Her long legs have browned in the Florida sun over the past couple of weeks, and she's wearing a pair of shorts and a white tank top with a sun hat.

"Left it all: keys, money, cell phone, I.D."

"Watch," Leanna says, pointing at Jake's wrist.

"Oh. Right. Can you take this, Holly?" Jake unfastens the watch and hands it to her. "So how are they going to react to me already being here?"

Leanna scans the horizon, squinting. "We're having the other eleven contestants brought in on three boats. They'll be mixed in with equipment, so when everyone is busy getting unloaded and acquainted, we'll bring you out of a tent to join them. No one will care who came in on which boat, so everyone will assume you were on a different boat than they were."

"Sounds foolproof."

Leanna shrugs. "It'll work. And we eliminate four people within the first forty-eight hours, so they'll all be focused on winning competitions and staying on the island." She shuffles through the papers on her clipboard. "Here's a list of the first hurdles you need to clear—I need this back before the boats get here. You're in that tent right there," she says, pointing at a tent with the canvas flap tied back. "Why don't you go in and read this over for a few minutes."

Holly follows Jake into the tent and sits next to him on the edge of the cot. "Is that a list of the competitions?"

"I think so," he says, scanning the stapled pages. "Looks like the first thing we'll be doing is getting paired up with tent partners, and then tonight there's a team scavenger hunt as the sun is setting."

"Do you think the other people get a heads-up on what the schedule looks like?" Holly asks, picking at her cuticles and trying to sound uninterested. "I mean, is it fair if you know what's happening ahead of time?" Beyond the flap of the tent, Leanna and Wayne are huddled at the edge of the water with a cameraman and another crew member. Holly watches them as they point down the beach and talk animatedly.

"Probably not." Jake runs a finger down the page as he reads.

"Do you think they're trying to help you win?"

"No. I don't think so." Jake flips the pages over and tosses them onto the cot. "I think they want me to stay in the game, but I'm not supposed to let anyone know that. I don't think it's going to be super-cushy or anything, but I feel like I might get a few advantages."

Holly picks up the stapled schedule and glances at it.

"You all done with that?" Wayne is at the opening of the tent, one hand held out to take the schedule.

Holly gives him a close-mouthed smile and hands over the papers.

"First boat's approaching. Holly, why don't you come out and blend in with the crew?" Wayne walks away as he's asking the question, no doubt assuming that Holly is following his directions like the rest of his crew would. She stands.

"So." Holly looks down at Jake. For the first time since she'd seen his pleased smile on Halloween night, a flicker of uncertainty crosses his face. He rests both elbows on his knees as he sits on the cot, his gaze far-away. He looks like a little boy whose mother is about to leave him at summer camp. "You'll be okay, right?"

The hesitance on his face melts into mild annoyance. "Of course. It's not like I'm leaving home or anything. I'm still here, I'm just sleeping on the beach for a couple of weeks."

"Maybe more," Holly reminds him.

The little boy at camp face comes back. "Dammit."

"What?" Holly reaches out a hand and sets it on his shoulder.

"I've never been good at breaking with routine. And I was always the kid who got homesick after a few days at my grandparents' house and wanted to go home. What am I doing, Hol? I hate stuff like this."

"Heyyyy," she says soothingly, running her hand up his neck and onto the back of his head. She trails her fingers through his short, dark hair without even thinking about the intimacy of it. "You're going to be great. I'm rooting for you."

Jake looks up at her as she stands next to him and their eyes meet in the dim tent. Her hand is still in his hair. "Yeah?" he asks, voice raspy. In the silence that follows, Jake sets his hand on her bare thigh—gently, hesitantly. "Even now that..."

Holly is about to answer his open-ended question when Wayne pokes his head in. "Holly, we've got a game plan here—let's roll." The smile on Wayne's face does nothing to mask his irritation at having to come back and fetch her.

"Sorry. I'm coming." She gives Jake's head a casual scruff, but the playfulness of this move doesn't jibe with the seriousness still hanging in the air between them.

Holly steps away from Jake and follows Wayne out of the tent without looking back.

* * *

As planned, three different boats speed toward the shoreline at staggered intervals. The captains cut their engines and drift up to shallower waters, dropping contestants and equipment into the smaller boats the crew have paddled out to meet them. The set-up—while entirely unnecessary, given the fact that Christmas Key has a perfectly good working dock—does make it seem as though the contestants are being dropped off in the middle of a barren paradise.

The first boat yields four contestants and several black boxes of camera equipment. The second boat drops three more competitors, a man who steps into the smaller boat with several garment bags in his arms, and a huge wooden crate with 'PASTA & RICE' stamped on the side in black stencil. The third boat delivers four tattooed contestants. One of the men is wearing a ripped and shredded t-shirt that reveals a giant Confederate flag tattoo emblazoned across his torso.

"Chuck Cortwell." Confederate Flag Guy steps forward on the sand after climbing out of the small boat and sticks a hand out to shake Holly's. She pauses, uncertain; no one has prepped her about what to say to the contestants. Her only plan is to blend into the crowd of crew members like she belongs there.

"Nice to meet you," Holly says, deciding on the spot that she won't give her name or too much info to anyone.

"Hi, Chuck," Leanna says smoothly, stepping in and offering her hand. "You made it."

"Sure did." He eyes Holly again, looking her up and down. "Do I get to pick which filly I'll be sharing a tent with?"

"We've pre-selected that for you, Chuck. And there won't be any gender-mixing when it comes to sleeping quarters. Yet." Leanna winks at him. "Oh, and this filly isn't a contestant," she says, tipping a head in Holly's direction. "Your fellow competitors are the ones coming off the boats. The crew is already here on shore."

As Chuck and the others circulate, shaking hands with each other and the crew members, Holly notices Jake in the mix. He's materialized in the middle of the crowd and is greeting people and looking around as if he's never seen the island before.

"He's a natural, isn't he?" Leanna leans in to Holly, talking out of one side of her mouth like someone might be able to read lips. "And don't worry—I'll keep my eye on him for you."

"Oh—no. Jake isn't my...I mean, we aren't..." Holly shakes her head.

Leanna narrows her eyes, no doubt trying to reconcile the blush on Holly's cheeks with the words coming out of her mouth. "Okay. Got it."

Holly stands away from the crowd as Wayne gathers the contestants in front of the tents. There are three cameras filming everything for special behind-the-scenes footage to air online and in later shows, and Leanna is watching through the screen of her iPhone as she circles behind the group, making a video of everything so they have some raw-looking footage to mix in as well.

Aside from Jake and Chuck Cortwell, there are ten other contestants of various ages, heights, sizes, and hair colors. One of the women looks to be in her late forties with hair that fades from coral to tangerine to apricot like her head is on fire. Both of her arms are covered in full-sleeve tattoos made of interlaced flowers. There are a couple of guys in their twenties who have the trim physiques and chiseled faces of male models or wannabe actors, and an angelic-looking girl of nineteen or twenty whose brown hair falls in perfect ringlets to her waist. Her eyes are wide and blue, and when she smiles, her face lights up like she's looking at the most beautiful thing she's ever seen.

Holly takes in the anxious, intense, curious faces of the competitors, her eyes finally landing on an Amazonian goddess. She's got the tousled blonde hair of a girl who travels with a hairstylist, and the shiny, tanned limbs of a tennis player who's spent her life in the sun. Her skin is flawless, her body a perfectly carved hourglass. In a bikini, she'd easily be *Sports Illustrated* swimsuit issue material. Holly can't tear her eyes away.

"So, you can come back over and check things out as we're filming," Leanna says in a stage whisper, zipping her phone into her fanny pack. "Normally we wouldn't give quite this much access to someone who isn't part of the crew, but I know we'll need to pick your brain as this progresses and find out more about the island and the area."

Holly nods, still watching the blonde model as she moves to stand next to Jake.

"Hey, I forgot to have you sign something…I've got it right here," Leanna says, turning a few pages on the clipboard. "It's no big deal, really. Just a non-disclosure agreement about the show while we're filming. And after." She uncaps a ballpoint pen and hands it to Holly. "Right here. And your initials over here." Leanna holds out the clipboard and taps two spots on the page.

Holly looks down at the legal document in front of her. "Non-disclosure agreement?"

"It says you won't talk to anyone about what goes on behind the scenes, or give any spoilers to the press or anyone else before the show airs. And you won't do any interviews afterward unless they're approved by us."

"Oh, right." Holly scans the page quickly before dragging the pen across the signature line. She adds her initials at the bottom.

"Thanks. Anyway, we're going to get started here, so why don't you text me next time you're thinking of visiting the set, and I'll let you know if it's a good time?" Leanna's body is positioned strategically between Holly and the campsite, blocking her view of Jake.

So suddenly a trip to the quietest beach on the island requires permission via text? And walking on the sand of her own island is now known as a "visit to the set"? Holly tries to keep an even smile on her face, but she's completely unprepared for the way relinquishing a portion of her island makes her chest seize up with anxiety.

"Sure. Of course." Holly retreats a few steps. "Thanks for letting me be here today."

"No problem!" Leanna has already turned her back on Holly.

Behind the wheel of her golf cart again, with the sound of the ocean breaking in the distance beyond the sand dune, Holly sits and stares at the palm trees and at the road stretching out ahead of her. She doesn't turn the key to kick on the cart's power, but instead lets the gentle breeze push her light brown hair around as she thinks.

Jake's hesitation in the tent brought out a protectiveness in her that she hadn't felt towards him in a while, and the sleek, blonde lion who'd nearly swallowed him whole hadn't done much to put Holly's mind at ease. The scene in the tent plays over and over again on a loop in her mind, and Holly pictures her hand in his hair. A pang of something uncomfortable—something that feels icky, like guilt mixed with regret—runs through her as she sees his face looking up at her again. What bothers her more than his obvious discomfort, and more than her strange territorial response to the gorgeous supermodel competitor, was the way she'd been so ready to comfort him. She'd cupped the back of his head in her hand and looked down in his eyes, ready to say…to say…

And that's what really nags at her: she has no idea what she'd been about to say.

Chapter Nine

After a full day at the B&B, Holly slips a yellow notepad into her purse and grabs her Yankees cap from the hook by the door. She makes a kissing noise at Pucci, who's been sitting calmly on his dog bed in the corner all day. He rises and gives a full-body shake, then follows Holly through the front lobby and out the door. They meander the few steps up Main Street to Jack Frosty's, where Holly stops and looks down at her trusty companion.

"You have to wait out here, buddy," she says to Pucci, pointing at a spot on the sidewalk outside the open air bar. The late-autumn sun is already low in the sky, and the temperature has taken a dip. Holly pulls her arms through the white cardigan she's had tied around her waist all day as she walks up the steps to Jack Frosty's.

"Over here, lady!" Fiona calls from the counter. She's already bellied up to the bar on one of the high stools, a cold drink sweating at her elbow.

Holly swings by the jukebox and picks a Springsteen song before climbing up onto a stool at the bar. When he hears her song choice, Buckhunter stops what he's doing and bobs his head to the beat.

"Hey, doc. How goes it?" Holly settles in next to her best friend.

"Pretty damn good." Fiona picks up her drink. "You gonna order before we start? You look like you could use a drink."

"Could I get a Sidecar, please?" Holly says to Buckhunter's back as he works behind the bar. She takes off her hat and lays it on the counter.

"That's an interesting choice," Buckhunter says to his niece. The napkin he sets on the counter in front of her has a print of a snowman holding two frothy mugs of beer in its stick hands stamped on it. Holly smiles, running her fingers over the name of the bar and the words 'Christmas Key, Florida' under the snowman.

"Well, I'm an interesting girl," she says.

· "No argument there." Buckhunter pulls a clean glass from the shelf and fills his shaker with ice.

"So?" Fiona makes a *tell me everything* motion with one hand. "What's going on? Have you been back to the set?"

"No, not yet. I felt weird about how Jake and I left things the other day."

"Why—how did you leave things?" Fiona swivels on her stool so that her whole body faces Holly; her knees touch the side of Holly's thigh.

Holly smiles at Buckhunter as he sets the drink on the cocktail napkin. There's a wedge of orange resting on the rim of the glass and she takes it off, tearing at its sweet, citrusy flesh with her teeth while she thinks about how much she wants to share.

"I don't know. It was strange to see him acting like he was a real competitor on the show."

"But isn't he?"

"Yeah, I guess. And we had this *moment* in his tent before the other contestants got there—"

"*No*," Fiona says. Her eyebrows shoot up, mouth rounded into a perfect O.

"No—not *that* kind of moment," Holly assures her, holding her glass in one hand. "I guess it could have turned into that kind of moment... but it didn't."

"We need to get River out here, stat."

"Ooooh, doctor talk—I love it when you say stuff like *stat* and *doctor's orders.*"

"You know what I mean. If you're thinking about having a quickie in a tent with Jake, then maybe Bonnie is right."

"About?"

"About us chipping in to buy a plane ticket for your boyfriend. We need him to make a cross-country trip as soon as possible."

"Why is this being discussed?" Holly takes her first drink of the Sidecar; the cognac slides down her esophagus, leaving a warm trail behind it.

"We're worried about you, Hol." Fiona leans in closer, talking into Holly's ear so that Buckhunter won't hear. "This whole Cap situation is ridiculous, and then there's a film crew on the island on top of that. I don't want to see you internalizing all of this without an outlet—it could jeopardize your health."

"Okay, that's *definitely* doctor-talk," Holly says, bumping Fiona's shoulder playfully with her own. "But I thought you were a general practitioner, not a shrink."

"I minored in abnormal psych." She pats Holly's leg. "Knowing a little about crazy people has helped me survive on this island," she says with a laugh, picking up her drink. "And it's definitely helped me to understand *you.*"

"Glad I could serve as a case-study for you, Fee," Holly says with a mock pout.

"Oh, no…" Fiona's looks at the entrance to the bar.

"What?" Holly turns on her stool: there, on the top step, are Cap and Wyatt Bender. They're wearing matching t-shirts, and with their marked differences in height and stature, they look like some mismatched comedy team from a movie. Holly makes an annoyed sound and takes another sip of her Sidecar.

Cap and Wyatt wave casually at neighbors and friends as they cut through the center of the bar, and Cap stops to shake hands with Ray and Millie Bradford. Ray sets his cheeseburger in its basket and stands up, brushing crumbs off the legs of his khaki pants before he takes the hand Cap offers.

"He never stops campaigning, does he?" Holly turns her back on Cap and Wyatt and shakes her half-empty drink lightly, knocking the ice cubes around in the glass.

"Ladies," Wyatt says, approaching the bar. Holly can feel him standing directly behind her, but she doesn't turn to greet him.

"Nice shirts, Wyatt." Fiona rolls her eyes.

Holly finally turns around—as slowly as possible—and glances at his chest. "'Cap's Your Chap—Vote For Duncan.' Very clever," she says without emotion, turning back to the bar.

"We thought so." Wyatt puts a rough, weathered hand on the counter next to Holly's drink.

"Mayor!" Cap says jovially. "Fancy meeting you here. Like our shirts?" He looks down at the front of his too-tight white t-shirt, a smug smile on his face.

"Where did you get those made so quickly?" Fiona holds up a finger to get Buckhunter's attention.

"Ordered 'em online," Wyatt says. "It's a wonder what a body can do with a computer and a credit card."

"Well, I declare," Fiona says sarcastically, sounding bored. She pushes her empty drink across the bar at Buckhunter.

"You two lovelies working on something in particular?" Cap asks. The gold hoop in his ear catches the reflection of the twinkling Christmas lights hanging around the bar.

"Oh, we're just writing a steamy romance novel together in our free time," Fiona says, stirring her fresh drink with a straw. "It's about a crusty old pirate and his oil tycoon lover. Very hot—it's kind of a twenty-first century thing."

Cap frowns, hand poised over his white goatee. He and Wyatt exchange a confused look. "Sounds like a doozy."

"Say," Wyatt interrupts, glancing around the bar. "Is that saucy redhead here tonight?"

"Nope." (Holly makes a mental note to tell Bonnie that Wyatt was asking for her.)

"I was kind of hoping she would be," he says, disappointment written all over his handsomely lined face.

"I'm sure you were. Now, if you'll excuse us." Holly turns around again so that her back is to the men. "If I were a betting woman," she says to Fiona once Cap and Wyatt are out of ear shot, "I'd say that Wyatt Bender doesn't give a rat's patooie about Cap being mayor."

"You're probably right. I can totally see that." Fiona grabs a fistful of shelled peanuts from a bowl on the bar.

"Exactly. He just wants to get under Bonnie's skin."

"Okay, let's ignore them for now and focus on your main points for Wednesday's meeting," Fiona says, sitting up straighter. She crosses her legs and folds her hands on the bar, her face suddenly serious. She looks like a reporter who's ready to get down to business. "I'm going to listen objectively, and then I'll decide whether I feel confident enough in your platform to give you my vote."

"I hope you're pulling my leg," Holly says, getting her notepad and pen out of her purse. She sets the legal pad on the bar.

"I'm still undecided." Fiona picks up the notes and looks over Holly's bullet points. "You know," she shrugs, "Cap's my chap, so it's hard to say —I *might* be voting for Duncan."

"What's it gonna take to get your vote, Dr. Potts?"

"Food. Lots of food."

"Buckhunter!" Holly shouts down the bar. "We're going to need an order of chili fries, and two baskets of chicken strips."

"Don't forget the onion rings," Fiona says. "We have some serious work to do on this speech."

"And onion rings!" Holly calls out, a smile spreading across her face.

She and Fiona spend the next two hours eating greasy food, laughing, and covering Buckhunter's bar with crumpled up napkins and wadded pieces of paper. In the end, they deem having a campaign slogan "too cheesy" and instead select a few of Holly's successes to highlight at the meeting. Buckhunter stops by every twenty minutes or so to offer his input and listen to their ideas, and at some point, Cap and Wyatt leave the bar. The women don't even notice.

When they finally step out onto Main Street well after dark, Holly feels prepared for Wednesday's meeting. She gives her best friend a hug. "Thanks, Fee. I couldn't have done this without you. I think I'm ready."

"And I think I've got a stomachache—that was *a lot* of junk food." Fiona sticks out her tongue. "Call me tomorrow?"

"Will do." Holly waves at Fiona. There's a light breeze as she walks down the sidewalk, breathing in the ocean air. It's a beautiful night on an even more beautiful island, and she feels the warmth and happiness of companionship after her evening with Fiona. This is the calmest she's felt in a while, and for a moment she's able to forget that there's anything amiss in her life. Holly feels a lightness in her heart about the mayoral race against Cap; maybe she actually needs this little political shake-up? Maybe being called on the carpet is what will give her an edge and help her to see the holes in her own approach to progress?

She swings her bag as she walks, but stops when her mind skips to Jake: Jake, who isn't her boyfriend; Jake, who is definitely not her concern; Jake, who she can't seem to keep out of her mind. She'd just like to get through one day without having him pop up in her thoughts. She'd like to have *one day* where she thinks of River more than she thinks about Jake.

As she stands there, the light breeze turns into a sharp gust of wind that pins Holly's skirt tight against her thighs. Her sweater blows open, whipping wildly as she clutches her purse. Holly wraps her arms around herself on the sidewalk, waiting for the wind to pass.

Chapter Ten

The B&B's dining room is nearly filled to capacity, and there's an electric hum in the air. November sixteenth is the coldest day of the year so far. Ladies all around the room are wearing shawls or shirts with sleeves that cover their browned and freckled shoulders, and some of the men have switched from shorts to long pants (mostly of the plaid variety, undoubtedly left over from years spent on the golf course).

Heddie Lang-Mueller is seated next to the podium with a sweater knotted around her narrow shoulders, hair in a tight bun. She's got her paper and three pens arranged on the table and she's tallying islanders in her head as they enter the room.

"Sorry!" Fiona mouths to Holly as she ducks into the dining room. Fiona stops at the third row from the front and scoots past knees and purses to reach the only open seat she can find, holding the edges of her white lab coat so they don't flap around and hit people as she steps over them.

Holly smiles nervously. She can tell Fiona ran out of her tiny doctor's office at Poinsettia Plaza—probably between appointments, though no one would have been scheduled to see her during the village council meeting anyway—and raced over to the B&B to be there for the meeting. Buckhunter is leaning against the back wall, arms folded, an unlit cigar clamped between his teeth. He winks at Holly almost imperceptibly, following it up with a few blinks of his lids so that it almost looks like he has something in his eye.

The only other person Holly would like to make eye contact with before the meeting starts is Jake, but he's on set with the rest of the cast and crew. The past five days have been filled with this mayoral nonsense between her and Cap, and on top of everything else, she's been talking to a festival coordinator from Tampa who has some ideas for seasonal events that she'd like to bring to Christmas Key. It hasn't left a lot of time to get permission to "visit the set," and so Holly's done her best to just keep her head down and stay focused.

"If we could call this meeting for November sixteenth to order, please," Holly says into the small microphone on the podium. "My apologies—we're nearing standing room only. Please find a spot wherever you can." She looks around, nodding at the empty chairs sprinkled throughout the crowd so those standing along the walls can find seats.

Wyatt Bender stands up at the back of the room and politely holds his cowboy hat out to to Bonnie, indicating that she should have his seat. Bonnie's face goes pink as she lifts her chin an inch or two, but she takes Wyatt's spot anyway, giving him a sidelong glance as she does.

"We've got several items on the agenda today, so I'd like to get started," Holly says, bending forward slightly to speak into the microphone. The crowd settles, and voices are lowered as people whisper to their neighbors. Finally, the room falls quiet. "Okay, first of all I'd like to thank you for coming, and to ask for a show of hands of registered voters in attendance."

Hands go up around the dining room and Heddie takes a full head count.

"Thank you. Now, if you'll indulge me, I'd like to get some of the smaller items checked off the agenda for this month before we get to the big ticket item." A surge of chatter ripples through the room. "First off,"

Holly says in a louder voice, hoping to talk over the voices and keep things moving. "Ellen Jankowitz has put forward a motion to approve the introduction of a new species to the island."

Heads turn all around the room as people search for Ellen. She and Carrie-Anne have closed the shop to be at the meeting, and they stand up now, Carrie-Anne with a large piece of poster board in her hands and Ellen with a sheet of paper.

"Come on up and present your request, ladies." Holly waves them to the front of the room. Carrie-Anne stands next to the podium and turns the poster board around so it faces the crowd. "Is this an actual photo of our potential new resident?" Holly prompts, widening her eyes to let Ellen and Carrie-Anne know they should start talking.

"It is," Ellen says, clearing her throat. The women are both wearing knee-length denim skirts and blouses, and Ellen's wild, curly mane of hair has been tamed with two clips. "This is Madonna, and she lives in Colorado."

"Did she say 'Madonna'?" Mrs. Agnelli asks loudly from the front row. "As in Our Lady? Is this a biblical donkey? Are we talking Abraham and Jacob and Moses here?" She squints at the picture glued to the poster board.

"I think it's more like the Material Donkey,'" Carrie-Anne pipes up, looking at Ellen for confirmation. "As in burning crosses, pointy bras, and Sean Penn."

Mrs. Agnelli's frown deepens as she turns to Iris Cafferkey for clarification.

"So," Holly hurries to move things forward, "tell us more about Madonna the donkey—or Madonkey, if you will." The crowd titters.

"Good one, Holly," Ellen says, laughing appreciatively at Holly's attempt to lighten the mood. "Um, she's from Colorado, and she currently lives in a shelter that searches for families who want to adopt displaced animals."

"How does a donkey get displaced?" Joe Sacamano calls out from the center of the room.

"Is this a riddle?" Jimmy Cafferkey says to him, turning his upper body to face Joe. "Like 'why did the chicken cross the road?'"

"Nah, it's a legitimate question, but if you feel a limerick coming on, then I'm all ears, Cafferkey." Joe scratches his whiskers and turns back to Ellen and Carrie-Anne. "Is he from a zoo?"

"She," Ellen corrects. "Madonna is a girl donkey."

"Of course—my mistake," Joe says expansively, a hint of amusement in his voice. "And why does Lady Madonna need a home?"

"Lots of animals around the country suffer from abuse, abandonment, and neglect—not just cats and dogs." Ellen consults the paper in her hand. "Donkeys are less likely to find homes than horses and even pot-bellied pigs, but they're curious and smart, and they can be trained."

"Where are we going to put Madonkey?" Buckhunter shouts from the back of the room. His arms are still folded across his chest, but he's taken the cigar out of his mouth. From the mirth on his face, he looks to be on the verge of laughter.

"Well, most of you have correctly identified November as Poe Month at the coffee shop, and the funds from all of my crafts will go towards Madonna's adoption costs, and to build a pen behind our cottage."

Cap stands up from his seat in the front row, right at the center of the dining room. He's clean and shaved, and looking as sober as a newborn. For the first time in a long time, he resembles the old Cap—the one who didn't barge into village council meetings drunk and decide to upend the local political infrastructure on a whim.

"Question for you, ladies," Cap says politely. His face is wiped clean of the scowl he'd worn at Mistletoe Morning Brew the last time he and

Holly had confronted one another, and he's looking at Ellen and Carrie-Anne as though he's never been inebriated enough to offer to show them what they've been missing by taking men off their dating menu. "What do we do if Madonna gets here and doesn't take to all of us? Or if we don't take to her?" He looks at the crowd, palms turned to the ceiling. "I'd make an off-color suggestion here about the things we could do to rid ourselves of an unfriendly donkey, but that would be unseemly behavior for a man who's about to ask for your vote."

The women in the crowd cover their mouths and shake their heads, and some of the men look like they've just been offered a whiff of burning garbage.

"That won't happen," Ellen says firmly, visibly steeling herself to square off with Cap. "Donkeys are loyal and strong, and Carrie-Anne and I will take full responsibility for her care and well-being. I think the issue at hand is simply getting approval to bring a new animal onto the island, not whether anyone is interested in trying donkey kabobs if it doesn't work out."

"Ellen and Carrie-Anne have a solid plan in place for Madonkey," Holly says, addressing the crowd again and stepping in to stop Cap from responding. "As mayor, I'm confident they've done their research and are prepared for the responsibility. I've also looked into the pros and cons of having a donkey on the island, and frankly, the fact that she'll eat up our weeds like they're candy far outweighs any of the negatives I could come up with."

"Donkeys are really wonderful to have as pets," Ellen says, pointing at the poster Carrie-Anne is still holding up. "Look at those sweet eyes. She'll be our pet, but you're all welcome to come and see her anytime you like."

"Okay then." Holly clasps her hands on top of the podium. "Let's start with a verbal yay for those in favor of introducing a donkey to

Christmas Key via the adoption of this lovely girl here." She holds a hand in front of the poster like she's introducing a grand prize on a game show.

The crowd gives a loud, synchronized "Yay."

"And those who are opposed, let's do a verbal nay." Holly looks out into the crowd, waiting; there are no dissenters. "That was easy." She smiles at Carrie-Anne and Ellen. "Congratulations—looks like you two are going to be donkey moms."

Carrie-Anne and Ellen hug each other excitedly.

"So everyone swing by Mistletoe Morning Brew this month and pick up a set of coasters and a latte to support Madonkey's adoption," Holly says in closing.

Heddie is furiously scribbling notes in shorthand on her paper as Holly talks. "I'm not sure we got 100% verbal confirmation," Heddie whispers up to her from her seat next to the podium. "But there were zero who spoke up as not in favor, so shall I just say it was a full consensus?"

Holly covers the microphone with one hand. "Works for me. What's up next?"

"New business proposition," Heddie says, scanning the agenda with the eraser of her pencil and tapping the next item on the docket.

"Right." Holly uncovers the microphone and looks out into the crowd again. "Next up, we have a proposition for a new business here on Christmas Key, and I believe all of the documents and bank paperwork are in order, correct?" She looks at Heddie again.

"Everything is submitted."

"Ray and Millie Bradford would like to open a salon on Main Street in the empty corner suite in Poinsettia Plaza. Millie, did you want to give us a brief overview?"

Millie stands in front of her chair on the right side of the room. "Good morning," she says, taking in the crowd with an easy smile. "Ray and I would like to open a salon called Scissors & Ribbons. We'll offer full hair services as well as manicures and pedicures, and we're hoping to add massages to the menu at some point." Millie's auburn hair is cut short, and she wears small gold knots on her earlobes. Because she owned a salon in Pennsylvania for more than twenty years, she's already the island's go-to hairdresser when anyone needs to color their grays or get a trim. No one questions the idea of Millie running a salon, and several of the women actually break out in soft applause. "Bringing a masseuse to the island is something that will take time, but we feel like there's definitely a call for basic services right now," Millie says. "I'm excited to get the salon up and running."

"Thank you, Millie." Holly notices the crowd shifting and looking restless in front of her. It's not as if they aren't excited at the prospect of donkeys and professionally permed hair, but most of the islanders are eager to see the real show, and Holly knows it. "New businesses don't need to be called to an official vote, particularly when all the paperwork is in order. If anyone has a substantial objection to the business or the idea, this is the time to speak up and carry on a productive discussion. If not, we'll move on with the meeting and Ray and Millie will move forward with Scissors & Ribbons. Questions or objections?"

Holly looks around the room, her hands resting on both sides of the podium. Everywhere she looks, people are nodding their heads. No one objects to the business idea, and Millie sits back down next to Ray, who puts his arm around her shoulders and leaves it there.

"Okay, that brings us to the last order of business, which is the upcoming mayoral election." The words stick in her throat, but Holly is determined to forge ahead. "As you all know, I've served the island as mayor for nearly three years now, and Cap Duncan has decided to challenge my seat." Most of the faces in the crowd are blank, but Holly knows in her heart that she'll have the majority of their votes. Her eyes seek out Buckhunter and Bonnie and Fiona for reassurance. She goes on. "It's required that we campaign for a full thirty days after publicly declaring the race, so I'll call for a vote at our next village council meeting, which is December twenty-first."

Cap stands and approaches the podium. As incumbent, Holly's going to step aside and let him speak first.

"Cap's going to give a brief speech about his intentions now, and then it will be my turn to appeal to you all as neighbors and voters." She hesitates, not sure she really wants to cede the floor to Cap. He's been such a loose cannon lately, and it feels risky to give him a microphone and an audience, but Holly knows it has to happen.

"Thank you, Mayor," Cap says, eyeing her suspiciously as she takes just a moment too long to step aside. "I'd like to talk to you all about my plans, and I can assure you that this speech will be brief, because I *have* no plans. Unlike our current mayor, I would prefer to see nature take its course. If someone wants to come to Christmas Key and contribute, let 'em. But going out and trying to recruit people to come to the island is pure hogwash. I don't believe it's in our best interests to pursue this course of action any further, and in fact, I think it's doing our island great harm." Cap punctuates this thought by holding up a forefinger and staring down the front row. "Having a bunch of cameras and television people here is the fastest way to spoil the purity of this place."

"What I want to know is when the rest of us are going to get to be on camera," Mrs. Agnelli says, her voice laced with indignation. "When Holly told us these people were coming, we were led to believe we'd all get to be a part of this big production. But so far Jake is the only one who's getting famous."

The crowd erupts. There are shouted questions, loud opinions, and open conjecture volleying around like a courtroom where the judge has lost control. Holly takes it all in, wondering whether she should boot Cap out from behind the podium. Instead, she steps up next to him and bends toward the microphone again. "Okay, okay," she says, holding up both hands. "If you'll all quiet down for a second, I'm happy to address your individual concerns."

"I promised my grandson he'd see me on television, and he's already told all his friends I was going to be on this show. I can't let him look like a liar," comes a voice from across the room. Holly is trying to see who's talking, but before she can respond, Cap bends forward into the microphone, nearly knocking her out of the way.

"If you'll all remember, I was the one who spoke the truth the first time those television people came to the island. I told you all right here in this room that we were in for trouble, and you didn't want to hear it. Now I'm here again to offer my guidance, and I think it's high time you heed my words." Cap grips both sides of the podium with his big hands and nearly swallows the microphone when he leans in even closer. "You've got another month to sit on your hands and wait for this show to turn you all into stars, or you can object to them monetizing our island and potentially destroying the very things that make us special. They'll rip apart our island and our friendships, and it'll be because *we* invited them here to do it." Cap looks right at Holly when he says this. "So if you want to stop this freight train of progress from mowing us all down, remember to vote for Duncan—Cap's your chap!"

Cap's words are swallowed by the noise from the crowd, but it doesn't matter, because he's successfully stirred up doubt about Holly's ability to make good choices as mayor. She looks around in a daze. Everything she's planned to say to her neighbors is forgotten as she watches them talk animatedly. But it isn't really necessary for her to share her plans or what she'd do as mayor, because they already know she's in favor of progress and growth. Her follow-up speech—her only chance for a true rebuttal—circles the drain as everyone debates amongst themselves.

With a weak smile, Holly takes back the podium. "Meeting adjourned," she says softly into the microphone. No one hears her.

Chapter Eleven

"I guess I didn't think it would be like *this*," Holly admits. Buckhunter is driving them to the *Wild Tropics* set in his beat-up golf cart the next morning. Because he'd been involved in showing the crew around when they first visited Christmas Key, and because Buckhunter and Holly own equal parts of the island, Leanna has agreed to let him visit the set today.

Holly shifts around on the cart's ripped vinyl seat, her purse in her lap. Buckhunter's shirt is unbuttoned, his narrow torso covered with a thin layer of tanned skin. Holly glances at the tattoo on his wrist: it's a slightly faded eagle, and she realizes there's still so much about her uncle that remains a mystery. Of course, she only found out they were related three or four months ago, but beyond the fact that his mother was a nurse who had an affair with her grandfather and then died of cancer when Buckhunter was in his twenties, there isn't much about him that Holly *does* know.

"There was really no way for you to guess how it would be, kid," he says, cranking the wheel with his rough hands. Holly points at a sand dune and he parks behind it abruptly, shutting off the cart's power. "But I still believe you've got something great on your hands here, and I guarantee people will see that when it's all said and done."

"Didn't you hear them yesterday?" she moans, putting her head into her hands. Buckhunter stays behind the wheel, laying an arm casually over the back of the seat as he listens. "They were fired up—*really* fired up. I haven't seen people in that much of a tizzy at a village council meeting since Mrs. Agnelli asked if we could hold a pole-dancing class in the B&B's dining room."

"Oh yeah, I forgot about that one," Buckhunter says, smirking into the distance. "Remind me again where she came up with the idea of aging hips on stripper poles?"

"I don't know. Some *Dateline* episode about middle-aged women taking pole-dancing lessons in the suburbs." Holly waves dismissively. "But this was different—this time they turned on me."

"Come on," Buckhunter says. "What about that Madonkey bit—you were completely on your game there."

Holly smiles at him. "Yeah, I was. That was off-the-cuff, too."

"They'll come back around. Let's not worry until we actually have something to worry about, huh?" Buckhunter chucks her on the shoulder gently with the hand he's been resting behind her on the seat. "Wanna go and check out this dog and pony show?"

"We probably should. Leanna wants us to blend in with the crew as much as possible so we don't distract from their taping. Let's find someone who looks official and hang with them." Holly pulls her Yankees cap out of her purse and puts it on. "Ready?"

"I forgot a hat. Am I incognito enough?"

Holly gets out and stands next to the cart, looking at Buckhunter. "You will be once you put your pecs away." She points at his open shirt. "And don't talk too much."

"Gee, okay, Mom. Can I have a cookie if I behave?" Buckhunter buttons his shirt.

"Yeah, yeah, yeah. Let's go."

There's a massive metal tower on the beach, and a man sits at the top of it on a chair, a huge camera in front of his face. He's talking into a walkie-talkie, and farther down the beach, Wayne is holding his own walkie-talkie to his ear. The tent flaps are all tied shut, and a member of the crew attends to the smoldering fire pit in the distance.

"So this is it." Buckhunter surveys the scene. "Huh."

Holly looks around for the competitors. She spots them as they bob to the surface of the water, emerging in snorkeling gear and bathing suits. The woman with the colorful hair is the first out of the water, a mesh bag full of shells tied around her waist. She's beaming and shouting something at the people behind her.

"Wow, look at all those shells," Holly says quietly, admiring the woman's ocean loot. Holly's been collecting shells from the beaches for most of her life, and for the past year or so, on the nights she hasn't been able to sleep, she's mixed up a batch of grout and carefully affixed her favorite shells to the exterior wall of her house that's covered by the lanai.

"Bet you could do something with those," Buckhunter says, nodding at the other contestants as they come out of the water with their own bags of shells. Given the close proximity of their houses, he sometimes sees Holly on her lanai late at night, lights on, music playing as she pads around barefoot, wiping sweat from her brow with the back of a mortar-covered hand as she focuses intently on her shell wall.

Before Holly can say anything, Jake steps onto the sand. His dark hair glistens with water, and his skin is a deeper brown than usual. Although it's been a while since she's seen him shirtless, she can tell his muscles are more pronounced, his abs leaner. The waistband of his swim trunks rides low on his pelvis, and a trail of hair from his bellybutton disappears into the navy fabric of his shorts like a path leading into a dense forest. Holly swallows hard and tears her eyes away.

Not ten seconds later, the Amazonian blonde emerges from the surf, pushing her goggles onto the top of her head as she laughs hysterically. Streams of water run over her almond-colored skin. Jake stops and reaches out a hand to her, pulling her forward and closer to him so that her young, firm breasts press against his strong arm. They run to shore together, racing for some unseen finish line.

"Well," Buckhunter says, tilting his head to one side. "This is more interesting than I thought it would be."

Holly whacks his arm. "This is more *naked* than I thought it would be."

"Everyone's covered." Buckhunter shrugs. "Looks harmless to me."

Holly ignores him and marches forward. She sees Leanna and slows her aggressive approach, thinking of what she wants to say.

"Holly! Leo!" Leanna waves at them, calling Buckhunter by his first name. "It's sandcastle day, and the contestants are paired up." Leanna pulls the headset she's wearing off her head and lets it dangle around her neck. "We've already sent the first four home, so now we're down to eight." Chuck Cortwell—with his giant Confederate flag tattoo—remains, as does the docile-looking angel with the waist-length waves of brown sugar hair. The flame-haired woman is paired with one of the generic male models, and the other contestants are on their knees in the sand, hard at work on what will obviously be sprawling sandcastles.

"Things are working out exactly the way we'd hoped," Leanna confides. "Jake is doing great, and he and Bridget have a natural chemistry. The camera *loves* them."

Holly bristles. Jake hasn't noticed her because he's clearly engrossed in the competition at hand—and in Bridget. Holly lowers her chin, watching from beneath the brim of her baseball cap.

"Looks like fun," Buckhunter interjects awkwardly, filling the silence when Holly doesn't say anything. "What happens when someone wins this competition?"

"They have three hours to construct and decorate. We brought in two of the world's professional-level master sandcastle judges—"

"Wait, there's such a thing as a 'master sandcastle judge'?" Holly looks away from Jake and Bridget.

"Of course. They even have their own union," Leanna says, pointing at a squat man in a Panama hat, and a tall, thick-legged woman with a puff of gray hair. "The boat dropped them off at dawn, and they'll be leaving again after we film this segment."

"Oh." This makes Holly feel strange. And helpless. How could two more strangers have landed on her island without her knowledge? What would the other islanders say if they knew how little control she actually has over this reality show?

"Anyway," Leanna continues. "After the judging, the winning team gets to eat a candlelit seafood dinner prepared by an award-winning chef from Miami. We're getting everything set up in the pleasure tent over there." She stretches one long arm, pointing at a large tent that's been constructed from two smaller ones.

Buckhunter snorts. "The 'pleasure tent'?"

"Mmhmm." Leanna is distracted as distant voices crackle in the earpiece of the headset around her neck. "Hold on." She puts the headset back on and listens for a minute, frowning. "Okay," she says, taking it off again. "Just some minor details."

"So, this dinner," Holly says, redirecting the conversation back to the pleasure tent.

"Right. Johannes Comedreu came by boat with the sandcastle judges," she says, turning her attention to the big tent.

Holly sways on her feet; the tally of unknown strangers on Christmas Key now stands at three.

"He's prepping right now if you want to take a peek at the tent," Leanna says, running a hand through her loose hair. "But if things run as long as they normally do, we might keep him here overnight. We promised him a room at the B&B, and I'm assuming there's still somewhere we can stick him? You can throw it on our bill," she adds hastily, not waiting for Holly to confirm whether or not they have a room for Johannes Comedreu. The Apple watch on Leanna's wrist buzzes, pulling her attention away from them again. "Anyhow, have a look around. But try to stay out of the way—we don't want to distract the contestants." Leanna is already staring at her watch and walking away from them, scratchy voices blaring from the headset as she goes. "Oh, and text me about the room at the inn!" she says over her shoulder, shielding her eyes from the sun.

Holly gives her a half-hearted thumbs-up.

"Shall we take a jaunt over to the pleasure tent, Mayor?" Buckhunter asks in a faux British accent. With a sigh of defeat, Holly falls into line behind him, following in the loose footprints his Birkenstocks leave in the sand.

"I think you should start referring to me as 'Mayoral Candidate' instead of 'Mayor,'" she says loudly. "Or maybe 'The Artist Formerly Known as Mayor,' because I've obviously lost control of this situation."

"Aww, don't be so hard on yourself, girl." Buckhunter tosses her a backwards glance. "Maybe Johannes Comedreu will give you a crab cake or something to cheer you up."

"Ha." Holly ducks under the flap of the giant tent behind Buckhunter and immediately stops in her tracks: an intimate table for two is set in the middle of the tent. It's covered with a snow-white table cloth, and gold-rimmed china rests on both place settings. The center of the table is filled with vanilla-scented candles and a tight bunch of ivory roses clipped short and studded with rhinestone stickpins. A gleaming guitar rests against a stool in one corner of the tent, and a sparkling chandelier is suspended from the tent's metal beam over the table. The delicate setting is a sharp juxtaposition to the ruggedness of the canvas tent, but it's so elegantly done that Holly half expects Martha Stewart to pop her head into the tent and ask if it needs a few more roses. The dreamy set-up is breathtaking enough to be a private wedding feast for a bride and groom, and in a heartbeat, Holly knows who will win the sandcastle challenge.

The clanging of pots and pans and a string of frustrated words in French rise from behind a modest partition in the tent. *"Mon dieu!"* a man shouts, slamming something metal.

"Let's go." Buckhunter grabs her elbow. "Johannes Comedreu sounds like he's not parting with any of his crab cakes, even for a Yankees fan." Holly holds onto her hat defensively as Buckhunter yanks her out of the tent and back onto the beach.

"So, do you want to stick around and watch these yahoos build Versailles out of sand, or should we split?" Buckhunter asks, hands on his hips as he looks around at the competitors digging in the sand.

"We should split, please. And get coffee."

"As you wish, madam." Buckhunter leads the way again. The crew is all heavily involved in filming the scene, and Leanna and Wayne stand shoulder to shoulder on the sand near the competitors and their creations.

Holly sneaks one last peek at Jake and Bridget just in time to see Jake jokingly hit Bridget on the butt with a firm cake of sand. They fall into one another, laughing. Holly's mouth drops open as she watches Bridget raise one hip alluringly and look over her shoulder at her own perfectly shaped, sand-dusted bottom.

"Keep walking, chicklet." Buckhunter follows her gaze and reaches out a hand to take hers and steer her away from the scene. "One foot in front of the other—there you go. Coffee awaits."

He leads Holly all the way to the cart and then drives her directly to Mistletoe Morning Brew. She stares into the distance the entire way, not saying a word.

Chapter Twelve

Bonnie's bungalow is tucked in behind a stand of palm trees, and the yard is staked with pink plastic flamingos in Santa hats. The inside of the house is layered in shades of yellow from butter to sunshine, and the walls are covered with framed black-and-white pictures taken by Bonnie's youngest son. A leopard-print throw rests casually over the arm of the couch in her front room.

"Now don't get your tinsel in a tangle over this, sugar," Bonnie advises, clearing a stack of cookbooks off the island in the middle of her kitchen so Holly can sit down and rest her elbows on the black quartz countertop. "I can see it all over your face, and going down this path is only going to get you into a whole heap of trouble—trust me." Bonnie sets the tea kettle on the stainless steel stove and twists the knob to turn on the burner.

"Please don't judge me, Bon. I never knew I had this, this—" she flails around for the right words, "—this ugly, jealous *beast* living inside me. This girl can't be more than five years younger than me, but when I look at her, suddenly I feel like an over-the-hill spinster. I'm a wrinkled old troll with teeth like yellow kernels of corn. And you should see her in a bikini—she's practically a Victoria's Secret model."

"Now you listen to me, and listen good," Bonnie says sharply, snapping a placemat in the air and setting it in front of Holly. "I would never judge you, honey—I think that goes without saying." Bonnie opens a white cabinet and chooses a heavy ceramic mug for the tea. "But you've got to find some peace with this." She searches for a suitable saucer and brings them both over to Holly, setting them on the placemat.

The kettle whistles and Bonnie pulls it off the burner. She hands Holly a container full of individual tea bags with flavor names like Passionate Peanut Butter Pie and Orange Jelly Donut.

"Are these flavors for real?" Holly picks one called Pineapple Papaya Margarita.

"Pretty much. Aren't they more fun than a barrel of monkeys?" Bonnie wrinkles her nose and sets the boiling water on a trivet in the middle of the island. "Milk or sugar?" she offers.

"No thanks." Holly chooses a packet of plain mint tea.

"I do think it's worth pointing out," Bonnie says, arching an eyebrow as she fills her own mug with hot water, "that what you're feeling right now is probably exactly what Jake was feeling when he saw you running around with River this summer."

Holly keeps her eyes on the tea bag as it bobs around in the cup of steaming water. "I tried my best not to rub his face in it. That was never my intention, you know."

"I know." Bonnie pats her hand. "And I'm sure they weren't engaging in foreplay on the beach today just to taunt you, honey. Jake probably used his manners and waited to untie her bikini top with his teeth until after you left."

Holly pushes her tea aside. "Well, that paints a nauseating picture."

"Good thing you chose the mint tea then, sugar, because I'm about to make you feel a little more queasy."

"How?" Holly's mood shifts from despondent to wary in an instant.

"Cookie?" Bonnie shoots her a nervous look, snapping the lid off the Tupperware container full of oatmeal raisin cookies that she's holding out like an olive branch. Holly takes one and sets it on her saucer. "Okay, you aren't going to want to hear this." Bonnie reaches across the island and takes Holly's hands in her own. "But your mother called today while you were out with Buckhunter."

"You're right," Holly says quickly. "I can taste the vomit already."

Bonnie holds tightly to both of Holly's hands. "She heard about Cap running for mayor, and she says it's one more sign that you aren't cut out for this. She thinks someone else could do it better, and she wants to come down over Thanksgiving to talk about the resort that's still interested in buying the island."

Holly lets go of Bonnie's hands and stands up, leaving her tea and cookie untouched. "But I know what I'm doing, Bon—why doesn't *anyone* think that I know what I'm doing?" She rubs her forehead with one hand, the other clamped on her waist below her ribcage, rubbing at the sudden pain shooting through her side. "I've got this handled."

"Okay, hon," Bonnie says soothingly, picking up her own cup by the handle and sipping the hot tea. "I believe in you. One hundred percent —you know that."

Holly knows Bonnie isn't pulling her leg, and she's grateful for the un-conditional support from her friend. "I have you, and I have Buckhunter and Fiona on my side, and…"

"And a lot of people." Bonnie sets the cup down on the saucer a little too loudly. "You've been running this island like a pro since your grand-father passed away, and no one has had any complaints to speak of until Cap got a bug up his butt about this whole mayor thing. Speaking of which, we still need to get to the bottom of his big secret," Bonnie says, wagging a finger as she talks. "The tantrum he threw at the village council meeting a couple of months ago about everyone having big se-crets has not been forgotten. At least not by me."

Holly relaxes, breathing through the stitch in her side. "Thanks, Bon. I know you've got my back."

"Of course I do," Bonnie insists. "We just need to eat this elephant one bite at a time."

"You're right." Holly sits down at the island again. "So what's the first bite?"

"Bite one is getting your hiney out of my kitchen and onto the beach." Bonnie points at Holly's beat up Converse tennis shoes, abandoned on the tile floor by the front door. Holly, Mrs. Agnelli, the triplets, and—recently—Bonnie, have been taking an early morning walk on the beach every Thursday since New Year's. They've postponed it until sunset today because of Holly's morning visit to the set, and Holly and Pucci have come by in the golf cart to pick up Bonnie. "Get your pup off my porch and let's do this, otherwise I'm sitting down on my lanai with a mystery novel and I'm not getting up again until bedtime."

"I'm ready." Holly takes one long sip of her tea and sets the cup and saucer in Bonnie's sink. "I need to get cussed out by Maria Agnelli like I need another man in my life, but let's do this."

The women leave the ceiling fans spinning throughout the bungalow. The back door to the lanai is open to let in the evening breeze, and the sound of rustling palm fronds fills the house.

Pucci hops onto the rear-facing seat of the golf cart and settles on the bench as Holly backs up onto the road, head craned to look over her shoulder.

"We're gonna get you some fresh air to clear your head, sugar. And then I want you to hurry on home and do that naked Skyping thing with old Slugger, you hear me?"

Holly's foot eases off the gas pedal as a surprised laugh overtakes her; it's the first real, easy feeling she's had all day. She looks over at Bonnie, whose face is one of complete innocence.

"I'm serious, sugar. In thirty years you two will be sitting in front of your computers in your birthday suits, and it won't be the same pretty picture as it is now." Bonnie sweeps a hand up and down in the air in front of Holly's body.

"Never in my life have I Skyped naked!" Holly says through her laughter. "I can't even imagine."

"Oooh, girl, you need to try it!" Bonnie pats Holly's thigh. "It can be *very* sexy."

"Wait—are you telling me..." Holly trails off. She can't even finish the sentence or the thought.

"I'm not telling you anything, Holly Jean—a lady never gives away her own secrets." Bonnie crosses one leg over the other, sitting as primly in the passenger seat of the golf cart as anyone ever has.

Holly casts a look in her friend's direction. "Well, well, well," she says, a knowing smirk on her face. "Wyatt Bender is one lucky man!"

A hint of horror passes across Bonnie's face. "You bite your tongue, missy. Wyatt Bender is most definitely *not* on the receiving end of a Skype call from yours truly."

"Oh?"

"But there are gentleman of a certain age in various parts of this fine country who've seen various parts of *my* fine anatomy, and that's all I can say about that."

"Well, Bon, that's good, because I think that's about all I can handle."

Chapter Thirteen

"I definitely *don't* want live turkeys!" Holly shouts down the hallway toward the back office of the B&B. She's rifling through the drawers behind the front desk, looking for the extra master key that opens every room in the hotel. "Make sure you tell them they'd better send us birds that are ready for the oven!"

Bonnie is still on the phone with the grocery store in Tampa, and her surprised laugh tells Holly everything she needs to know. She shuts the drawer and walks back to the office.

"So what's the verdict?"

Bonnie sets down the phone and pokes the end of her ballpoint pen into the pile of red curls on top of her head. "Well, sugar," she smiles sweetly, "looks like we're going to have some company for Marco."

"I don't think parrots and turkeys are natural bedfellows," Holly says, her brow creasing. "But my bigger concern is how we're going to turn ten live turkeys into Thanksgiving dinner by Thursday."

"Oh, honey, you got me there." Bonnie shakes her head. "The manager at the store said their organic farm specializes in shipping live birds, so the mistake has to be ours."

"Who would ever want live fowl showing up on their doorstep?" Holly walks to the window and stares out at the street. "Okay, we have to think." She rubs her forehead. "The boat gets here this evening, and we need to be prepared to take the shipment. So where should we put these birds while we figure out what to do?"

"I think you ought to go down and see Carrie-Anne and Ellen."

"Because I'm in the middle of a caffeine shortage?"

"No—I mean, a coffee wouldn't hurt at this point, but I was thinking about the pen they've been building for that damn donkey. I'm pretty sure it's done, and they might let you store your gobblers back there until we work something out."

Holly is already in the doorway by the time Bonnie stops talking. "You're right! Madonkey won't be here for a few more weeks. I'm on my way over. Want me to grab you a latte while I'm there?" She plucks her denim jacket from the hook by the door.

"Definitely. And pick up a couple of donuts, will you? I need some carbs and sugar, and it might be a good idea to run up a bill there before you ask them to be foster moms to ten turkeys."

"Good thinking."

Holly is out the door and down the street in under a minute, but she comes to a halt outside of Mistletoe Morning Brew when she spots Cap and Wyatt at a table under the awning.

"Top o' the mornin' to ya." Cap lifts his chin in her direction. He's sitting hunched over an iPad with Wyatt at his elbow. There are two cups of coffee on the small bistro table, and Marco is perched on Cap's left shoulder. "You ever seen one of these, Mayor?" He holds up the device for her inspection.

"Yeah, it's an iPad, Cap. I've got one at home." Holly breezes past the two men without further comment. She doesn't mean to sound so abrupt, but the live, un-plucked, un-gutted turkeys currently bobbing across the Gulf of Mexico are pecking away at the back of her brain, and she needs to work out their accommodations—immediately.

"Holly! Good to see you," Carrie-Anne says. She's picking up plates from around the coffee shop, holding a stack of crumb-covered dishes in one hand as she wipes down tables with the other.

"Hi, Carrie-Anne." Holly shoves her hands into the pockets of her jean jacket. "Can I get two iced lattes to go, please? And two chocolate donuts." She pauses, remembering Bonnie's advice to butter up the women before trying to dump her livestock on them. "And one blueberry muffin…two biscotti, and three almond croissants."

"You got it." Carrie-Anne sets the dishes in the sink behind the counter and wipes her hands on her apron.

"Nice shirt," Holly says. Edgar Allan Poe is stretched across Carrie-Anne's chest, and he's holding a mug of coffee to his lips with the words "Go ahead and Poe me another" scrawled beneath the picture.

"Thanks. Ellen designed them."

"Does that woman ever sleep?"

"Not much."

"Listen, Carrie-Anne…I have a favor to ask." Holly takes her wallet out of her purse.

"Hence the giant pastry order?" Carrie-Anne looks at Holly over her shoulder as she fixes the coffee drinks. "Okay, lay it on me."

"You know how we're doing a full turkey dinner in the B&B's dining room for pretty much everyone on the island? And another separate dinner to be cooked and delivered to the *Wild Tropics* set?"

"You want me to bring the stuffing?"

"Actually, it's a slightly bigger favor than that." She pauses for a second before plunging ahead. "I want to know if you and Ellen would be willing to hang onto the turkeys until—well, probably until Wednesday."

Carrie-Anne snaps lids onto the two iced coffees. "I don't think our fridge is nearly big enough to help you out there, kiddo."

"Okay, well, this is where it gets funny."

Carrie-Anne is using a pair of tongs to pick up the muffins, donuts, and biscotti. She sets each item gently into a pastry box before giving a simple "Oh?"

"Okay, so the place we ordered the birds from in Tampa is sort of a… well, it ships live turkeys from an organic farm."

"Live turkeys?" Carrie-Anne's smile fades. "You have *live* turkeys being shipped to the island?"

"Yeah," Holly confirms, peeling bills off the pile in her hand. "Ten of them."

"Fully-feathered, gobbling, strutting-around *turkeys*."

"Right. But that's not even the worst part."

Carrie-Anne folds the lid of the box and tucks the tabs into the sides. "Let me guess: no one knows how to wring their necks and pluck them?"

"Someone might." Holly's eyes are wide. She shoves a wad of cash across the counter at Carrie-Anne. "But I don't."

"So what you're asking me is if you can store them in Madonkey's pen, right?" Carrie-Anne blinks a few times as she processes the situation. She's endlessly amused by Holly's nickname for their soon-to-be pet, and insisted on calling the donkey by her new name the whole time she and Ellen worked to clear an area in their grass and construct a fenced-in pen. She'd even goaded Ellen into ordering her a t-shirt with "Madonkey's Mom" on the front when Ellen was designing the Poe shirts.

"Yep. That's pretty much what I'm asking." Holly slides the pastry box across the counter and sets her two coffee drinks on top of it so she can carry it all.

"Huh." Carrie-Anne puts both hands on her hips. "I guess that would be fine. But I do need to warn you about Ellen: you know she's an animal-lover of the first order, and she'll have those damn turkeys named by sundown. Trying to get them out of her hands so you can chop their heads off isn't going to be an easy task."

Holly's face goes white at the mention of chopping off turkey heads. "Got it."

Carrie-Anne tips her head from side-to-side. "Okay. As long as you know what we're in for, then I think it's fine."

Holly lifts the box and the coffees carefully, holding them to her chest. "Carrie-Anne, I never know what I'm in for. But I promise I won't ask for a favor like this again." She backs up to the front door, stepping aside to let Joe Sacamano into the coffee shop.

"'*Leave no black plume as a token of that lie thy soul hath spoken!*'" Carrie-Anne says dramatically, flinging her towel around as she speaks. Her lined face breaks into an amused grin. "Pretty good, huh?"

"Not bad. Poe would be impressed." The pastry box and the coffees shift precariously in Holly's hands. "I'll see you later on at your place after I pick up my shipment at the dock."

"You got it, Mayor."

* * *

The usual Christmas decorations that festoon houses, golf carts, front lawns, and all of Main Street are enough to thrill even the most casual Christmas-lover, but as soon as Thanksgiving rolls around, the *real* decorations come out. Garlands are pulled from closets to drape over the doorways all up and down Main, and wreaths are fluffed and hung from nearly every front door. The palm trees on all of the busy streets are wound with strings of solar-powered holiday lights, and everyone pitches in to cart the five-foot-tall wooden Nutcrackers and elves from the storage space in Poinsettia Plaza so they can hold court on the sidewalks until after the New Year.

The decorating has begun in earnest as Holly drives around the island with her cell phone tucked between her ear and her shoulder. She slows to wave at Ray and Millie as they twist red and white strings of tinsel together like long candy canes to wrap around the lampposts, and beeps her cart's horn at Jimmy Cafferkey as he tests a string of lights outside Poinsettia Plaza. Holly's got the turkeys arriving in just a couple of hours, and she has a call from her mother to return. All thoughts of ducking over to the *Wild Tropics* set for a visit have flown the coop.

To get the call out of the way, she picks up her cell phone and dials Coco as she drives.

"Mom," Holly says. "What can I do for you?" She turns the wheel of her cart and passes under a thick bough of fake pine needles studded with colorful glass ornaments. Buckhunter is standing on a tall ladder, tugging on one end of the bough to make sure it's fastened tightly to the lamppost.

"You know my parents ran fiber-optic cable out to that island, right? The phones should be working just fine." Holly can imagine her mother simmering while she waited for a return call from her only child. "Or maybe that receptionist of yours wrote my message on a bubble gum wrapper and then lost it."

"Bonnie gave me your message," Holly says, gritting her teeth. "But it's been one thing after another around here all day."

"Well, I'm glad you could squeeze me in somewhere," Coco says coolly. "I'm coming down for Thanksgiving and I'm not bringing Alan, so I can just stay at your house instead of at the B&B."

Holly jams on the brake and pulls over to the side of the sandy road. She's not far from the Jingle Bell Bistro, but the thought of her mother sleeping just feet from her own bedroom makes her feel lightheaded.

"Uh, I'm remodeling," she says, blurting out the first thing that comes to mind.

"Remodeling what?" Coco demands. "Didn't you just remodel when you moved in a couple of years ago?"

"The guest room is a wreck. I'm re-painting, and I had to take the bed frame apart to get it out of the room," Holly lies easily. The guest room is, in fact, lovely and untouched, painted a soft gray with white crown molding. Its perfectly-made bed is piled high with decorative throw pillows.

"Oh, okay." Coco sounds dubious. "Then book me a room at the B&B, I guess. I'll be there on Wednesday afternoon, and I'll stay until Sunday."

"Sure, Mom," Holly says. "But why are you coming?"

"Other than the fact that it's Thanksgiving and I want to spend it with my daughter?"

"Right. Other than that." The breeze coming from the water nearby blows through the tinsel that's wrapped around Holly's golf cart and sends small drifts of sand skittering across the makeshift road.

Coco sighs loudly. "You know, it would be nice if we could have one holiday together where everyone gets along, Holly. Will we be having turkey with the whole island as usual?"

It's amusing to Holly to hear her mother refer to something on the island happening "as usual." For the entirety of her life, Coco has come and gone from Christmas Key like the seasons, and it's hard to believe she has any idea how things normally run on the island.

"Yes, we'll have dinner at the B&B like we always do," she says carefully, "and then we have to make a separate dinner for the *Wild Tropics* crew."

"And this would be the television show that I didn't have any say about welcoming to our island?"

"This would be the one." Holly closes her eyes and prays for patience.

"I see. And is this show still dividing the island?"

Holly isn't sure how to answer that. "Dividing" is a strong word—surely Cap is opposed, Wyatt has decided to amuse himself by supporting Cap's displeasure, and several islanders are wondering when they'll get to make their star turn, but...*dividing* the island seems extreme. "Not at all," Holly says, blowing off her mother's concerns. "We're really enjoying having them here. But they have a closed set on the north side of the island, so we don't run into them much."

"I'll be curious to see the set for myself," Coco says. "Please arrange a visit for me. And don't forget to put me in a room at the B&B so I don't interrupt your *remodeling*," she says pointedly. "I'll see you on Wednesday."

Holly ends the call and sits there for another minute, listening to the waves. She needs to head over to the bistro and ask Jimmy and Iris Cafferkey if they'll help her prep the turkeys for dinner (and by "prep," she means "take them from alive and gobbling to buttered and ready for the oven"). She's not looking forward to yet another retelling of the story about the ten turkeys set to arrive on the island with all of their feathers intact, but she really needs Iris and Jimmy's help.

For the time being, Holly has to forget that Coco is coming down for Thanksgiving. Getting food on the table for Thursday's dinner is top priority, and making sure Ellen doesn't fall in love with her turkeys and stage a PETA-worthy protest on Main Street to keep them alive is her most pressing issue. Everything else—including Coco—will just have to wait.

Chapter Fourteen

"I'm pretty sure this counts as a hostage situation," Holly laments over the phone to River. "Carrie-Anne did warn me that this could happen, but I honestly thought—for once—that everything might go smoothly." She's standing on the pool deck at the B&B, peering between the layer of foliage that separates her from Main Street where Cap and Wyatt are holding up signs on sticks that say: 'Our Mayor is Boggled—She Wants These Gobblers Gobbled!' They've attached pictures of the ten turkeys strutting around in the pen at Carrie-Anne and Ellen's house, and now Wyatt and Cap are standing on the sidewalk, shouting at anyone who will listen.

People are stopping by to admire Cap's handiwork in front of North Star Cigars, shaking their heads and moving on after they've seen the photos. Holly can't tell if the head shakes are for her callousness towards the turkeys, or for Cap's ridiculous protest.

"It honestly sounds kind of funny," River admits, chuckling on the other end of the line.

"Did I mention that my mother is coming tonight?" Holly snaps.

"A couple of times. Listen, Hol—I think you need to march out there and remind them that a Thanksgiving dinner made up of just potatoes and stuffing isn't really a Thanksgiving dinner at all—it's a vegetarian snack. And hold your ground. These people have eaten turkey every year of their lives on Thanksgiving, and they need to be reminded that all those birds started out as live, feathered fowl before landing on their plates under a pile of gravy."

"It feels like everyone is turning on me all of a sudden, and I don't know why." Holly chews on her lower lip, watching Wyatt Bender as he stops Fiona on the sidewalk and tries to chat her up. She waves him off and keeps walking. "Except Fiona, and Buckhunter, and Bonnie," she amends.

"Come on—there are more people on Team Baxter than you know. Give yourself some credit."

"It's still pretty tempting to put on a wig, pack a bag, and jump onto the ferry tonight as my mother climbs off. I could be in Key West by nightfall, in Miami four or five hours later, and then on a flight across country in time to have Thanksgiving dinner in Oregon tomorrow."

"But you won't," he says gently.

"But I won't," Holly agrees. Responsibility, commitment, and loyalty will always keep her tethered to the island in the middle of a storm, though her mind easily plays out the fantasy. And she has to admit: the picture in her head is a nice one. She's never been to Oregon, but she imagines a snowy Thanksgiving in a log cabin with a roaring fire, River's family watching football together in matching knit sweaters, and hot toddies for all the grown-ups as they bundle up to make snow angels in the moonlight after dinner. She sighs. "I have to stay here."

"I know you do—I'd expect nothing less." He pauses on the other end of the line. "So here's my hang-up with getting down there," River says. "I'm fishing next week in that competition I told you about, and then we've got a tournament with the foster kids the next weekend. So right now I'm looking at about December twelfth. Approximately."

"To come here?" Holly lets go of the leaves she's been peering through and they fall closed. She plops down on a chair next to the pool.

"I can fly down for a couple of days, or stay through the holidays— whatever you want. There's a fishing tournament in Bimini on December tenth and eleventh. I figured that would get me down there and then I could write off the trip, but other than that, I'm all yours."

"You have no idea how good that sounds right now." Holly puts her feet up on the lounge chair and examines her tangerine-colored toenails.

"Catching fish in Bimini?" River jokes.

"No, having you here for most of December. Can you stay until New Year's?"

"Let me map it out, but I think it's a real possibility," he promises. "But now you need to get out there and face the music. Go face Cap head-on. You've got turkeys to pluck, young lady."

Holly makes a choking-vomiting sound before hanging up. She flexes her toes in her sandals, wiggling them and listening to the Calypso music coming from the speakers on the pool deck. River is right, and she knows it. Even if she won't be plucking the turkeys herself, she needs to get her butt in gear and get out there. Cap can't win this race by bullying her into hiding, but he can certainly make her life miserable in the weeks leading up to the vote.

Holly stands up and slips her phone into the back pocket of her white denim shorts. She leaves the pool deck through the side gate, ready to hit Main Street with dignity and grace.

But just to make sure the dignity and grace are evident to all, she spits her gum into the trash can by the gate on her way out.

* * *

"I don't know about everyone else, but I'll have an extra serving of that delicious turkey, Mayor!" Joe Sacamano calls out, slowing his golf cart to a crawl as Holly walks down the sidewalk to Mistletoe Morning

Brew. "Don't let Cap fool you: he wants a slice of that bird like he wants a glass of scotch," Joe says, throwing Cap and Wyatt a sidelong glance as they wave their handmade signs at him.

"Thanks, Joe," Holly says. She smiles weakly. "I'm working on Thanksgiving dinner, and I'm waiting for Coco to get here this evening."

Joe grimaces. "Oh, jeez, kid. All this and your mother too?"

"Well, the holidays are a glorious time for family and fellowship," Holly doesn't break her stride, and Joe continues to roll along the center of Main Street, keeping pace with her.

"Well, let me know if there's anything I can do to help." Joe steps on the gas and waves as he drives on. He makes a left turn onto Pine Cone Boulevard and disappears from view.

Inside Mistletoe Morning Brew, Carrie-Anne is sitting at a table, filling metal boxes with paper napkins. She holds up a hand in Holly's direction. "Honey, you can't say I didn't warn you," Carrie-Anne says, shaking her head as she stuffs a napkin box.

"Oh, Holly, good—you're here," Ellen says breathlessly, hurrying out from the back room. She's wearing a light pink t-shirt with Edgar Allan Poe's face transposed onto a lumpy potato, mustache and all. The words across the top of the shirt say: "Poe-tay-toe, Poe-tah-toe."

"Ellen—" Holly starts.

"You can't, you just *can't*," Ellen pleads. Her eyes are watery, and her dark curls are pinned up in a loose pile on the crown of her head. The silver trinkets dangling from her earrings make a light tinkling sound as she shakes her head pitifully.

"They've got names," Carrie-Anne warns from her spot at the table. She clicks the front of the napkin dispenser closed, then opens another.

"They do!" Ellen says urgently. "Trixie and Troy and Godiva, and then there's Monty and Prince and—"

"Prince?" Holly interrupts. "You've got a turkey named Prince, and a donkey named Madonna?"

"We're adopting a turtle named Cyndi Lauper next month," Carrie-Anne says, still focused on her napkins.

"Seriously?" Holly snorts.

"No. She's joking," Ellen says with irritation. "But we need to focus on the turkeys right now," she begs. "Tomorrow is Thanksgiving!"

"I know, I know—that's why I'm here," Holly says in her most soothing voice. The older woman looks like she's on the verge of hysteria, and her words are high-pitched and frantic. Holly reaches out a hand to touch Ellen on the arm.

"We can't do this," Ellen says. "I've stood by and kept my mouth shut for years because I know people don't want to have some crazy vegetarian lady preaching to them while they eat their steaks and pork chops, but these are beautiful animals with *faces*, Holly. They've got *souls*." Ellen's eyes are warm and soft, her kindness radiating from within as she begs for the lives of a bunch of helpless turkeys. And just like that, Holly's resolve crumbles. The image of bloody feathers and skinned birds is actually making her a little sick, and she sinks into the nearest chair, ready to consider their options.

Ellen has both of her hands on the sides of her head, and her forehead has collapsed into an accordion of worried wrinkles. "I have other ideas. Will you just hear me out?"

Holly nods. "I'll listen, but I have no idea how we're going to make a vegetarian Thanksgiving dinner for the entire island *and* for the crew and competitors of the show. We only have twenty-four hours."

"Really? But you'll consider it?" Ellen sits in the chair across from Holly. The Poe-tay-toe face on her shirt stares at Holly with a haughty, judgmental glare that makes her look away; even in potato form, Poe is formidable, and she hates being judged by a dead guy who married his own thirteen-year-old cousin.

Ellen wastes no time laying out her plan. "Okay, I took the liberty of ordering enough ingredients the night you dropped the birds off at our place. Everything is coming on the delivery boat tonight. If we get together a small team of chefs, we can whip up something that will blow your mind—I promise! Oh, Holly, thank you for hearing me out on this!"

Holly isn't convinced that they're about to wow their neighbors with a Thanksgiving feast of beansprout loaves and chickpea rolls with meatless gravy, but she is worn down by the prospect of what will have to happen next if they plan on eating turkey. "No problem," she sighs.

"This is incredible!" Ellen shouts, clapping her hands together and standing up. "I hope the turkeys won't mind living with a donkey," she adds as an afterthought, already making her way back to the office behind the front counter.

"You do realize that we're now the proud owners of ten chatty birds that can live up to a decade if cared for correctly, right?" Carrie-Anne turns to Holly, resting her elbow on the back of the chair she's sitting in. "And we're about to add a donkey to our brood, which means we'll be running a mini-farm over at our place."

"You could probably classify it as a petting zoo," Holly offers helpfully. There's a part of her that's relieved to have the turkey drama over with, even though Carrie-Anne will give her a hard time about it for years to come.

"Ah, well, what are you gonna do?" Carrie-Anne smiles. Her eyes are tired, but it's obvious that she's amused by the whole situation. "Ellen loves animals. And a happy wife means a happy life, so…"

"Thanks, Carrie-Anne." Holly stands up and pushes her chair in. "I need to go and tell Cap to stand down with his 'meat is murder' sign, and then I have a boat to meet at the dock, which will be delivering both my mother and about two hundred pounds of Tofurkey."

Carrie-Anne laughs to herself, tearing the paper wrapper off another stack of napkins to load into the dispensers spread out before her on the table. "I'm not sure who has it worse right now, chickadee. I actually think it might be you."

Chapter Fifteen

"I don't know why you'd want to keep subjecting yourself to this chaos," Coco says, her hands covered in mashed sweet potatoes on Thanksgiving morning. Holly's brief vacation from all things Coco has ended abruptly (they'd essentially stopped talking after Coco's visit during the summer, and Holly has been referring all emails from her mother to her lawyer since then). But Coco had arrived on the ferry at five o'clock the night before, and she'd immediately demanded to be driven to Holly's bungalow to see the remodeling that was preventing her from staying with her daughter.

Knowing how important it is to stay one step ahead of Coco, Holly had dispatched Buckhunter to her house while she ran errands, and he'd handily dismantled the guest room bed frame, spread some tools around, and slapped blue painter's tape on the trim around the doors and windows. When she'd walked into the room with Coco in tow, Holly had momentarily forgotten that she wasn't really about to paint the room and blow out a wall or two.

"I keep subjecting myself to this chaos because this is my life, and it makes me happy," Holly says, reaching across her mother in the busy kitchen of the B&B to pick up a paring knife for the apples she's peeling.

Coco wipes her brow with the back of one hand, leaving a smear of rust-colored potato on her forehead. "But I could make all of this nonsense go away, Holly," she says through clenched teeth. "Why won't you even consider the idea of a resort coming in and taking over? Think of the *money* you'll walk away with…and the *freedom*."

Coco has wasted no time laying into Holly with her usual rhetoric about how ill-equipped a thirty-year-old woman is to run an entire island. It always comes down to that, and it's a battle they've engaged in more times than Holly cares to count.

"I don't want my freedom," Holly says stubbornly. A long ribbon of bright green apple skin falls into the silver mixing bowl she's using to catch the shavings. "I want my island."

"Tell me what's going on with the men in your life," Coco demands, shifting the subject. The sharp turn in the conversation doesn't fool Holly; this tactic will no doubt lead back to all the reasons why Holly needs to give up the island and focus her efforts on finding a husband and having a family.

"There's not much to tell." Holly walks to the end of the counter to dump the silver bowl into an open trash can. The kitchen is full of islanders in various stages of food prep. Ellen has—as promised—taken charge of the main course assembly, and Holly is keeping one eye on the "magic vegan loaf" that's coming out of the oven in bread pans and being doused liberally with mushroom gravy.

"Is Jake going to be at dinner tonight?" Coco takes her hands out of the bowl she's using and inspects her French manicure.

"No, Mom, he's not."

"Holly?" Maria Agnelli approaches the counter where Holly and Coco are working together. "What do you think of me making a few bologna sandwiches on the side? I'm not sure anyone is going to touch that garbage over there." She lifts her chin and nods at the cashews, cooked lentils, and chopped celery that Ellen is running through a food processor for her next vegan loaf.

"That might not be a bad idea, Mrs. Agnelli," Holly says kindly. "Why don't you run home and make those sandwiches, and we can have them on hand here in case anyone passes on the Tofurkey and vegan loaf?"

"Fine. That's what I'll do." She turns to Coco. "So, did you hear about this television program your daughter brought out here? Half-cocked show, if you ask me—they haven't even come and filmed any of us yet. I got people waiting to see me on TV, and I don't even know what to tell them," she complains, one shaky, veined hand resting on the stainless steel counter for support.

"Tell them your mayor is trying her hardest to do right by everyone," Coco says firmly, turning the bowl of sweet potatoes upside down and using a spatula to transfer them into a serving dish.

Holly stops what she's doing and looks at her mother with unmasked confusion. Is Coco *defending* her? Has the planet just stopped spinning on its axis and turned into a giant, glittering disco ball in the sky?

"Well," Mrs. Agnelli huffs. "*Jake* gets to be on the show. He up and left us with no cop to protect us, *and* he gets to be famous."

"There's absolutely nothing for Jake to protect you from, Maria, and I'm sure Holly has her reasons for whatever she's doing," Coco says calmly, covering the potato dish with aluminum foil. "Now, why don't you go and make those sandwiches?"

Mrs. Agnelli stands there, looking back and forth between Holly and Coco like she isn't sure what to say. Finally, she totters off to repeat her complaints about the reality show to Bonnie and the triplets.

In the silence that follows Mrs. Agnelli's departure, Holly pretends not to be surprised by her mother's support. "Thanks," she says casually, going back to peeling her apples for the Waldorf salad.

"I don't have to agree with what you're doing around here," Coco says. "But if anyone's going to henpeck you and call you an idiot, it's going to be *me.*"

Holly smirks to herself as Coco walks the potatoes over to the industrial-sized refrigerator and sets them on a shelf.

"Sugar!" Bonnie shouts from across the kitchen. She's standing with Glen, Gen, and Gwen, chopping and assembling side dishes as rapidly as possible. "Your phone is ringing!" Bonnie's hands are covered in a paste of water and dried flour, but she nods her head at Holly's cell phone, which is resting on the windowsill in a patch of early morning sunlight.

Holly drops the apple she's working on and wipes her hands on the front of her jeans as she hurries to answer her phone. It's Leanna.

"Hello?"

"Happy Thanksgiving! How's the feast coming?" Leanna sounds annoyingly cheerful.

"Great. We've been in the kitchen since six this morning, and there are about twelve of us working on sides and the main dish."

"The turkey? Will it be camera-ready? Because I'm thinking we should get it all set up on the table and get a long shot from one end. The perfectly cooked turkey will be the focal point. God, it's making me hungry just thinking about it, and I know the contestants are *starving.* But let's not carve it until we get the shot, okay?"

"About the turkey…" Holly glances at the fourteen vegan loaves cooling on a baking rack. "There's been a change of plans."

Leanna is silent on the other end of the line.

"Anyway," Holly says, filling in the gap. "We're trying something new this year: a healthy, vegetarian Thanksgiving." She sounds like a hostess on a late-night infomercial: *New, improved, great for your health and your waistline—a VEGETARIAN THANKSGIVING!*

"But, *Holly.*" Leanna sounds perplexed. "The contestants have been living on rice, nuts, and beans for almost two weeks now," she says flatly. "We promised them a full Thanksgiving dinner with all the fixings. Not to mention the crew. We need a turkey."

"I'm sorry. There were some unexpected obstacles here." Holly doesn't want to bring up the fact that ten perfectly good turkeys with names like Trixie, Prince, and Godiva have narrowly escaped becoming the glistening, cooked birds Leanna is envisioning on the dinner table in her perfect shot and are now happily ensconced in a donkey pen on the island.

"That's disappointing," Leanna says, pausing. "Okay." She changes gears optimistically. "Let me try to spin that. And while I have you, I really need to talk to you about Jake."

"Oh?" Holly glances around the kitchen, feeling guilty because of the way her heart leaps at the mention of Jake's name. She looks at her feet.

"Yeah," Leanna puts a hand over the receiver, muffling the sound. "Hold on, Holly, let me walk a few feet away here."

With a sharp knife, Bonnie scrapes some chopped herbs from her cutting board into a bowl on the counter. It's a bright, sunny Thanksgiving morning, and the light streaming in through the windows over the sink glints off the edge of Bonnie's knife.

"Things are getting heated with Bridget and Jake," Leanna says excitedly, her voice lowered. "It's going even better than we'd hoped. But I need some info on Jake that we can use, and I feel like you're my gal."

"I don't know if I really have any of the information you'd want." Holly closes her eyes as she stands there, preparing for what she knows is coming next.

"I bet you do," Leanna counters. "Do you have a key to his house?"

"What?" Holly sucks in a sharp breath. "No, I don't have a key." She doesn't mention the fact that someone locking their house on Christmas

Key is almost unheard of, and that she could simply walk through the front door of Jake's house if she wanted to.

"I need some pictures of his life: his family, his house, what's in his fridge. High school or college diplomas—anything we can feed to Bridget so they'll find even more common ground than they already have."

The room brightens considerably in her field of vision, and Holly feels faint. Nothing about this sounds right. Bonnie has stopped what she's doing and is staring openly at Holly. "I don't...I can't..."

"Holly," Leanna's says curtly. "I'm about to tell a group of starving, homesick, overtired adults that the juicy slab of turkey they've been promised is now a pile of rice and beans with steamed asparagus on the side. I'm going to cover your tail with the network when we have to readjust our expectations on a dime, and now you're telling me you can't help me out with a little information?"

"But that's his private life," Holly argues.

"I'm not asking you to take pictures of his bank statements or his un-derwear drawer. You aren't 007, you're just walking in and snapping a few shots of the pictures he keeps on his dresser." Leanna's words are tinged with the defiance of a woman who isn't used to hearing the word *No*. "I really need you over to the set by ten o'clock with some informa-tion I can use."

"I'm at the B&B working in the kitchen now," Holly says, as if the Thanksgiving prep can't go on without her.

"Fine. So hand someone else the potato masher, and drive over to his place. Break a window or something. The network will pay to have it re-placed before he leaves the set. He'll never even know it happened."

But I'll know, Holly wants to say.

"Look, this is how it works, Holly. You scratch my back, I'll scratch yours. You bring me a picture of Jake and his favorite sister, and I'll tell the network that a vegetarian Thanksgiving dinner is a great opportunity for them to approach Gardenburger or Kashi Foods about running ads during this episode. That way everybody gets what they want, and there's no love lost. Got it?"

Holly nods, unable to speak.

"See you over here at ten?"

"Okay. See you at ten." She ends the call.

* * *

There's a stillness in the house that makes Holly want to throw the windows open to the salty ocean air. Against all of her better judgments —against the voices screaming at her inside her head *not* to do it—she's let herself in through Jake's sliding back door, and she's standing in the middle of his tidy living room, looking around. The air is off, as are the ceiling fans, and the only sound is the hum of the refrigerator in the kitchen. All of his curtains are closed, and it feels wrong to disturb Jake's house any more than she has to.

Even with Leanna's assurance that they aren't expecting 007-level spy tactics, Holly still feels like she's doing something that might get her into serious trouble. She creeps into the hallway and back to Jake's room, holding her breath the entire time. The bed is made, and she stands in the doorway, staring at the leopard-print pillowcases that match the sheet she wore as a Halloween costume not even a month ago. On his night-stand is a book, and she lifts it gently in the dim room.

The book she's holding is a hardcover copy of John Grisham's latest. She flips it over to read the back cover; it's typical Jake reading. She sets it down again. On top of his dresser is a wooden box with a broken lock. Holly already knows this is where he keeps his most valuable possessions, but she opens the lid reverently with both hands anyway, looking in at the items he's carefully laid inside.

Holly takes out the large, gold ring that belonged to Jake's grandfather, inspecting the words etched on the metal that would have touched Grandpa Vito Zavaroni's skin. In a light, worn-down cursive script are the words *It Was Ever Thus*. Holly traces the lettering with the pad of her index finger before she sets it back inside the box. Next to the ring is a broken watch. The heft of it—the weight of the cool metal—is heavy in Holly's palm as she inspects the cracked face. The hands rest eternally at 5:13. This is the watch that Jake's best friend Adam had on his wrist when he was killed in a car accident just before their high school graduation. Holly knows that Adam's mom gifted it to Jake when he decided to join the police academy, telling him that it was his reminder to stop as many drunk drivers as he could. Jake's decision to become a police officer had, in fact, been inspired by Adam's loss, and she knew the watch meant everything to him.

She sets the timepiece back in the box and pulls out a stack of black-and-white photos, faded polaroids, and concert ticket stubs. There's a photo of Grandpa Vito and Grandma Louisa on their wedding day, the gold wedding ring visible on Vito's left hand. The polaroids are of a young, tanned Jake playing and riding his bike in front of his stucco house in Miami with his brother. There's a high school dance photo tucked into the pile that shows Jake with thick, wavy hair and shiny black shoes, looking sharp in a white tuxedo while his blonde date places her manicured hand protectively on his lapel. The girl is pretty: tall, with toned legs and a shiny, mint-green prom dress. She looks like the kind of girl who would have been Jake's first love. Holly shuffles the photos, smiling at the ticket stubs from Green Day, the Beastie Boys, and (inexplicably) Goo Goo Dolls concerts.

Holly arranges the keepsakes just the way she found them and sets them back into the box, closing the lid.

In the kitchen she quietly opens and closes cupboards, mentally cataloguing the half-eaten box of Raisin Bran, the unopened bag of Doritos, and the collection of mismatched drinking glasses on one shelf. Holly hates herself for being in Jake's house uninvited, but Leanna's tone made it clear that her visitation rights to the set could easily be revoked if she didn't make her Thanksgiving dinner snafu right by digging up some usable information on Jake. Which she still hasn't done.

In the living room is a stack of newspapers and magazines. Holly pulls her phone out of her purse and spreads the copies of *Sports Illustrated* and *Popular Science* across the coffee table. She snaps a picture before putting the pile back together. She's always been amused by Jake's wide interests, and she flips through an issue of *Popular Science*, noting that he's folded over the corner of a page with an article about robots.

For good measure, Holly circles back and takes a picture of the John Grisham book on Jake's nightstand, and another of the Christmas card photo of his sister's kids on the front of his refrigerator. There's so much more to Jake than this small collection of cute nieces and nephews, reading material, and pantry items, but there's no way she's going to tell Leanna anything that's truly important about Jake. Nothing about this mission feels right to her, and she tries to squash the feeling in the pit of her stomach that's been nagging her since she stepped through his door.

* * *

Leanna latches on to Holly's elbow the second she steps onto the sand. "What did you get?" she hisses, guiding her away from the cast and crew.

Holly stumbles as she tries to keep up with Leanna. "I didn't really…"

"I need to give Bridget *something* she can use to connect with him." They duck behind a tent and Leanna holds out a hand for Holly's phone. "Did you get pictures?"

"I got a couple, but I don't think there's anything interesting. He's a pretty boring guy."

Leanna snorts. "Boring? We've got some footage of him and Bridget down by the water the other night that didn't seem boring at all, if you know what I mean."

Holly knows what she means. Memories of a steamy summer slow dance she shared with Jake at the water's edge outside the Ho Ho Hideaway flood her mind. And then the guilty reminder that she's semi-al-most-completely attached to River follows closely on the heels of the first memory. Why does she care so much about Jake and Bridget? She doesn't—she *can't*. Holly squares her shoulders, ready to give Leanna something she can cut her teeth on.

"Okay, he's not completely boring, but there are no skeletons in the closet, so to speak. He reads stuff like John Grisham, he likes cereal, and his favorite movie is *Scarface*."

Leanna is listening intently.

"He likes to walk around the house shirtless after work, and he snores when it gets too hot in the bedroom. He hates to balance his checkbook, and he loves to chew on the ice at the bottom of his drink." These random details are tumbling out of her mouth before she even realizes that she's giving bits and pieces of Jake away.

"Ice…I can use that," Leanna says. She rests her long fingertips against her lips. "And the rest of it is good, too. How about other weird things— quirks or eccentricities?"

"Quirks?" Holly pretends to ponder the question. She desperately wants to stop giving Leanna info about her ex-boyfriend, but the vision of dry vegan protein loaves drowned in a grayish vegetable gravy instead of a juicy turkey for the cast and crew snaps her back to reality. She needs to hold up her end of the bargain so Leanna will smooth that over for her—or she at least needs to *pretend* to hold up her end of the bargain. "Well, I don't know if you'd consider this quirky, but he does like to visit this lady named Lola whenever he's in Miami—she lives in Little Havana," Holly says, warming up to the idea of embellishment.

"Okay. Go on."

"She's a psychic or something—maybe a card-reader. He won't talk about it, but he swears she's helped him make some of his biggest life choices."

"So he's into metaphysical things. I didn't see that coming," Leanna says as she stares off into the distance.

"Oh, and he loves the Bee Gees. And the Carpenters." She's hesitant to stretch it too far. "Really any 70s music." In truth, Jake despises the music that reminds him "of being a kid in the backseat of a station wagon, listening to AM radio and getting carsick." In his book, that means anything from before about 1985.

"The Carpenters," Leanna says, puckering her lips. "Okay. If you say so. From the things you're telling me, he sounds more...I don't know—"

"Quirky?" Holly offers.

"Yeah, I guess he's more quirky than I thought."

"Quirky is his middle name!" Holly gives Leanna a big, sunny grin. "Plus, he always plays the same numbers in the lottery, he can't go to bed without tapping on his nightstand three times, and he thinks it's bad luck when the Yankees win, so he won't leave the house the next day just in case something falls on his head."

"So he's superstitious?"

"Oh, very. A real odd duck, that one." Holly isn't sure why this need to throw a protective forcefield around Jake is so strong, but she's going with her gut here.

"Okay," Leanna says. "This is good info—thank you." She starts to walk across the sand, assuming that Holly is going to follow. "They're over there in that little patch of forest—it's where we let the competitors hold their tribal council meetings."

"Ah," Holly says, as if she has any clue what a tribal council meeting is. She imagines it vaguely resembles the island's village council meetings —only the participants are clad in loincloths and warpaint instead of cardigans and BenGay. "What time is dinner?"

"We've got the table set up over there." Leanna points at a long dining room table covered with a pumpkin-colored tablecloth that's rippling in the breeze. Centerpieces and silver dome-covered dishes anchor the fabric so that it won't blow away. "All we need is the food, so you tell us what time we're looking at and we'll make it work."

Holly consults her watch, keeping one eye on the area where the tribal council meeting is taking place. "When I left the kitchen it looked like things were in full-swing. It's almost eleven now, so how about if we aim for three?"

"Sure." Leanna pulls out her phone and starts texting.

"We can bring everything out here, but where are the contestants going to think it all came from? I thought we were promoting the illusion of a deserted island."

Leanna sends her message and waves a hand through the air. "They're so hungry they probably won't even ask. Most of them have only had rice for the past four days, so they might be hallucinating by this point anyway."

Holly's heart sinks. After four days of rice, a succulent slice of juicy turkey smothered in rich gravy would have hit the spot for these people. But even though he might be starving now, after it's all said and done, Holly knows Jake will be at least mildly amused by the fates of Godiva, Trixie, Prince, and the rest of the turkeys.

"Got it. Buckhunter and I will bring it all over, but I'll text you first—we can meet you where I parked today," Holly says, pointing into the distance. "And then we can help you carry it in. They've seen both of us before, so that should be fine, right?"

"That works," Leanna says, motioning to the cameraman who's setting up near the dinner table. "I'll wait to hear from you." Holly takes her in from head to toe: hair wavy and un-styled, feet bare in the sand, the ever-present waist pack slung over her narrow hips. Less than a month on Christmas Key and she's already morphed into an island girl. "Oh," Leanna turns back, sun glinting off the lenses of her shades, "thanks again for the info!" She gives Holly a thumbs-up.

Holly sticks her own thumb up in response, but it feels false. She may have thrown Leanna off for a little while, but she knows this business with Jake and Bridget is far from over.

Chapter Sixteen

After a day of mad prep and crazed scrambling to make sure every-thing is hot and ready to order, Holly and Buckhunter drive the loaded-down golf cart to the set of the show. They carry twenty-four separate dishes over the sand and to the dining table on the beach, and explain to the hungry and disappointed crew members that it's a meat-free dinner.

By four o'clock the sun is sinking low over the water and Holly is ex-hausted. And sweaty. Her hair is plastered to the sides of her head, and she's already regretted wearing jeans about eighteen different times since the day started.

"Drop me off at the B&B," Buckhunter says, his knee sticking out the passenger side of the golf cart as he rides along. "You run home for a quick shower. I'll tell everyone you forgot to leave the serving spoons with the food and you had to go back."

"You'd lie for me?"

"What are uncles for?"

"I'm still trying to figure that out."

Buckhunter pats his niece on the knee as she drives. "Same here. Now go."

After a quick date with some hot water and a bar of soap, Holly puts on a floor-length dress and tops it with a denim jacket. She rolls up the sleeves and adds a few silver bangles to her wrists.

"You think this'll work, Pooch?" she asks Pucci, who sits on the rug near the foot of her bed. His golden head rests on outstretched front paws, and he raises one ear in response.

Since it's Thanksgiving, Holly adds the diamond stud earrings that belonged to her grandmother, and a pair of sandals. As she swipes on light pink lip gloss, she stares at her own reflection in the bathroom mirror. There's a strange moment of uncertainty—a disconcerting unfamiliarity with the face that looks back at her. Who *is* this woman? If she'll walk into her ex-boyfriend's house—uninvited—and invade his personal space to save her own tail, then who is she at her very core? There's a part of her that wants to sweep the whole incident under the rug, to forgive a minor (God, she hopes it's minor) transgression like shuffling through Jake's belongings when, in the end, she's only trying to protect him with a few harmless lies while she figures out Leanna's end game.

In the short term, at least, it's obvious that the producers of the show want to manufacture a romance between their two most attractive competitors, but what will that mean for Jake in the long run? If only the term "romantically savvy" applied to him, then Holly would back off and let it play out organically—but Jake's not suave and calculating when it comes to matters of the heart, not in the least—and it hurts her to picture him being used and thrown away when they're done with this particular plot line.

She tosses the lip gloss into her make-up drawer and runs a hand over her smooth forehead. Things had seemed complicated with both River and Jake underfoot during the summer, but somehow they seem even more complicated now when neither of them is even within arm's reach. She shuts the drawer with her hip and runs a finger along the side of her mouth to pick up a stray dab of lip gloss.

"Be good while I'm gone, Pooch!" she calls to her dog from the driveway as she puts the cart in reverse. Pucci stands next to his silver water dish on the stairs, pink tongue hanging over the side of his mouth expectantly as his mistress backs up over crackling leaves and shells.

"Stay here, boy—I'll bring you back some pine nut loaf and a side of quinoa stuffing!" Holly shouts. Pucci sits down on the top step, his head sinking onto his front paws again as he takes up his position as sentry on the front porch.

* * *

"Honey, it all looks delicious," Bonnie says, looping one arm through Holly's as they enter the B&B's dining room together. Thanksgiving dinner is spread on a table on the far side of the room, buffet-style. The table is laden with gleaming serving dishes and clean china and flatware, and the round tables are topped with cream-colored tablecloths and gold runners. In the center of each table is a cut-glass vase with a miniature palm frond and a few tropical flowers. It's simple, but lovely.

"Even the Tofurkey?" Holly nudges Bonnie's arm with her elbow.

"I don't know what the hell a Tofurkey is made of, doll, but even that mess looks at least reasonably palatable."

"Hey, reasonably palatable works for me," Holly says, waving at Fiona, her silver bracelets jingling as she does. Fiona is talking to the triplets near the buffet table. Holly spots Coco making small talk with a couple of people near a window and turns her back on her mother so that they can't make eye contact. "Is Cap here?" she asks Bonnie in a low voice. But before Bonnie can answer, Cap himself lumbers into the dining room, shaking hands and cracking jokes with everyone he sees.

"Holly!" he says, approaching her with Wyatt Bender at his side. "Happy Thanksgiving." Cap offers her a hand. She hesitates briefly before accepting it. It's Thanksgiving, and she won't be unsettled by Cap on a day when she should be breaking bread and sharing joy with her neighbors.

"You too," she says, trying not to feel guarded.

"As I say every year, this feast is one of my favorite ways to celebrate island life and my wonderful neighbors, and I thank you for coordinating it and putting it on." His tone is jovial and sober, and he sounds entirely like the old Cap—the one who didn't slosh around the island, pickled in gin and ready to lash out with a sharp tongue.

"You're welcome," she says, giving Cap a long look before turning to Wyatt. "And Mr. Bender, how long will we be enjoying your company this year—for the whole season?"

"Oh, you know me, Mayor, I'm just like every other snowbird in the Sunshine State. I migrate down here on October first like clockwork, feather my nest until Easter, then head back to Texas to check on my grandkids and my land. Been doing it every year since 1993, and I'll keep doing it until the good Lord calls me home."

Wyatt is holding his cowboy hat over his heart earnestly. His salt-and-pepper hair is combed back with some sort of tonic that makes it look slightly wet, and his aftershave smells expensive and woodsy. The look on Bonnie's face has gone from steely to seductive in under ninety seconds, and Holly can tell that her friend has caught a dangerous whiff of Wyatt's cologne and pheromones. Holly reaches over and grabs Bonnie's forearm casually to keep her from falling face-first into Wyatt.

"Anyhow," Cap interjects. "I wanted to let you know that all talk of politics and civil unrest is suspended for tonight. This is a holiday for all of us."

When Holly doesn't answer right away, Bonnie bumps into her subtly.

"Right. Yes. Happy Thanksgiving," Holly says, nodding at both men as they walk away.

"Well, I'll be damned, sugar. Cap Duncan just acted human for the first time in six months."

"He was almost like the old Cap," Holly says. "Almost—but not quite."

"Maybe if we steer him away from the sauce and keep him sober all night, he'll stay civil until the pumpkin pie is served," Bonnie says.

"I say let's enjoy it while it lasts."

"Ladies!" Fiona says, a glass of wine in each hand as she approaches. "Happy Thanksgiving. Everything smells wonderful."

"Who knew you could throw a bunch of vegetables and some walnuts into a blender, slop it into a meatloaf pan, and turn it into dinner?" Holly says, taking the glass of wine that Fiona offers her.

"I only had two hands, Bon. Let me grab you a glass of wine," Fiona says, ready to go pour another glass.

"No, doll, I'm fine. Listen, I forgot to mention something to Mr. Bender about his Coco Plum bush—it's so overgrown that I can't see around it when I try to turn onto Ivy Lane. I nearly ran smack into Heddie with my cart the other day! I'll catch back up with you ladies in a bit." She winks at the younger women and saunters away, holding up a hand to get Wyatt's attention from across the room.

"And off she goes to get a little more face-time with Mr. Oil Tycoon himself," Fiona says, pressing her arm against Holly's as they stand to-gether. They watch Bonnie sidle up to Wyatt at the table they've set up like a mini-bar. He picks up a bottle of white wine and pours a glass for himself and one for Bonnie, smiling at her indulgently. "It's funny how a woman with eyes for every man suddenly only has eyes for one man when October rolls around and Wyatt sails into town."

"Hey, can I talk to you?" Holly asks, changing the subject without warning.

"What's up?"

"I think I did something crazy."

"Wouldn't be the first time, but lucky for you, I like crazy." Fiona clinks her wine glass against Holly's and takes a sip.

"It was slightly more crazy than usual." She fills Fiona in on all the details about Jake and Bridget, and about Leanna's request for information that might help Bridget get closer to Jake. She explains why she broke into Jake's house, and tells her about Leanna's "deal" to smooth things over with the network after the less-than-delectable Thanksgiving dinner as long as Holly gives her the info she wants.

Fiona swirls the wine around in her glass. "That sounds like blackmail, Hol. And not even good blackmail." Her upper lip curls in disgust. "She really asked you to do a B&E and betray your ex just because you decided not to slaughter some turkeys? That seems extreme."

"I know. It was dumb—I see that now. I mean, what's the worst they could have done to me? They're already here and filming, so it's not like they'd pull the show over a lackluster Thanksgiving dinner. I panicked. What should I do now?"

"You should watch out for her. And don't let her hornswoggle you into doing anything else you don't feel good about, because if there's one thing I know about this island after being here for a couple of years, it's that we take care of our own. And even if he's not *yours*, Jake is still *ours*."

Holly nods grimly. She knows Fiona has hit the nail on the head.

"Now let's get in line with everyone else and fill our plates with bark chips and gravy, then when all of these people have gone home, we can make bacon and eggs in the kitchen like we did on Halloween, and I can tell you how great things are between me and Buckhunter."

Holly throws an arm around Fiona's shoulders and makes a face like she can't bear to hear anything too gooey and romantic about her own uncle.

"Oh, come on, you big lug," Fiona teases, looking up at her tall friend. "If we hurry, maybe we can score a table all the way across the room from your mom."

"Dr. Potts, you're my hero," she says in the adoring voice of a love-struck teenager.

Fiona wrinkles her nose as they fall into the line for the buffet that snakes through the dining room. "Did you seriously tell her that Jake goes to a psychic and listens to the Carpenters? Because he would die if he thought anyone had him pegged as a mystic with a collection of cheesy 70s vinyl."

"Hey," Holly says, holding up her wineglass in a little toast to her own creativity. "A girl's gotta do what a girl's gotta do. On this island, we look out for our own."

Chapter Seventeen

Rather than trying to have a conversation at Mistletoe Morning Brew on the Saturday after Thanksgiving, Holly picks Coco up at the B&B and drives her back to the family property. She's invited Buckhunter to join in on the meeting, and they've privately kicked around their potential responses to what will surely be a contentious discussion with Coco about selling the island.

"I don't know how you can stand that second house being so close to the main one," Coco says as they pull into Holly's sandy driveway. The tall palm trees lining the road sway overhead, and the morning is mild and cool.

"It's not bad." Holly skids to a stop in front of her bungalow. "Ready?"

Coco swings her knees daintily to the right so she can set both feet on the ground at the same time like the queen stepping from a horse-drawn carriage. She's not as dolled-up as she gets for dinners at the B&B, but she's certainly not dressed for roaming the unpaved streets of a desolate island in the middle of the Gulf of Mexico.

"Nice ensemble, Mom," Holly says, eyeing her mother as they walk up the front steps to her house. Coco is dressed in a pair of culottes with a bold orchid print, an off-the-shoulder wrap top in a purple that matches the flowers on her pants, and a pair of cream-colored wedge sandals. She's carrying a small purse over one arm, and her nails and toes are painted a glossy fuchsia. After becoming a teen mom, Coco's Act II had been a stint as a traveling cocktail waitress who visited her young daughter on Christmas Key only when her own parents demanded it. Her third act has been a long-running gig as a well-heeled corporate wife. Coco has taken on this latest incarnation with verve, and her plumped, waxed, smoothed, toned, tanned, and entitled exterior never cease to both amaze and intimidate Holly.

Inside the house, Coco sets her purse on the table next to the front door and immediately begins examining every room without invitation.

"I never asked what color you were painting this room," she calls out from the hallway, flipping on the light to the guest room.

Holly kicks her sandals off in the kitchen and walks through the house to find her mother. "Either coral or lime green," she says, standing behind Coco in the doorway. At this point, with Buckhunter's work to take everything apart and to line all the windows with painter's tape, Holly figures she might as well put down a drop cloth and open a gallon of paint. In fact, she's already imagining the room in a bright, tropical hue before she remembers that the remodeling is all a ruse to keep Coco at the B&B and away from camping out at her house.

"Too cliché," Coco decides, resting one narrow shoulder against the doorframe. "How about a light, toasty brown—like sand?" She walks into the room, her wedge heels clicking against the wood floors. "And you could do a really crisp, white duvet and pillows, with green accents throughout the room. It would remind your guests of palm fronds and sandy beaches. You could even bring in a couple of small potted palms to add some foliage. I can see a framed print over here," she walks over to a wall, spreading both hands out to show how big the artwork should be, "and maybe a headboard made of driftwood."

Holly nods, breathing in deeply through her nose as she silently counts to ten.

"This is fun!" Coco says, clapping her hands together. "You could let me pick everything out. In fact, that's what I'll do. When I get back to New Jersey, I'll talk to my decorator and get a few drawings and samples to FedEx to you—"

"Hello? Anyone home?" Buckhunter's voice rings through the house. "Holly?"

"Coming!" Holly says loudly, walking down the hall toward the kitchen. She's thrilled to have Buckhunter interrupt the onset of Hurricane Coco. Dealing with her mother's ideas about redecorating her house on top of whatever discussion they're about to have is already wearing her down.

"Mom, Buckhunter brought breakfast," Holly shouts down the hallway, taking the waxy bag from his hands. Buckhunter sets a cardboard drink carrier that holds three hot cups of coffee on the counter.

"Good morning, Leo," Coco says without much enthusiasm. She's picked up her purse in the front room and is holding it over the crook of her arm again as though she doesn't trust its safety now that there's a third person in the house.

"Hey, Coco. Hope you like bagels and cream cheese," Buckhunter says, offering her a steaming cup of coffee with a lid. "And I got you a latte."

"Thank you." Coco takes the coffee from him and watches as Holly puts the half-dozen bagels on a small platter. There are two wheat bagels, a jalapeño, a blueberry, one onion, and a garlic and sesame seed. Holly takes the plastic lid off the tub of full-fat cream cheese and sets the container on the platter. She hands it all to Buckhunter and nods at the lanai.

"I'll meet you out there," Holly says to Coco and Buckhunter. She grabs a cutting knife for the bagels, three butter knives, three small plates, napkins, and placemats. She looks around for Pucci and finds him hiding under the little table in the hallway, his body so big that his paws hang out from one end, his tail from the other. "I don't blame you, buddy," she coos. "She won't be here long, I promise."

Out on the lanai, Coco is brushing at the seat of her patio chair, still holding her purse in one hand. "I see dog hairs on this," she says, fluffing the throw pillow and turning her head away as if the offending stray hairs will fill the air around her like a dust storm. "You know I'm allergic."

"Yes, I've heard." Holly sets the placemats and napkins on the table and lays the knives and plates out. "Pucci is in the back of the house—he won't come out here and bother you."

Coco sniffs and perches on the edge of the chair, her purse settled near her feet. "This is an interesting wall you've got going here," she says, holding her coffee with both hands and staring at Holly's half-finished shell wall. "Maybe my decorator can think of a creative way to…fix this. I'll ask him."

"I don't need it fixed, Mom. I need to finish it."

"Huh," Coco says, eyebrow arched. She sips her coffee. "So, let's talk about the matter at hand."

"I vote for the jalapeño," Buckhunter says.

"Pardon me?" Coco sets her cup on the edge of her placemat.

"Breakfast is the matter at hand for me. I thought we were voting on who got which bagel," he jokes, reaching for the platter to offer first choice to his half-sister.

"No," Coco says, holding up a palm. "Too many carbs. But thank you."

Buckhunter holds the dish out to Holly and she chooses the garlic and sesame seed.

"Fine, now breakfast is settled. What do you want to talk about?" Buckhunter slices his bagel and reaches for the tub of cream cheese.

"It's been several months since I broached the topic of selling the is-land with Holly, and I understand that we've all seen legal documenta-tion as to the division of assets here," Coco says stiffly, avoiding eye contact with her father's illegitimate son. A frost settles over her attrac-tive features that makes her look like she's carved of ice.

"Yeah, we all share things equally—got it." Holly takes a bite of her bagel and the thick cream cheese sticks to the roof of her mouth as she chews.

"Well, not entirely equally," Coco says pointedly. The ice behind her almond-shaped eyes immediately melts in a puddle of hot anger. The color rises on both of her cheeks. "For some reason, your grandfather thought that dividing the island up three ways and giving you one per-cent more ownership than he gave to his two children—" Coco pauses here, swallowing hard like she has to physically digest the idea that Buck-hunter is also her father's child. "He thought this uneven split made sense. Honestly, I think all it does is make a point: he preferred you, and he always did."

"Mom, come on," Holly coaxes. This isn't the time to analyze or hy-pothesize about what Frank Baxter's intention might have been. It is what it is, and in Holly's mind, the only message her grandfather was trying to impart with the uneven split was that he'd groomed Holly to take over where he'd left off. And he *had* groomed her for the job. He'd even left her his thoughts, plans, and dreams for the island in the form of a typed prospectus.

"No. *You* come on, Holly." Coco slams a palm against the glass table top. The three cups of coffee jump, and the cutting knife falls from the edge of the bagel platter, clattering loudly against the glass. "We have an opportunity here to make serious money with the sale of this *albatross*, and you're fooling around here with, with—" she splutters.

"With what, Mom?" Holly's tone remains the same in spite of her mother's visible anger. She places her elbows on the table as she searches Coco's face.

"With ridiculous elections and buffet dinners like you're running a retirement home." Coco sits back in her chair, manicured hands folded in her lap. "With reality shows about Lord only knows what," she says meanly. "With donkeys and turkeys and no police officer protecting the streets."

"We have Jake," Holly protests.

"Jake is busy building a hut out of coconut shells," Coco says. "Or trying to win an extra cup of rice for building a sand castle on the beach."

"But, Mom—we don't really need a full-time cop here. We've never been invaded by pirates or alligators, and crime is nonexistent on Christmas Key." Holly sits back in her seat, trying to keep her face impassive. Coco is way closer to the truth on this one than she wants to admit.

"Now that you mention it, there are some snakes and smaller lizards we could use protection from," Buckhunter says, cutting a second bagel for himself. "But we can probably run them off the island ourselves." He smiles directly at Coco and reaches across the table for the cream cheese.

"Look, there are going to be serious long-term ramifications if we keep this island on the books, and the two of you obviously don't see that. When this population of pensioners starts dying off and leaving you with rotting bungalows and no money to fund operations, you're going to wish you'd listened to me."

"Is that really how you see the people who helped to raise your only child?" Holly asks in a near whisper. "As 'pensioners' who've got one foot in their graves? These are the men and women who taught me about life, Mom. They're the people who still talk me through things, who roll up their sleeves and make sacrifices so that we can live in paradise. They're family to me."

"Well," Coco says, sounding unapologetic. "They're family who aren't going to live forever."

"Coco," Buckhunter says. "I understand why you want to sell Christmas Key—I really do. But your daughter has a real passion for this place. This is her home."

"You don't understand anything, Leo. You're an interloper here, no matter what my father's will says."

"Okay, you're entitled to that opinion," he says. "But Holly works night and day to create something that would make our dad proud." Coco rolls her eyes dramatically at the use of the term "our dad" to describe Frank Baxter. "She's got big plans, and a ton of support here. This nonsense with Cap Duncan will blow over, if that's what's got you concerned. The man started drinking last summer and he hasn't stopped since. Everybody knows it."

"He speaks for others on the island, I'm sure," Coco says, looking directly at her daughter. "It must feel ridiculous for some of them to think that their fate is in the hands of a girl who lives her life like Huckleberry Finn."

"That's enough." Buckhunter stands up. "We're not gonna come to an agreement, so we might as well end this before it gets ugly."

"Are you kicking me out of my own parents' house?" Coco demands incredulously. She doesn't move.

"He's not, but I am," Holly says, rising from her chair so that she and her uncle are both looking down at her mother. "I think we're out-voting you again, Coco."

Coco shakes her head, looking back and forth between the two of them. "This is ridiculous. All of this." She tosses her napkin on the placemat and stands, lifting her purse from the ground as she does. The three of them stare at one another like chiefs from different tribes. "I guess the next time you'll hear from me is when my lawyer contacts you with a dollar amount."

"A dollar amount for what?" Holly asks.

Coco glares at them both. "For you to buy out my stake in the island." She reaches the door that leads back into the house before she turns around, her hand resting tentatively on the doorknob. Her dramatic exit has hit a snag. "Leo, will you please drive me back to the B&B?" she asks, obviously remembering that she has no way to get back across the island on her teetering wedge heels. "I'm sure my own daughter couldn't be bothered to drive me over there—it kills her to do me any favors."

Holly sinks back into her chair as Buckhunter follows Coco through the house. The front door slams behind them. She can hear his cart rolling down the driveway, and finally, the silence of the morning surrounds her. There is no doubt in her mind that Coco means what she says: there will be contact from a lawyer, and an astronomical dollar figure will get bandied around like a tennis ball. It also goes without saying that she and Buckhunter won't have the resources to buy Coco out, but it will still cost them some money in legal fees.

As if the air in the house has changed with Coco's exit, Pucci pokes his nose through the door leading from the lanai into the house. He glances around, then ambles out, his big, golden retriever body swaying from side-to-side.

"Come here, boy," Holly says, dangling a hand over the arm of her chair. Pucci walks to her and sits; his head fits neatly under her hand and she pets him. "How did you know I needed cheering up?" She runs one of his silky ears through her hand.

Holly looks at the half-finished shell wall, admiring the varied shapes and sizes of the shells she's collected over the years. The wall represents all of her pent-up energy, sleepless nights, and dedication to creating something with her own bare hands. By insulting the wall, Coco was really insulting the effort and energy that Holly's put into Christmas Key, and she feels strongly that somehow, Coco had known that. It's always been her mother's nature to criticize first and worry about the fallout later.

"Let's go for a drive, Pooch." Holly stands up and gathers the food from the table so she can take into the kitchen. "Get your tennis ball, dude," she orders, pointing at the basket in the living room where she stores dog toys. "Let's hit the beach."

Holly slips her sandals on and picks up her Yankees hat and cell phone from the kitchen counter. Pucci leads the way to the golf cart, jumping up into the passenger seat next to her with his tennis ball clenched in his jaw. He drops it onto the patterned fabric of the seat and lets it roll over and rest against Holly's thigh.

She gets to the end of the driveway and is ready to turn left onto Cinnamon Lane and head for Pinecone Path when her phone rings. It's Wayne Coates.

"Holly, can we talk? I'm at the B&B." Wayne's voice is crisp, his words to-the-point. "It's about Jake."

"Sure. I can be there in five minutes." Holly places her hand on Pucci's warm head as she ends the call and wedges the phone between her thighs. "Change of plans, pup, but you can come along for the ride." She cranks the wheel to the right and points her cart in the opposite direction onto Cinnamon Lane. "Duty calls."

* * *

"You want him to *what?*" Holly frowns at Wayne Coates across her desk in the back office of the B&B. "I don't think he'll do that."

"Why not? He's single, she's single…and frankly, we wield a lot of power over someone when we withhold food and sleep," Wayne says, legs crossed as he sits comfortably in Bonnie's wicker desk chair. He picks at the knee of his cargo pants, smoothing one clean hand over the fabric.

Holly takes off her hat and runs a hand through her long hair. The morning already feels like it's been three days long. "I just—I don't know. It kind of feels like psychological warfare," she admits, setting her beloved baseball cap on top of the desk between them.

Wayne huffs. "It's standard reality show mechanics. We manipulate the players and then edit the show to tell the story we want to tell." He laces his fingers together and wraps his hands around the knee that's resting on top of the other one. "Surely you didn't imagine that a television network would invest millions of dollars in a program where they just rolled film and watched a bunch of people bumble around and do whatever they wanted to."

"I'm not sure what I imagined, but…it wasn't this," Holly admits. The stuff she's seen on-set so far looked like standard reality show competition fare, but the manipulations of the players' personal items that she'd seen before the cast arrived, and the request to have background info on Jake in order to force him and Bridget into a pseudo-relationship have her feeling concerned.

"Listen," Wayne says, his smile widening to reveal a mouth full of white teeth. "Nothing that's going on here is out of the norm—I can assure you of that. And the network loves this island; the dailies we're sending back are knocking their socks off," he says, square hands held up in surrender, his smooth palms facing Holly. "You all have a great thing going here, and we can't wait for the finale when we bring the last two competitors over to this side of the island. It's going to make for great

TV when they see Main Street and have a romantic dinner on the patio at your little bistro."

"How do you know it's going to be romantic?" Holly asks defiantly.

"Because, Holly, we know how this is going to end," Wayne says firmly, dropping his own chin in response to her movements. It's an interesting show of body language between them, and Holly refuses to be the first to look away as they stare at one another across the desk. "And it's *going* to end with a proposal between Jake and Bridget."

"So you're asking me to do what?"

"I'm asking you to arrange an engagement party at that bar on the beach."

Holly shakes her head and looks out the window. Saturday morning on Main Street is as busy as any other day, and she watches as Ray Bradford parks in front of North Star Cigars and steps inside. Through the big picture window of Cap's store, she can see him step from behind the counter to greet Ray, Marco perched on his shoulder as usual. She looks back at Wayne.

"It feels weird. And wrong."

"It feels like what you agreed to, Mayor." Wayne pats the top of her desk. "Look at it this way: you help us make a great show—I mean, really compelling TV—and we'll edit the show to make this island look like the paradise that it is. You stand to reap the rewards of us making a hit, which was your goal all along, no?"

Pucci stands up from his dog bed and slinks across the office to sit at his mistress's feet.

Holly shrugs. "I suppose so, but this feels like the wrong way to do it. What happens when the cameras stop rolling and the show is over?"

"Ideally we'll have a follow-up wedding to televise, but if not, we'll at least end this show with a blowout surprise engagement that will leave the audience completely satisfied."

"And these two humans whose lives you've doctored just to get ratings?" Holly asks, picking up her hat and folding the bill between her hands absentmindedly. "What happens to them?"

"Bridget is an actress, Holly. She's in for a penny, in for a pound here," Wayne says confidently. "And Jake is a grown man who can handle himself. Besides, who are we to say it won't work out between them?" He offers this bon mot as if it ties the whole package up in a neat bow.

Holly opens her mouth to protest, but instead ends up stammering incoherently.

"Think it over—weigh the pros and cons," Wayne urges, pushing back from the desk and standing. "This isn't some devious, evil plan to ruin the lives of unwitting innocents," he says, slipping one hand into the deep pocket of his cargo pants. "Anyone who gets involved with a reality show knows the risks and the expectations. We're creating entertainment here; performance art, if you will."

Holly tosses her Yankees hat back on the desk and sets her elbows on the chair's armrests.

"Just swing by the set and have a look. If anyone appears to be under duress, I'll let you off the hook and handle it all myself." He looks at Holly with dark, flashing eyes full of challenge and amusement. "But if you see that everyone is there competing freely, then I'd ask you to consider lending a hand. It'll pay off in the end for you, I promise." Wayne looks at her for a long minute before he turns and walks out the door.

Chapter Eighteen

The chosen space for Ray and Millie Bradford's salon, Scissors & Ribbons, is the site of a former denture shop inside Poinsettia Plaza. So few of Christmas Key's residents wore dentures that the shop never really took off, but H. Gerald Biggins had always hoped that it would. Finally, with the passing of his old friend Frank Baxter and at the behest of his eldest daughter, he'd decamped to Maine and left his equipment behind. Now, there's a big, empty room to be filled with all the accoutrements of a beauty salon, and a small area in the back that can be turned into an office just as soon as the Bradfords get the denture fitting and repair machinery removed.

Millie has invited Fiona to stop by after closing up her own office in the building on Wednesday evening, and she's also asked Holly, Bonnie, Iris and Emily Cafferkey, and the triplets to come over and check things out with her. The women of the island have been eyeballing the empty storefront eagerly ever since Millie announced her intentions at the last village council meeting, and they can't wait to hear her plans.

"I'm so excited about this," Millie says, smoothing her hands over the thighs of her jeans. "I want the hair dryers to be lined up along that wall," she says, pointing at the far wall that she'll share with Fiona's doctor's office, "and a mani-pedi station over in this corner." Millie paces across the room and stops, indicating the spot where she'll set up a table for her nail polishes and acrylic supplies.

"I'm sure the men of Christmas Key will thank you, darlin'," Bonnie says, observing the empty space. "When's the last time a gent around these parts got to pass an evening with a professionally coiffed woman in his arms?"

Glen giggles and pats her own neat, blonde bob.

"Not to mention the pedicures," Holly adds. "There are way too many sandals and flip-flops running around this island for us not to have a callus grinder and a foot soaking tub on hand."

"And you'll do big business at Mother's Day and Christmas, doll," Bonnie says. "The men will line up to buy gift certificates."

Millie grins, her eyes full of possibility as she looks around the big, empty room. It's been years since she's had her own storefront, and the hustle and bustle—the creativity and companionship—will be good for her and for the island.

"How long do you think it'll take to get this all set up?" Fiona asks, walking over to the dusty floor-to-ceiling window that looks onto Main Street. She rubs a spot on the glass until she can see the B&B's front door across the street.

"I'm not sure," Millie admits. "I need to make sure my licensure is all set up in Florida, and I'll have to think about hiring someone to work the front desk. And then there's the issue of whether I want to do everything myself, or hire someone to move out here and offer services with me."

"You mentioned massage," Bonnie points out. "Are you licensed for that?"

"No, that would be something I'd have to hire out for. Maybe I could get someone to come over once a week and do a full day, you know? I bet that could work." Her face is flushed with excitement.

"This is going to be awesome, Millie," Holly says. "I don't think we should put off the celebration one second longer." She pulls a foil-wrapped bottle of champagne from her tote bag. "Do you have the cups?" Holly turns to Bonnie and holds out a hand.

"Of course—I wouldn't fall down on an important job like that," Bonnie says, handing over a stack of red plastic cups from the B&B's kitchen. Holly passes them over to Fiona to hand out.

"Then let's make a toast," Holly says, struggling with the bottle as she unwinds the wire cage that surrounds the cork. With a small twist and a grimace, Holly manages to get the cork to pop. "I didn't even spill!" she crows, setting the mouth of the bottle over the cup that Gwen holds out to her. Holly moves around the small circle, making sure everyone has champagne frothing in their plastic cups. "Okay," she says. "We want to welcome Scissors & Ribbons to the island, and to offer our love and support as you open your new business here on Main Street." Holly holds her cup in the air.

"Yes, let's all thank Millie for making us sexy again!" Bonnie hoots, holding her cup of champagne aloft next to Holly's. "I mean, let's thank her for making the rest of y'all sexy—I've been that way all along," she says, breaking into a hearty laugh.

The women give a whoop of joy. Holly and Bonnie touch the lips of their cups together knowingly, watching as Millie goes back to showing everyone around the room, describing her imaginary set-up in detail once more.

"We're doing it, Bon," Holly says quietly. "Every day is a new step on the path to a bigger, better Christmas Key."

"Don't I know it, sugar." Bonnie drains her champagne. "Got any more of that bubbly?"

"I do. Why don't you share it with everyone and make sure Millie gets home safely in case she gets tipsy."

"Where are you off to?" Bonnie's looks at Holly over the rim of her cup.

"I need to run to the set this evening."

"Everything okay over there?"

Holly pauses. She wants to tell Bonnie that yes, everything is wonderful, but between Coco's short visit (she'd left the island on the supply delivery boat without another word to anyone on Saturday), Cap's aggressive mayoral campaigning, and her discomfort over getting roped into the network's manipulations and orchestrations with regards to Jake and Bridget, the truth is that things aren't fine.

The other women are oohing and aahing over talk of shampoo bowls and semi-permanent hair colors, so Holly drags Bonnie over to the doorway where they can talk out of earshot.

"I'm not sure how I feel about this," she starts, looking around as if the walls might have ears.

"What, sugar? What is it?"

"Well…they're trying to create a relationship between Jake and this, this—*woman*," Holly says. "And it really bugs me to see him being used like that."

"How do they 'create' a relationship, doll? Either there is one or there isn't."

"That's what you might *think*," Holly says, holding up a finger, "but then you'd be wrong. In the world of reality television, all they have to do is starve you and deprive you of sleep, and then they can get you to do anything they want."

"So, wait just a cotton-picking minute here and let me get this straight: are you telling me that these fancy TV people are doing something to make Jake fall in fake love?"

"I don't know. I guess he could be falling in real love." Her face is serious. "But that's not my business. I just don't want them to use him and throw him away like he's not a real person."

"I know, sugar: you don't want them to make him look like a fool."

"At least not any more than I already have," Holly adds softly.

"You did no such thing, Holly Jean Baxter. You two were good and broken up when River came to town. Don't go around trying to take the weight of the world onto your own shoulders—there's no call for that," Bonnie says reproachfully. "Now what proof do we have that they're using Office Zavaroni as a made-for-TV love machine?"

Holly snickers at Bonnie's description of Jake. "Well, they basically *blackmailed* me until I agreed to break into his house and find some juicy details they can feed to Bridget so that she can reel him in."

"Ooooh, sugar. That's not good," Bonnie says in a stage whisper. The triplets are circling the room, and Holly moves in closer to Bonnie. Both women have been on the island long enough to know that even your closest neighbors and friends can carry a torch of gossip and start a wildfire without meaning to.

"Want to take a walk?" Holly nods at the door leading onto Main Street.

"Sure, let's tell Millie we're going."

The women toss their champagne cups in the trash and give Millie congratulatory hugs before heading out into the autumn evening.

"So, how in the world did they blackmail you? I've never known a person with less dirt to dig through than you," Bonnie says.

"It's dumb. They acted like the network was going to be furious that I ruined their picture-perfect Thanksgiving dinner by giving them vegetarian food instead of a giant turkey to put on the table."

"Wait—that's it? That *is* dumb," Bonnie agrees. "I'm surprised that was enough to convince you to hand over details about Jake's personal life."

"I already feel like an ass, so thank you for confirming it."

"Honey, I'm not trying to make you feel worse." There is concern on Bonnie's face. "Don't beat yourself up over this."

"Nah, it's okay. You're allowed to tell me when I'm being an idiot. But now I have to make it right," Holly says definitively. "I can't let these people swoop in here and play Jake for a fool just to get ratings."

"Are you thinking what I'm thinking?"

"I think I'm probably thinking what you're thinking," Holly ventures with caution. "But not if it involves Wyatt Bender doing belly shots off you on top of the bar at Jack Frosty's."

Bonnie stops on the sidewalk and reaches for Holly's arm as she throws her head back and hoots. "Oh, sugar! The things you come up with, I swear." Bonnie bends forward at the waist, one arm holding her stomach as she laughs. "Me on top of a bar—that'll be the day!"

"You can't honestly tell me it would be the first time."

"Well," Bonnie says, breathless as she tries to compose herself. "Between you, me, and the fencepost, Holly Jean—I might not say no to a little whisky-and-Wyatt combo, but there'll certainly be no body shots, doll. And I'm not confirming or denying whether or not this derrière has ever been on top of a bar." Bonnie pats her round behind with a mischievous smile.

"Hey, you can't blame a girl for having an imagination." Holly puts an arm around Bonnie's shoulders now that she's finally stopped laughing. "Okay, what were you really thinking?"

"Before you got me all hot and bothered thinking about cowboys and booze?"

"Am I really supposed to believe you didn't already have cowboys and booze on the brain?"

"Good point," Bonnie says as they start to walk again. "Anyway, I know you're thinking what I'm *really* thinking."

They look at each other and nod. "Emergency village council meeting," the women say in unison.

"You got it," Bonnie confirms, serious once again. "Let's get this ball rolling."

"Perfect. I'll swing by the set first thing in the morning to see what's going on," Holly says.

"And I'll call a meeting for Friday morning. Sound good?"

"Not as good as cowboys and booze," Holly cracks, "but better than what I've got so far."

"It's a deal, sugar. Now go on home and do your naked video chatting thing with that hunk from Oregon." Bonnie gives her a light shove.

"Oh, Bon." Holly rolls her eyes as they peel away from one another at the B&B. Holly's parked her cart in the lot at the inn, and Bonnie's golf cart is just down Main Street in front of Mistletoe Morning Brew. "This 'naked video chatting' business is definitely a figment of your imagination."

"Hey," Bonnie laughs as she turns on the sidewalk to face Holly. "You can't blame a girl for having an imagination!"

* * *

Holly walks up the path to the set of *Wild Tropics* around ten-thirty the next morning. She's left her shoes on the seat of the golf cart so she can trudge through the cool, powdery sand barefoot.

Wayne Coates nods at Holly from his director's chair by the fire pit. He's got a clipboard resting on his crossed legs, and he's holding a walkie-talkie to one ear. This visit is unplanned, and Holly is surprised at how casual everyone is when they see her. The cameramen give her familiar smiles, and even Leanna glances over and waves as she sets up a shot inside one of the tents.

At Wayne's behest, Holly had visited the set over the weekend to see if anyone appeared to be acting against their will, but the competitors had been off shore, paddling furiously in two-person kayaks when she arrived. Holly had shielded her eyes, staring at the primary colors of the boats on the horizon, a little skiff with a motor following close behind to catch the action on camera. With no Jake and no Bridget to observe, she'd made a perfunctory tour of the set, saying hello and asking polite questions about how the crew was enjoying the island before leaving the beach and Wayne's smirking face behind.

Now, with the competitors kicking a soccer ball around in the sand, doing yoga stretches, and ducking in and out of tents, Holly pulls her Mets hat lower over her eyes and approaches the closest crew member—a guy named Ryan with gangly limbs, smooth skin, and the dark, floppy hair of a teenager.

"Hey. You here to drop off more tofu and bran disguised as real food?" Ryan asks, one side of his mouth turned up. He's winding an orange extension cord around a spool, his tan forearms lean and roped with veins.

"Nope, no fake food this time. I'm just here to visit," Holly says, digging in the sand with her right foot. She reaches for the back of her baseball cap and holds her palm flat against her head. "Hey," she asks, voice low and confidential. "Let me ask you something. Do you think the contestants are weirded out when a strange face pops up here?"

"Nah, not really." Ryan squints at the six competitors who are still in the game. "They know we all stay in a separate crew area, and that there are some people there who edit and do computer work all day and night.

For all they know, you're an editor coming up for air." He shrugs and keeps rolling the cord.

"Huh." Holly shoves her hands into the pockets of her jeans. "Well, I'm trying not to call attention to myself when I come over here."

"Put this on." Ryan sets his spool on the sand and pulls the timer he's wearing on a cord around his neck off over his head. He puts it over Holly's head, but it gets stuck on the brim of her hat and they laugh, trying to free her cap from the cord. "There." Ryan steps back and looks at her. "Oh, and maybe this." He pulls a pad of paper and a pen from his back pocket and gives it to her.

"Do I look official now?"

Ryan's eyes crinkle at the corners when he smiles. "Pretty much. Just pass that stuff off to me before you leave, okay?" He runs a hand through his loose, glossy hair.

A layer of gray clouds is rolling in off the water, and with it comes a cooler-than-usual breeze. Holly shivers as she walks into the fray, watching as two crew members rig up a light so they can keep shooting even when the sun disappears later that evening.

"Hi, Holly," Leanna says, approaching her. "Nice stopwatch." She points at the timer from Ryan. "If you start looking too official, we might put you to work."

"I wouldn't mind. Right now, this is way more fun than being mayor."

"I heard the scuttlebutt about the cigar shop owner wanting to run against you—ouch." Leanna winces sympathetically. "Is it getting ugly?"

"Not too ugly." Holly pulls a quick, unconvincing smile. "He's the one who was opposed to you guys coming in the first place."

"Right—the guy who spoke up at the meeting when we visited last summer. I remember."

"Anyhow, it'll work itself out; things always do." Holly glances at Jake as he drops and starts doing push-ups in the sand. "But it's important for me to know how things are going here, and to make sure you guys have everything you need to make your stay here comfort—"

As Holly is speaking, the flame-haired female contestant races between her and Leanna, ducking and rolling in the sand like a martial artist escaping from a dangerous opponent. "Whoa!" Holly jumps back, startled. "What's everyone working out for?"

"The competition tonight involves some hand-to-hand combat."

"Combat?"

"It's gentle—don't worry. We're still talking family-friendly television here, you know."

"What do you win if you beat everyone else to a pulp?" Holly's eyes scan the beach and land on Bridget; she's wearing white yoga pants that hug her smooth curves, and a sky blue t-shirt with an orange sun on the back. Bridget lunges into warrior pose and gazes intently in Jake's direction.

"It's a *Hunger Games*-style battle to grab all the food they can. We're taking them to a drop spot in that jungly area on the west side of the island so they can fight for apples and ears of corn. I think there might be a couple of bags of rice, and maybe some beef jerky."

"Intense." Holly notices the way Bridget's ribs poke through her thin cotton shirt. And Jake—who is normally muscled and definitely more bulky than lean—appears drawn and narrow. His kneecaps protrude sharply from under his ragged khaki cargo shorts, and his backside looks flatter, leaving his shorts saggy and oversized.

"Yeah, it's intense. But at this point in the show, the audience wants to be able to root for their favorite competitor, and the harder we make them work, the more the audience invests in them."

"Right. They make an investment," Holly parrots back, nodding as she watches the stretching and kickboxing and yoga posing. "But all this working out is for corn and and apples?"

"Part of that is intentional," Leanna says in a near-whisper, guiding Holly toward the former "pleasure tent." They step inside, and Holly sees that the table has been cleared out, leaving a desk covered with messy piles of paper and an open laptop. Boxes and bins litter the tent. "We keep them hungry so we can keep them on task," Leanna explains. "But there's something sexy about having your final competitors looking lean and angular as they frolic in skimpy clothes. That's a ratings boost, too."

"So…ratings," Holly says, biting her lower lip. "Everything is always for the ratings, not the people?"

"The people *are* the ratings," Leanna counters, frowning. "They're what keep us on the air."

"No—not those people," Holly clarifies. "I mean the people who are here, on the beach, smacking each other around for a piece of beef jerky." Her words come out with a bite, so she softens her tone before going on. "I guess I just worry about *those* people, too."

"They're okay, Holly. You need to let go and trust that we know what we're doing here." Leanna sets her phone on the desk and shuffles through some loose paper. "Everyone on this set is an adult, and they're not here under false pretenses." Holly wants to object, but as she opens her mouth, a soccer ball rolls in through the open flap of the tent and stops at her feet. "Think of it like a one-night stand: you go into it hoping to have a good time, but you know there's just as good a chance that you'll wake up the next day a little hungover and filled with regret. You don't always win, but it doesn't stop you from playing."

Holly reaches down to pick up the soccer ball, but before she can touch it, a dark figure fills the opening of the tent and she stands up again. It's Jake, one hand on his hip, panting slightly.

"Hey," Holly says automatically. She's torn between reaching down for the ball and reaching out to him to make sure he's still the Jake she's always known. His eyes look bigger than usual, and a rough layer of whiskers covers his tanned face, but other than that and the obvious weight he's lost, he looks essentially the same.

Jake stands in the doorway, and there's a moment of awkwardness as he looks at Leanna before responding. "Hi," he says finally.

"You all ready for tonight?" Leanna asks him. She pops the top on a cooler next to the desk and pulls out a can of Diet Coke. Jake eyes the cold soda in her hand as he nods. "We'll leave here as soon as we get the shot we need of you guys before tonight's competition." Jake nods again, and his eyes move back to Holly. "Holly's just visiting us to see how things are going—things are good here, right, Jake?" Leanna prompts.

He moves into the tent cautiously. The combination of his lean physique and his watchful eyes remind Holly of a panther. He continues surveying his ex-girlfriend carefully as he reaches for the soccer ball.

"I don't suppose anyone would know if I slipped you a Diet Coke, would they?" Leanna asks rhetorically, handing the can of soda to Jake. "Go ahead. Drink. The kick of caffeine will do you good."

Holly stands there, serving as one angle of this odd triangle inside the tent. Jake takes the can from Leanna and pauses, obviously considering whether or not he should drink it.

"Go on," Leanna says, waving it away.

"So, the jungled side of the island," Holly says, clearing her throat. "That's where I live. And it's where the Ho Ho Hideaway is. What if one of the contestants goes too far in the dark and ends up on my doorstep?"

"Won't happen." Leanna shakes her head, gathering up papers from the desk and straightening them. We have crew members stationed at the outer edges of the area we've chosen, and we already asked the owner of the Ho Ho Hideaway if he'd shut down for the competition and turn off all the lights. And your house is way past the perimeter we've set up, but it would be much appreciated if you felt like keeping the lights off."

The image of a darkened Ho Ho Hideaway flickers through her mind; Joe had probably agreed to shut down the bar and take a night off without much convincing, but Holly isn't sure she feels like sitting around in the dark all evening. If all else fails, she'll just pack a bag and head over to Bonnie or Fiona's.

Jake cracks the tab on the can of Diet Coke and tips his head all the way back, pouring the cold soda down his throat thirstily. Holly watches as his Adam's apple bobs with each swallow, and it isn't until Leanna taps the edge of her pile of papers against the desk loudly that she realizes she's staring at him.

"So, Jake—" Holly starts.

"Is about to finish that soda and get back out there," Leanna interrupts. "He's got food on the line tonight, and I think the camera crew is about ready to set up our shot."

Jake hands Leanna the empty can and wipes his mouth with the back of his hand. Even his fingers look knobby to Holly, and she shoots him a look of sympathy as he ducks under the flap of the tent. Leanna has already turned her attention to the phone she's picked up from her desk, so she's not watching as Jake pauses on the threshold of the tent and turns his head over one shoulder, catching Holly's eye. He gives her a weak smile and holds up a hand, fingers splayed. It's a simple greeting and an even simpler good-bye, but Holly knows it's his way of saying that he's okay.

Only she knows that he isn't. His dark head disappears beyond the other tents lining the sand, and Holly watches the space between the canvas, hoping to catch one more glimpse of him as he goes.

* * *

The buzz in the room is almost tangible. There hasn't been an emergency village council meeting called since a small fire broke out at Mistletoe Morning Brew in 2013, causing a short closure and a widespread panic over the Coffee Situation, as it came to be known. The coffee conundrum of '13 was ultimately remedied by setting up a rotating, color-coded schedule for various islanders to host morning coffee gatherings at their houses while Iris and Jimmy ordered extra coffee beans to be shipped to the Jingle Bell Bistro. It had been a beautiful showing of teamwork and cooperation, and Holly hopes for nothing less now as she's standing before them at the podium in the B&B's dining room on Friday morning.

"I'd like to call to order the emergency village council meeting of December second," she says, nodding at Heddie Lang-Mueller, who is seated—as always—at a table to the right of the podium. Heddie's ink starts flowing as she begins jotting the meeting minutes.

It takes longer than usual to get everyone seated and calmed, and Holly watches like an elementary school teacher waiting patiently for her pupils to gather themselves and fall silent. Maria Agnelli, short as she is, hunches over at the waist and scurries to her seat in the front row like she's in a movie theater and might be blocking the views of the people behind her.

"Thank you for coming on such short notice," Holly says. "I need to ask for your help with something, and I want to preface it by saying that there is absolutely no cause to be alarmed."

Naturally, this causes alarm. Faces in the room are marked with concern, and mouths drop open expectantly.

"I'm not sure how to say this, because I don't want to misstate what I see as the issue here." Holly pauses, looking around the room.

"Just rip it off like a band-aid, lass," Jimmy Cafferkey says from the crowd, one arm around his daughter Emily's chair. Emily waves at Holly with her fingers, smiling encouragingly; Holly waves back at her. It's not easy to admit that she's second-guessing herself, but as she looks at the faces of the people she's known her entire life, she realizes that there's no better group of people to ask for help.

"I know that we were somewhat divided on the issue of having the reality show come to the island," Holly says, trying hard not to glance in Cap's direction. "And I still think it will ultimately be a great thing for our exposure. That said, I have some…concerns."

The crowd breaks out into a loud discussion. People turn to their immediate neighbors and start talking. Some shout out in Holly's direction; others turn to Cap and start speaking loudly. From his position standing against the wall at the side of the room, Cap smiles smugly.

Holly lets the debate rage for about a minute, then lifts the pink marble gavel that Bonnie had given her for Christmas one year as a joke. It's smooth and cool in her hand, and its weight carries the gravitas she needs to lead this discussion. She raps lightly on the gavel's sound block and the heavy clicks ring out in the B&B's dining room like a final verdict. The room goes quiet.

"I still say those folks should be filming us—we're the *real* stars of this island," Maria Agnelli says loudly from her seat, arms folded across her ribcage. "They've got all manner of young, sexy people over on that beach, and visitors are going to be sorely disappointed when they show up here and find a bunch of old geezers in golf carts."

"Holly's got a plan, Maria," Joe Sacamano tempers, speaking up from the center of the room. "We all need to have some patience and wait this one out."

"Thanks, Joe," Holly says, still holding the gavel in her right hand. "Anyway, as I said, I know that we have different views on what will come of the show, and at least a couple of us were pretty opposed to their filming here in the first place, but I have a more immediate concern."

The islanders are calm again, waiting to hear what Holly is going to say. With a shiver, Bonnie pulls her cardigan around her body. An unusual cold snap rolled over the island the night before, bringing morning temperatures in the upper forties. The crowd in front of Holly is a sea of sweatshirts, windbreakers, and brightly colored sweaters.

"Right now I need to ask for your help with one of our own."

Eyes widen all over the room.

"As you all know, Jake is competing on the show, and I've gotten wind of the fact that they'd like to, well, match him up with a fellow contestant." Holly looks around at the faces staring back at her. "In a romantic way," she adds. People turn to one another again, this time keeping their voices at a low whisper. "I've visited the set a number of times as a kind of quality control measure, and what I've gathered is that the producers have a hand in the outcome of the competitions and the show."

"Hell, I'm an old woman, and even *I* knew those reality shows were fake," Maria Agnelli says with disgust.

"I don't think it's all fake," Holly backpedals, "but there are some behind-the-scenes manipulations going on to give certain contestants advantages. I've seen them trying to force Jake and another contestant together, and I've even heard them mention a televised wedding."

"What?" Carrie-Anne shouts from the third row. "That doesn't sound like Jake, diving headfirst into something like this. I mean, look how long it took him to propose to you." She gestures at Holly.

"Right," Holly says, clearing her throat. Her face burns. The last thing she wants is for everyone to think that she's interfering with this because she's jealous of Jake moving on. She's not jealous, just worried. "Anyway, I've seen him up close on the set, and he definitely looks like they're not feeding him enough. When I was there on Wednesday evening, the contestants were about to fight over some fruits and vegetables, and Jake seemed really quiet and…not himself. Not at all."

"Well, you would know what his real self is, doll, and if you say he's acting funny, then I believe the man is acting funny." Bonnie stands up, pulling her shirt down over her hips as she speaks. "I can't stand the thought of people coming here and preying on someone's weaknesses for entertainment's sake," Bonnie says, touching her wavy, red hair with one hand. "Especially when it's one of our own."

"That's my point exactly," Holly says, diving back in. "You all know where I stand with Jake on a personal level, and his love life is certainly none of my business, but this just feels wrong. Forcing a relationship to happen to get ratings, and then potentially leaving him behind with all of the legal entanglements of a marriage that was never meant to last…" She trails off, imagining Jake's humiliation. "We don't agree on everything around here, but the one thing we always do well is look out for our own." The room is as quiet as a library. Holly's office phone chirps in the distance, through the lobby and down the hallway, but it goes unanswered. She stares at her neighbors, conviction filling her chest. "And that means we have to pull together, make sure *Wild Tropics* shows Christmas Key for what it really is, and—most importantly—keep Jake from being used like a prop on the set."

"Here, here," comes a voice from the side of the room. It shatters the silence, and Holly's eyes dart over to its source like a heat-seeking missile. It's Cap, and he's nodding at her firmly. "All disagreements aside, we take care of each other *first*," he says.

Holly smiles, her eyes lingering on Cap. She tears her gaze away from him and looks out at her fellow islanders: Iris Cafferkey is wiping her nose with a crushed tissue; Maria Agnelli is holding her purse in her lap, clutching it with both hands; Buckhunter winks at her, arms folded over his chest.

"Show of hands of those willing to pitch in to help with Operation Jake?"

Every hand in the room shoots up, and within thirty seconds, small groups have started to congregate to begin organizing tactical missions and to discuss ideas. Holly sets her pink marble gavel down and steps away from the podium.

Chapter Nineteen

There are five contestants left following the *Hunger Games*-style mission, and Jake and Bridget are two of them. Chuck Cortwell is still there with his Confederate flag tattoo, the orange-haired woman with yoga-toned arms and full sleeve tattoos is hanging on, and one of the muscular, semi-attractive guys who looked like a cross between a male model and an aspiring actor has narrowly escaped being sent home as well.

Holly sets her binoculars on the sand in front of her and turns to Fiona. It's Saturday morning, and they've spread a blanket out behind a small dune that blocks them from the cameras, cast, and crew of the show. Fiona is wearing jeans and a bubblegum pink hoodie sweatshirt with 'Northwestern' embroidered across the chest in thick white lettering. It's still chilly outside, but the sky is clear and blue. They're on their stomachs, propped up on elbows as they watch the happenings on set through matching binoculars.

"So what do we know about the other competitors?" Holly asks, rolling onto her back and looking up at the sky.

"Okay, Chuck Cortwell introduced himself to you by name. That made him easy."

Holly exhales audibly. After the emergency village council meeting the day before, everyone had offered ideas and signed up for tasks—even Cap and Wyatt. Fiona's task had been internet research to find out anything and everything she could about the other contestants, and even about the crew members.

"Chuck is fifty-three, and from Beaufort, South Carolina. He's part-owner of a military-themed karate studio."

"A what?" Holly frowns. "Like you have to salute before you chop a block of wood in half with your bare hands?"

"Maybe. Or you have to march and sing cadence before you can do the crane on top of a wooden post at the beach." Fiona sets down her own binoculars and rests her chin on her forearms.

"I think you're making up a movie in your head that's half *Platoon* and half *Karate Kid*," Holly says, lacing her fingers on top of her stomach as she watches a seagull fly overhead.

"Probably, but I'd watch it. Anyway, Chuck is divorced, has three adult children, and a family history with the KKK."

"As in the actual KKK?" Holly recoils.

"That's the one. But nothing recent. We're talking grandfather, great-uncle, cousins. That sort of thing."

"But that Confederate flag tattoo…"

"Yeah, who knows. Maybe a youthful indiscretion." Fiona pops back up on her elbows and turns to Holly. "The orange-haired chick was pretty easy, too. There's an acting agency in Portland that only reps tattooed and pierced talent. Their website is pretty much wall-to-wall hipsters."

"And?"

"And she's on there. Violetta DuBois. Enjoys yoga retreats, chai tea, and Deepak Chopra."

"So basically exactly what you'd expect."

"Pretty much. I looked her up on Facebook. Grew up near Seattle. Has a cat. Nothing too exciting."

"That leaves the bland actor-boy and Bridget." Holly looks at her best friend's face. "And we really have nothing to go on with them."

"Right. Actor-boy could be any one of thousands of dudes trying to break into the biz, and Bridget-with-no-last-name is kind of vague in terms of doing research."

Holly puts one arm over her eyes and thinks for a second. "So what can we do now?"

"We can keep observing the action on the beach, but I've got one other piece of news," Fiona says. "My college friend Amanda is dating this guy Henry from New York."

"Okay…"

"And Henry's sister moved to L.A. a few years ago to live with her boyfriend. Anyway, the sister's boyfriend is the personal assistant to a reality show producer from ABC."

"That seems like kind of a stretch," Holly says dubiously.

"It's not. The guy is super-nice, and when I emailed him yesterday, he responded right away. He said it wouldn't be too hard to find out through the grapevine which actors were working on which reality shows. Hollywood is actually a pretty small town, you know."

"I wouldn't know about Hollywood, but I know Christmas Key is a small town, and if I screw this up, I'm never going to hear the end of it." Holly rolls back onto her stomach and picks up her binoculars again. "So basically Amanda's brother Henry's friend is going to get back to us?"

"No, Henry's sister's boyfriend is getting back to us," Fiona clarifies, her shoulder touching Holly's. They both squint into their binoculars and watch as the contestants haul long pieces of wood across the sand with their bare hands.

"Got it," Holly says. "And thanks for doing all the legwork. I hope we can find out something useful about Busty Bridget."

"No problem." Fiona pulls her binoculars away from her eyes. "Wow. You're not kidding about Bridget, but isn't it kind of cold to be dragging giant logs around in a bikini top?"

"Must not be fifty degrees in TV-land," Holly says dryly. Jake and the other young guy are shirtless, but the crew members are wearing jeans and sweatshirts like Holly and Fiona. "Let's head back to the B&B; there's not much to see here."

"I don't know about that," Fiona says, wrinkling her nose as she looks through the binoculars again. "Shirtless guys carrying big pieces of wood across the beach isn't a bad view for a Saturday morning."

"Come on, Fee," Holly says, getting up onto her knees. She gives Fiona's denim-clad backside a loud whack. "You can beg Buckhunter to take off his shirt and drag his wood around in the sand later."

Fiona cackles as gets up on her knees. "Okay, okay. Back to headquarters we go, boss."

* * *

"I've done everything you asked me to, sugar," Bonnie says from her stool at the Ho Ho Hideaway later that evening. The sun has set, taking with it any semblance of tropical warmth. To combat the chill in the air, Joe Sacamano has two tall patio heaters running: one near the open steps leading into the bar, and the other at the top of the wide plank steps that lead down onto the beach. A good-sized Saturday night crowd has gathered, and the men with the least hair are wearing stocking caps or red Santa hats over their balding pates, while the ladies are wound in hand-knitted scarves and clutching their drinks with gloved hands.

"Thanks, Bon." Holly takes a warm mug from Joe Sacamano. "What is this?" she asks him, putting the drink to her nose and sniffing.

"Salted butterscotch hot chocolate," he says. Joe's wearing a thick black sweatshirt that makes his snowy white curls stand out even more than usual. At almost seventy, his face is still tan and handsome, and there's a twinkle in his eyes. "It's got a shot of scotch in it."

"Holy smokes," Holly says, tasting the sweet drink. "This is amazing."

"Thank you kindly, Mayor," Joe says with a small bow. He disappears to serve two more mugs of the hot drink to the Cafferkeys at the other end of the bar.

"I got Jake's mom on the phone," Bonnie goes on, holding her own mug delicately between her manicured fingertips. "And I told her the whole family is invited to the wrap party here at the Ho Ho when the show is over."

"Perfect."

"She knew about the show, but said she hadn't heard from Jake in a couple of weeks, so I told her that the network forbids contestants from having any contact with the outside world during the course of the show."

"Which is basically true," Holly says, taking another drink of her butterscotch cocoa. "I felt like Leanna was letting me get a peek at him the other day, but I could tell she didn't want him to talk to me. And the most bizarre thing about it was that he *obeyed* her. His eyes were strange —it wasn't him, Bon."

Bonnie puts a hand on Holly's arm. "I believe you, sugar. I do. You know Jake better than any of us, and if you say he was acting funny then he was."

The unmistakable opening notes of Bobby Helms singing 'Jingle Bell Rock' blare over the speakers, and Buckhunter pulls Fiona onto the dance floor.

"How 'bout it?" Wyatt Bender asks, appearing between Bonnie and Holly. He holds out a hand to Bonnie. "I know we're on different sides of the political fence, so to speak, but I'd love to take a fine lady like yourself for a spin on the dance floor if you'd oblige me." Wyatt takes his cowboy hat off politely.

Bonnie and Holly exchange a look. "My mother told me never to say no to a man who gets up the nerve to ask for a dance," Bonnie explains to her friend. "It's bad manners, and Southern girls are nothing if not well-mannered."

"Hey, no explanation necessary," Holly says with a smile, holding her drink in her hands to warm her fingers. "Enjoy." She watches as Wyatt leads Bonnie to the center of the room. They just get settled into one another's arms and find a rhythm when the short song ends and Ella Fitzgerald starts singing 'Let it Snow! Let it Snow! Let it Snow!' Holly turns on her stool and watches them together.

After a few minutes, she takes her drink and ambles over to the steps that lead down onto the beach. Joe has wound strings of large, multi-colored bulbs around the railings of the stairs, and the palm trees on either side of the bar are already festooned with holiday lights from the ground all the way up to the fronds. The patio heater is radiant at her side, and the waves crash in the darkness beyond the bar. This combination of lights, music, cold winter weather, and the warm drink conspire to wrap Holly in the comfort and cheer of the holiday season.

When 'Santa Baby' starts playing, Holly knows she'll turn around and find Bonnie lip-synching and acting out the words. Sure enough, she's up on the little stage that Joe uses when he plays his guitar for the locals, and the crowd is watching Bonnie do her silly Earth Kitt impression. It's an annual favorite, and everyone laughs and cheers her on as she trains her eyes on Wyatt Bender, mouthing the words directly to him while his face goes pink.

Holly watches from the steps. It's beautiful to look around and see everyone mingling at the Ho Ho, and there's comfort in the knowledge that even in the face of disagreement and disillusion, the islanders can pull together and work as a team.

This shouldn't surprise Holly—after all, they'd come together in August to keep everything running while a tropical storm battered the island, and they've seen each other through illness, loss, and plenty of good times—but knowing that a bond of real love and respect runs through the people of Christmas Key brings Holly peace. And in this moment, nothing else matters, not even Cap trying to unseat her from her position as mayor. Her eyes mist over as she watches these people she loves. They're all her family, and without them, she wouldn't be who she is—in fact, this island could never *be* at all.

From the plummy darkness of the beach beyond, the rustic shack on the water twinkles with colorful lights and the buttery warmth of electricity while a woman sits on the steps alone. And as the sounds of the season mingle with the echoes of the crashing waves beyond the bar, the diamond-sharp stars in the sky blink high above the little island, clear and bright in the cold winter night.

Chapter Twenty

Holly stops and looks at the front window of Mistletoe Morning Brew at six-thirty on Monday morning, one hand resting on the door handle. The large pane of glass facing the street is covered with an intricately painted scene of a snowy city street. There's a horse-drawn carriage in the center of a cobbled lane, and a glowing street lamp with a holiday wreath hanging beneath its lantern. She pushes the door in, and the cacophony of sleigh bells that Carrie-Anne and Ellen have tied to the door sends a cascade of sound careening around the coffee shop. Inside, the store is decorated for December, and all of the Poe paraphernalia from November has been sold or packed away. Delicate paper snowflakes dangle from invisible fishing line, and a holiday carol played on Scottish bagpipes fills the room.

The temperature on the island has shot back up by about twenty degrees, so even with the pink skies of dawn outside, Holly is comfortable in cut-off jean shorts and a flannel button-up shirt over her tank top, along with her Yankees cap and Converse. She walks over to where Heddie Lang-Mueller sits at her favorite table, a cup of coffee resting on a saucer next to an open book.

"Morning, Heddie," Holly says, hanging her purse over the chair back. She takes off her hat and shoves it into the purse. "Looks festive in here." Holly fishes her wallet out of her purse and looks at a glossy poster on the wall. It's got a drawing of an old man in a nightshirt, and he's hunched over, carrying a candle dripping with melted wax.

Ellen is waiting behind the counter in a ruffled red-and-green checkered apron. "Up and at 'em early, huh?" she asks Holly, one hand on her hip.

"I am, but did you ever go to bed, or did you stay up all night painting that front window?"

"Guilty as charged," Ellen admits, looking at the window with pride. "I hear you and I both have late night projects to work on when we can't sleep."

"True, but mine is nothing compared to the stuff you do here," Holly says. "I just slap a few shells on the wall of my lanai late at night. You work magic while the rest of us sleep."

"Thank you kindly," Ellen says, ducking her head modestly. "I can't sleep when I'm in the middle of creating something."

"It's pretty impressive. Hey, how are the turkeys doing?"

"Oh, they're running the show. We've been working on another pen so we have a place to put Madonkey when she gets here—which should be soon." Ellen pulls a pen out of her apron pocket and taps the end of it against the counter. "What can I get for you this morning?"

The chalkboard behind Ellen's head has been rewritten and decorated for the holidays, and Holly scans the list of seasonal items. "Hmmm, the Mr. Lillyvick Latte? The Rose Maylie Mocha? I'm sensing a theme here…" Holly scrunches up her forehead, thinking. "Ahhh, I got it! Copperfield Cold Coffee—it's Charles Dickens!"

"Yay!" Ellen claps, clearly pleased that Holly has guessed correctly. "You got it."

"I'm going with plain coffee this morning," Holly says, picking up an empty ceramic mug from the counter.

"On the house today," Ellen says, putting a hand in her apron pocket. "You and Heddie are our early birds, so you get the good stuff." She nods at the big carafes of coffee on the counter that runs along the wall. "Help yourself."

Holly fills her mug with a steaming vanilla-nut blend, then tops it off with half-and-half and a sprinkle of cinnamon.

"So," she says to Heddie, setting her full coffee cup on the table gently and pulling out her chair. "You wanted to meet me here before the sun is even up, so you must have something good to share." Holly settles into the tall chair at the bistro table and looks at Heddie expectantly.

Heddie—as ever—is sitting ramrod straight in her chair, gray-blonde hair smoothed into a neat bun at the nape of her neck. The former German film star is known for carrying herself regally at all times, and six-thirty in the morning is no exception. Heddie closes a bookmark into the crease of the book she's been reading.

"I do have something to share," she says, her flawless English flavored with her native accent. Heddie picks up the spoon she's left on the saucer and sticks it into her cream-lightened coffee. She stirs slowly. "It's about Cap."

Holly nods carefully, moving her own cup of coffee so that it rests directly in front of her. Her movements are measured; Heddie is like a horse she doesn't want to spook. The bagpipe carols end and a jazzy rendition of 'God Rest Ye Merry Gentlemen' begins. They are still the only customers in the shop.

"Some time ago," Heddie begins, "when you were still a very small girl and paid no mind to us old people, things were different than they are now."

"How so?" Holly ventures, picking up her mug.

"Well, for starters, Cap Duncan wasn't an old pirate whose only companion is a feathered nitwit." Heddie glances at the door. "And for another thing, he was quite handsome."

Holly chokes on her coffee.

"Yes, it's true," Heddie assures her, "he was tall and kept his hair short, and he wasn't wearing that ridiculous earring yet."

Holly leans back in her chair, waiting for more.

"Not only was he handsome, but he was a good dancer, and he'd read every book you could think of. Quite an interesting person to pass an evening with."

"I did dance with him once—in his shop this past summer," Holly says, remembering the time he'd insisted on taking her in his arms and dancing to Bob Marley. "He was pretty good."

"Indeed he was. And then—as with all things—time changed him." Heddie looks at Holly, her eyes serious. "We spent time together on a regular basis, and at some point I realized that it wasn't working."

"Meaning…you broke up with him?" Holly asks tentatively.

"I suppose you could say that," Heddie says. "He was drinking again —this has been his life-long battle, you understand—and becoming less predictable. And I do *not* do unpredictable." Heddie wags a long, slim finger back and forth in the air as she shakes her head.

"That would have been my guess," Holly jokes, one side of her mouth curling into a smile. She reaches for the Christmas tree-shaped sugar jar in the middle of the table and uses the miniature spoon sitting next to the jar to dump some into her coffee.

"I like routine. I like structure. I like control." Heddie straightens her shoulders, though they're already straight enough to balance trays upon. "I am offended by a man who drinks himself into a stupor and can't remember the things he did or didn't say to a woman."

"That's understandable."

"I have not forgiven him for some of the things that happened, but that is not why I want to tell you this—please let me be clear. It's because I am a fan of all you do and all you stand for when it comes to this island, Holly. Your grandparents were very dear people, and I think the choices you make always honor their intentions."

"Thank you. That means a lot." Tears well up in Holly's eyes at the mention of her grandparents; she swallows hard.

"I believe Cap is behaving foolishly, and much of what he's doing and saying comes from the place of a lonely, drunken man. That said, I want you to know what it is he might be hiding, though all I can do is point you in the right direction."

Heddie has her complete attention at this point, and Holly waits for more, her eyes wide with anticipation.

"It's been nearly twenty-five years since I spent time in Cap's apartment, but at one point I was a frequent visitor." Heddie pauses, pulling the folded napkin from beneath her saucer. She pats her lips with the napkin. "It was during this time that I discovered that Cap isn't really Cap."

"I always figured he had a real first name."

"Oh, yes—he does. And a different last name."

"What?" The room spins and Holly grabs the edge of the table to steady herself. There have been so many—too many—surprises in the past six months, and finding out that Cap isn't really who she's always thought he was might be the thing that pushes her over the edge. "Who is he?" She needs to hear this.

"His name is Caspar Braun. He is also German, but he will not want you to know that. There are secrets here, Holly, and you need to handle them carefully," Heddie warns.

Holly sits still, digesting this information. "But…Cap…he doesn't *sound* German," she protests, as if this answers any of the questions that are zipping through her brain like jolts of electricity through power lines.

"He spent many, many years sailing around the world, as he's told you. He speaks several languages," Heddie says. There is a note of protectiveness in her voice that surprises Holly. She's not sure if it's borne of national pride, or from a decades old romance that, perhaps, never really ended. "By the time he landed on this island, there was virtually no trace of the man he'd been before."

"How did he end up here? How did you?" Holly sputters. She is thrashing around, searching for meaning. From the corner of her eye, she sees Carrie-Anne come from the back room, tying her own holiday-themed apron in a bow behind her back. Carrie-Anne and Ellen talk quietly behind the front counter, discussing the day ahead in muted tones.

"How did any of us? And why?" Heddie asks gently, her thin eyebrows arched. "I fell in love with the wrong man once and came here for escape, then fell in love with the wrong man again. This must be my lot in life," she says, reaching a thin hand across the table and wrapping it around Holly's. Heddie's hand is cool, her crepey skin soft to the touch.

Holly nods, trying to understand.

"Please use this information wisely. It has the potential to hurt people." Heddie looks into her eyes, begging silently for agreement.

"I promise," Holly says, wrapping her own hand around Heddie's. She squeezes reassuringly, not tearing her gaze away. "I promise."

* * *

"I take it there's more," Holly says that afternoon, slinging her bag onto a stool at the slab of wood that serves as a counter at Jack Frosty's.

Buckhunter has two long pieces of sanded wood rigged up on the side of the bar that looks out onto Main Street, and when patrons feel like people-watching, they choose a stool facing the busy street so they can greet their neighbors as they snack or have a drink.

Fiona is already sitting on a stool, a glass of chardonnay catching sparks of light from the late afternoon sun. Next to her wineglass is a pair of big, black sunglasses and a notepad. She's wearing a black sweater and a pair of dark jeans.

Holly looks her up and down. "Are you dressed like Jackie O., or a Bond Girl?"

Fiona glances at her own outfit. "I was going more for *La Femme Nikita*," she says, frowning. "Serious sleuthing calls for serious fashion."

"That's a lot of black for the tropics, but you do look fabulous," Holly admits, signaling Buckhunter. "Are we drinking?"

"Is Rudolph a red-nosed reindeer?"

"Oooh, fashionable *and* on-theme. I'm impressed." Holly points at Fiona's wine glass and holds up her index finger so that Buckhunter will know she wants the same thing. "So whatcha got?"

"Well, a couple of things." Fiona grins wickedly. "But I feel like an order of onion rings would really help to jog my memory when it comes to the details."

"Isn't that what the notepad is for?" Holly gestures at the pad of paper.

"But the doodles don't make any sense when I start to get weak from low blood sugar," Fiona argues, fanning herself with a plastic-covered menu.

"I told you that's too much black. You're going to have a heatstroke," Holly says, picking up another menu and waving it at Fiona like a fan.

"It's December. And all I wore in Chicago was black. I can handle this."

"Suit yourself, doc." Holly shrugs and turns to look for Buckhunter. "Hey, barkeep—can we get an order of onion rings, two ice waters, and the fan turned on overhead, please?"

"Coming right up," Buckhunter says. Holly watches her uncle cut through the tables in the open-air bar, grabbing empty glasses and shouting out greetings to the handful of people who're sitting around at the low tables.

"Food is forthcoming. Now dish."

"So, I heard back from my Hollywood source, and apparently Other Guy—"

"As in the other guy who isn't Jake, Bridget, Chuck Cortwell, or Violetta the hipster?"

"The one who looks like he should be modeling boxers in a Sears catalog, and yet kind of like he might be mowing the lawn next door? Yeah, him." Fiona flips open her notepad and scans the notes she's written on the page. "Adam Hobson. Born in Maryland, moved to L.A. after dropping out of community college. Lifts weights at a Crossfit in Burbank, and met a producer at the Coffee Bean & Tea Leaf by his gym. Producer told him to audition for this reality show, and boom—here he is. Twenty-eight, single, possibly straight, possibly not. Who knows."

Holly smiles at Buckhunter as he sets a glass of wine in front of her along with the ice waters. The breeze picks up outside and blows through the open-air bar, lifting the ends of Holly's hair as she takes her first sip. "How did you find out all of this about Adam…Hopkins?"

"Hobson. And I told you, my Hollywood connection came through. He even sent me a clip of Adam's *Wild Tropics* audition."

"You're amazing," Holly says, setting the base of her wine glass down on the wooden counter with a clink. Fiona's resourcefulness is impressive. "So now that leaves us with Bridget, and we've got nothing on her?"

"Nothing *yet*, which is strange, but my guy is working on it. I'll get to the bottom of this—don't worry."

"I'm not worried, Fee, I'm just perplexed at how quickly life can go from 'Eh, everything is fine, no big deal,' to 'WHAT THE HELL IS GOING ON AROUND HERE?!'—it's kind of unnerving."

"You mean because of Jake?" Fiona reaches for the basket of onion rings as Buckhunter hands them over.

"Yeah. And Cap trying to oust me from office, and my mother wanting us to buy her out, and, well, all of it. I swear I had things under control and then one day I just…didn't."

"You do have things under control. Don't kid yourself. Who else whips the entire island into a frenzy trying to save Jake from himself?"

"But it's my fault he's—"

"Your fault he's what? Getting romanced by a supermodel? Going to be on national television? Come on, Hol," Fiona says sternly. "Pull yourself out of the equation here. It's not your job to save Jake or the world."

"Just the island," Holly says, and she knows this is the truth: saving Jake from possible humiliation and disappointment is really her way of saving the island. Of course she cares about him and his feelings—there's no question about that. But she suddenly can't think of a time when she made choices or took action without the best interest of Christmas Key at the center of it all.

No matter what's at stake, it always comes back to the island.

* * *

It's quiet inside of Holly's house. She's lying in her darkened living room, feet up on the armrest of her couch with Pucci sitting on the floor next to her. Her hand dangles off the edge and rests on the dog's furry back, her fingers tracing mindless circles as she pets him and stares at the television. It's late—almost midnight—and she's wearing sweats and a long-sleeved t-shirt, a crocheted blanket that her grandma made for her pulled up over her body. The things Heddie told her at the coffee shop have been flipping and diving through her brain all day, but she hasn't shared the information about Cap with anyone, not even with Fiona at Jack Frosty's that evening. Heddie's warning to tread lightly is something she takes seriously, and she'll weigh whatever she finds carefully before deciding what to do with it.

For the seventh time already since Thanksgiving, Chevy Chase is on her television stapling the cuff of his shirtsleeve to the gutter on the second story of his suburban house. Holly unwraps a Hershey's Kiss and pops it into her mouth, tossing the foil wrapper in the general direction of her coffee table. As Clark Griswold, Chevy fumbles on his ladder, falling backwards against a tree, then pushing his body upright again so he can finish hanging the Christmas lights. She's seen *National Lampoon's Christmas Vacation* more times than she cares to think about, but this year—as she watches Clark Griswold, the eternal optimist—she empathizes with him rather than just laughing at his hijinks. No matter how kooky his desire for an old-fashioned family Christmas seems, and no matter what lengths he has to go to in order to make holiday magic happen for his family, Clark Griswold plasters a smile on his face over and over. Every time something brings him down he pops back up again, ready to face the world.

Holly uses her free hand to dig into the bowl that's wedged between her hip and the couch cushions. She fishes out a fistful of popcorn and shoves it into her mouth, still petting Pucci with her dangling hand. Holly snorts as the Griswolds' yuppie neighbors doubt him at every turn. She watches as the people Clark invites into his home bungle his plans and try to talk him out of his vision, their own agendas disrupting the flow of Clark's plan for a perfect Christmas.

When the popcorn bowl is empty, Holly sets it on the coffee table with a thud and rolls onto her side, tucking a throw pillow under her ear.

She watches with amusement, laughing at Cousin Eddie and the slapstick jokes as she does every year. But when Clark's boss is delivered to his house wrapped in a bow Holly sits up, her blanket slipping to the floor. "This is it, Pooch. This is it *exactly*," she says out loud to the dog. Pucci looks up at her with big brown eyes, the crocheted blanket covering his hind legs and tail. "Even though Clark Griswold feels like everyone is working against him," she explains, holding out one hand at the television, "he keeps doing it anyway. And do you know why?" She looks down at her dog. Pucci puts his head on the rug under the coffee table, ears still perked up. "Because it brings him joy, and he knows that once everything comes together, it'll make everyone else happy, too."

Holly stands up and walks over to the kitchen counter where her phone is plugged in. She unhooks it from the charger and pulls up River's number. It's only about nine-thirty on the west coast, and she listens to the ringing as she waits for him to pick up. When he finally does, she blurts out, "I'm Clark Griswold. I'm him. He's me—I mean, we're kindred spirits." She digs the remote out of the couch cushions and clicks the television off. The light from the kitchen filters into the room, and the smell of the frozen pizza she baked in the oven for dinner lingers with the scent of microwave popcorn layered over the top.

"He's probably a little hairier than you are, but I'm listening." River sounds amused on the other end of the line.

Holly paces around her living room, the glow of her phone screen lighting up her face. The corner where she puts her Christmas tree every year is still empty, and she makes a mental note to dig out her decorations and start on the house. "I'm watching *Christmas Vacation*—"

"As one does at this time of year."

"—And I realized this time that I wasn't laughing at Clark Griswold because I actually *feel* for him. He's busting his hump trying to hang lights and make the perfect turkey—"

"Speaking of turkeys…"

"—Yeah, they're still alive. Stop interrupting," Holly says. "Now, listen. Sometimes people are against him, and sometimes he's his own worst enemy, but he always keeps his eyes on the prize."

"Okay…right," River says.

"And no matter what obstacles get in his way, he plays the long game."

"All right, I'm seeing the connections now. I am curious if you've been drinking, but I can agree that there is a certain Griswoldness to your laser-sharp focus when you decide to do something."

"Thank you," Holly says. As the words crossed her lips she wondered whether they sounded crazy, so it feels good when River gets her thought process. "And no, I'm not drinking. Hey, can you hurry up and get here already?"

"Next week, Griswold. But you have to swear you won't kick the crap out of a plastic lawn Santa in front of everyone, or I'm leaving again."

"No promises." Holly smiles to herself. It's all going to be fine: River will be there soon, and she'll figure out whatever it is that Heddie wants her to know about Cap. Somehow a plan for what to do with the wrap party that they've invited Jake's family to will materialize, and Fiona will dig up some information on Bridget.

And before she knows it, just like Clark Griswold, she'll figure out how to turn a hostage situation into a party.

Chapter Twenty-One

The old denture equipment has been removed from the space where Scissors & Ribbons is going in, and—thanks to Jimmy Cafferkey and his ladder—a week after the ladies met to sip champagne and celebrate the salon space, the windows are sparkling and clear. Eighteen people are gathered in the empty shop, its tile floors swept clean and mopped, the harsh florescent lights changed out for softer bulbs. Millie Bradford has a red bandana wrapped around her short hair, and she's wearing a yellow t-shirt and a pair of overalls flecked with dried paint.

"I chose this Tiffany blue color for the walls," she explains, one palm resting on the front counter that she's already sanded and repainted a shiny black. "And my shampoo chairs are black with stainless steel bowls. Black isn't very beachy, but I want it to be functional."

Everyone is gathered around, dressed in their own painting clothes, and ready to pitch in when Millie gives them the go-ahead. Cap has joined the group with his hair pulled back in a rubber band, and he's wearing one of his campaign shirts with the words "If you want it done in a snap, you'd better vote for Cap!" plastered across the back. On the front is a cartoon drawing of a profile that looks like Cap himself with a bird that's the spitting image of Marco sitting on the man's shoulder. It's utterly ridiculous, and Holly turns to Bonnie to give her an exaggerated eye roll.

"I thought Cap was the man who had no plan," Bonnie hisses to her. "What could he possibly be getting done in a snap?" They shake their heads and turn their attention back to Millie.

"I'd like to go all white in the bathroom," Millie says, pointing at the door to the public restroom at one end of the salon. "And I've already done all of the taping off of windows and trim. If anyone's not comfortable painting, there are lots of other things I'd love help with, so just let me know." Millie presses her hands together in front of her chest as if in prayer. "I really appreciate all of you, and your help and support. It means a lot to me and Ray to be a part of this community, and I'm really happy to be able to offer something to Christmas Key by opening this salon." Millie's cheeks are flushed with excitement.

"Here, here, Millie!" Joe Sacamano shouts, holding up a paintbrush for emphasis. "Let's get this job done!"

"Okay," Millie says, clapping her hands together. "Let's do this."

The islanders spread out, finding open cans of paint on the tarps that Millie and Ray have spread on the floor. Ray turns on the stereo and a calypso song with steel drums bursts from the speakers. Behind the front counter is a cooler full of soda and water and ice. People choose spots next to the friends and neighbors they want to talk to while they work, and within minutes, everyone is working to turn the beige walls blue. Holly dips her brush into the paint and makes her first swipe. With the window next to her, the strip of paint looks like a color swatch of sky held up next to its real life counterpart. Holly dips her brush into the can again and pulls it up and down the wall smoothly, watching her patch of blue spread across the old paint.

"Mind if I work here?" Buckhunter is standing next to Holly holding a can of paint by its wire handle. In his other hand is a well-used paintbrush.

"Nope. Join me," she says. "I'm just turning stuff over in my head here, so don't mind me."

"How are things going with Operation Jake?" Buckhunter sets his paint can on the tarp and pries off the lid.

"Eh. Fiona found out the backstory on all of the contestants except Bridget. There's really nothing there."

"What were you hoping to find?" he asks mildly, mixing his can of paint with a long stir stick.

"I don't know. Something, I guess. Maybe some dirt we could use on them somehow."

"Sounds pretty vague." Buckhunter is nothing if not succinct. Always unapologetically a man of few words, he's prone to making declarations and then sitting back to see what happens next.

"So what would you suggest?" Holly looks around. Bonnie and Wyatt Bender are painting next to one another on the other side of the room, and Cap is on his knees near the front door, dragging his own angled brush across the top of the trim that runs along the floor. Clearly they've suspended their campaigning while they paint (save for Cap's t-shirt), and Wyatt is using his free time to chat Bonnie up. Holly turns her attention back to Buckhunter.

"I'm not sure. But I do think you'd be better served by bringing Jake back to his senses than you'd be by trying to cut someone off at the knees."

Holly stops painting and stares out the window. The swags of faux greenery dotted with ornaments that stretch from one sidewalk over to the other all up and down Main Street are moving slightly in the gentle December breeze. "Hmm." She frowns, considering this. "So you mean we need to remind him he's not a television star and that this isn't Hollywood?"

"More than that," Buckhunter says, stopping to wipe at a drip of the robin's egg blue paint as it runs down his forearm, "I think you need to remind him what he loves about the island and about being a cop. I never heard him say he wanted to be a reality star, but sometimes when you feel like you don't have much going, you'll take whatever comes your way." His stroke on the wall is effortless, and he dips and paints easily, covering at least twice as much ground as Holly does.

She thinks about Buckhunter's words. Obviously her breakup with Jake is at the heart of Buckhunter's assessment of the situation, and without Holly and their future together, Jake really doesn't have much holding him back. Without being tied to her, he has no real reason not to have a fling with Bridget. She knows Buckhunter is right, but she doesn't know how to remind Jake that he's not anchor-less and adrift at sea—he's got the island. He's got her friendship. He has the support of everyone on Christmas Key.

"But I don't know how to make him see that."

"You'll figure it out. You're a resourceful gal." Buckhunter looks at her. He's got a smear of paint the color of a Tiffany's jewelry box in his graying blonde goatee. "But while you're thinking about it, would you mind grabbing me a Diet Coke?" He nods at the cooler behind the front counter.

"I thought *you* were the bartender."

"I'm currently off-duty." Buckhunter reaches over with his paintbrush and dabs it lightly against the tip of his niece's nose. The paint-covered bristles are cool and wet on her skin.

"Well, you don't have to paint me—you can just ask for the drink," she says, ducking to get away from him.

"I *did* ask for it." Buckhunter turns back to the wall and gives it another swipe of paint.

Holly laughs to herself as she walks over to the cooler. Fiona passes by the doorway to the salon in her lab coat with Mrs. Agnelli following close on her heels. The room is filled with the sounds of Caribbean jazz and friendly discussion, and the paint fumes are cut by the smell of the ocean through the open windows and doors.

Holly picks out two cans of Diet Coke from the cooler and shakes off the dripping water from the melted ice. She knows Buckhunter's advice is solid: finding a way to bring Jake back into the fold is the best way to fix this situation. Sharing someone's private information and embarrassing them doesn't feel like a good thing to do. It might have seemed like a necessary evil, but that certainly doesn't make it right.

With a loud grunt, Cap pushes himself up from his kneeling position on the floor. Since meeting Heddie two days before, all she's been able to do is hunt and peck around on a couple of ancestry websites looking for any mention of Caspar Braun, but she hasn't turned up anything earth-shattering.

As she watches him now, Holly realizes that she has to treat Cap the same way she treats Jake and the other contestants: she needs to make sure she doesn't use personal information to simply embarrass him as she tries to gain the upper hand. That would be a mistake—and one that she'd never forgive herself for.

Holly hands Buckhunter his can of soda and pops the top on her own. She takes a long pull and then sets the can on the windowsill so she can get back to painting.

* * *

After an evening of painting at Scissors & Ribbons, Holly is awake in her darkened bedroom while Pucci snores peacefully on his dog bed in the corner. She contemplates getting up and working on her shell wall on the lanai, but instead yanks on a mismatched bikini in the dim light from her hallway, covering it up with a sweatshirt and a pair of fleece pajama bottoms.

After a short drive through the night noises of the sleep-covered island, her fingers tucked into the cuffs of her sweatshirt for warmth against the cool winter night, Holly pulls into the driveway of the B&B. She tiptoes through the lobby and onto the pool deck, holding the handle of the door so that it shuts softly on its hinges.

Under the bright winter moon, she sheds her fleece pants and sweatshirt. The cool air raises goosebumps on her bare arms and legs. She dips a toe into the heated pool and shivers; the water isn't as warm as her bed, and for a second Holly hesitates, looking down at the steam rising off the water in the cold night. The pool is lit from beneath with lights, but two of the clear bulbs have already been replaced with red and green lights for the holidays. Holly stands next to the pool looking at the washes of color that spread through the blue like Christmas-themed oil slicks.

The water ripples and waves in the pool, and the hum of the heater fills the air around her. Without another thought, Holly points the toes of her right foot and steps over the water, arms wrapped tightly around her torso, face scrunched up to keep the water out of her eyes and nose. She slices through the water and plunges for the bottom. When her toes touch, she pushes off and glides back up, cutting the surface with the crown of her head and gasping for air. The frigid water on her already-cold skin has awakened her senses, and she experiences everything in macro: the pool heater is no longer a hum, but a saw-like buzz; the stars aren't just twinkling, they're flashing aggressively overhead like lighthouse beacons; the colored pool lights have morphed from watercolor washes of red and green to opaque blotches of crimson and emerald.

Holly loosens her grip on her upper body and lets her arms float around her like cooked spaghetti. She falls backward, her toes slowly lifting from the ground and rising in the water in front of her until she's lying on her back, her face and breasts bobbing above the water while the rest of her body is cocooned by the heated pool. The air is cold on her face, and from this position, she can see the lights of two of the guest rooms burning from the second floor. They're Wayne and Leanna's rooms, if she's counting from the end correctly. Holly watches the gauzy curtains that cover both windows, but she doesn't see any movement.

Underwater, the muted sounds of the pool filter and heater lull her into a hypnotic state. Every month feels like the most beautiful month on her island, and every season is her favorite when she's in the middle of it. But winter—and December—have a special feel that no other time of year can replicate. The Christmas decorations that cover the island all year long are amplified by what the islanders call their "winter weather," and the feeling of a winter night experienced while swimming under the stars is incomparable. Holly spreads her limbs like she's making a snow angel, dragging her arms in and out as she slowly treads water on her back.

She's hashed and re-hashed Buckhunter's advice all evening, trying to mesh it with the demands that Wayne made during their meeting at the B&B nearly two weeks ago, and she's still coming up empty-handed. The way she sees it, she's obligated to help the network throw a party as the show's finale, but she's also obligated to keep Jake from looking like a fool. On top of it all, she's got Cap to contend with, and they're only ten days away from calling a vote to determine who'll hold office as mayor for the next term.

Overhead, Aries is visible in the night sky. Holly counts the stars that make up the constellation, watching her own breath as it folds into the steam from the water and drifts away like smoke. She counts the pin-points of light again, but before she can even finish, she's got it: she knows what she needs to do to bring Jake back.

In one swift move, Holly swims to the stairs and climbs out, a sheet of lukewarm water running from her wet hair and trailing down her back. She grabs the towel she's tossed onto the lounge chair and wraps it around her head like a turban. The fleece pants go on over her damp skin, and she zips the sweatshirt over her wet swimsuit hurriedly. It's late—or maybe it's early, as it was nearly midnight when she left her house—but Holly knows she needs to go tonight or she risks losing her nerve.

Under the cloak of darkness, she flips the switch on her golf cart and rolls out of the lot, wet head still wrapped in a towel. When she gets to Jake's house, she cuts the headlamp on her cart and takes the towel off her head, setting her Mets cap on top of her wet, tangled hair instead. Then she zips her sweatshirt all the way up to the chin and pulls the hoody on over her hat. With a quick glance at the dark houses around Jake's bungalow, Holly runs to his lanai. She holds her breath as she pauses with one hand on the door handle. Slowly, exhaling as though even the slightest breath will set off an intricate alarm system, she slides open the glass door just as she'd done at Leanna's request on Thanksgiving morning. Everything is as it had been during her last visit.

Holly slides the door closed behind her and tiptoes through Jake's kitchen. She's inside.

Chapter Twenty-Two

Operation Jake has officially morphed from a mission to undermine to a search and rescue operation. The word has spread across the island that all previous plans to approach the camp site; to infiltrate the B&B and gather intel from Wayne and Leanna's rooms; or to otherwise bungle the reality show's operations, were to cease and desist. Carrie-Anne and Ellen had offered to loose the turkeys on the camp site at sunrise, Maria Agnelli had promised to bake cookies laced with castor oil for the producers (which led to much speculation about whether or not she normally adds odd things to her potluck dishes intentionally or as a side effect of senility, as they'd all assumed), and Cap and Wyatt had declared that a controlled fire upwind of the whole operation would produce enough smoke and debris to put the crew off filming for at least a day or two. And while Holly is thrilled with the creative ideas that had been the fruit of their emergency village council meeting, she knows she's got something even better now.

"Today's the day, sugar!" Bonnie calls out as Holly breezes into the B&B's office and hangs her bag on the hook by the door. She takes off her Mets cap and sets it on top of the filing cabinet.

"I know—I can't believe he's *finally coming back*," Holly says, dropping into her chair and lifting her sandaled feet off the floor. In one fluid motion, she sets her heels on the edge of the desk and laces her hands across her stomach. "I feel dizzy—I think I'm coming down with something."

"It's just the butterflies in your belly, you lovesick girl-child." Bonnie gives her a knowing look. "Did you shave your legs?"

"I always do."

"Above the knee?" She wiggles her eyebrows suggestively.

An impish grin spreads across Holly's face. "Yep. And I got Millie to give me a pedicure, even though she's not quite ready to open for business." She wiggles her bright red toes so that Bonnie can see.

"So I guess we won't see you for dinner tonight?"

"Probably not. But with any luck, you might see us tomorrow."

River's boat is scheduled to dock around three, and Holly has a romantic dinner for two planned on her lanai. She's already put in an order with Iris and Jimmy, and they'll have her lobster dinner for two boxed up and ready to go when she swings by later. As a special treat, Holly asked the triplets to order in a special bottle of Champagne Collet, and it's cooling in her fridge next to the bowl of passionfruit and guava that she's cut up for dessert.

"Ooooh, you devil!" Bonnie holds a flyer in one hand, and she reaches across the desk and uses it to swat Holly's bare calf. "You two kids have fun now, you hear?"

"That's the plan," Holly says, swinging her legs around and setting her feet back on the ground. She opens her laptop and hits the power button. "I guess I should do something around here to keep myself occupied until three, huh?"

"We've got a few irons in the fire we can check on. Want to work on January?"

The women pull up their calendars on their respective desktops and open the working documents they share to coordinate their plans for the upcoming months.

"Did you ever hear back from the Coast Guard?" Holly taps at her keyboard, pulling up her email.

"Sure did, sugar. They granted us a Special Local Regulation and Safety Zone for January 27th through the 30th. The only problem is that no one else can enter or anchor freely without permission during that time." Bonnie gets out of her chair and walks over to the giant whiteboard. She picks up a marker and uncaps it.

"That's fine. In fact," Holly says, turning around in her chair to look at her assistant, "it's preferable. With so many new people visiting, I think we want to have some sort of regulation of traffic."

Bonnie stands in front of the board, the felt tip of her marker poised to write. Her face melts into a dreamy gaze. "Just think of all of those men dressed as pirates with their eye patches and tight breeches, swashbuckling around with swords dangling from their belts…"

"That does sound a lot like a pirate festival," Holly says. She turns back to her laptop with a smirk.

"It's a brilliant idea—one of your best," Bonnie says encouragingly, snapping out of her mental montage of men in tights and buccaneer hats. She finally sets the pen against the board and drags it across the words 'Coast Guard confirmation' with a flourish, effectively crossing it off the list of things to do.

"I needed something brilliant to redeem me after the live turkey debacle, and after the reality show that's trying to turn my ex-boyfriend into a Stepford Wife and marry him off to a human Barbie."

"You're still letting this nonsense rattle you, doll," Bonnie says, capping the marker and sitting down in her own chair across from Holly's. "You've done nothing wrong here, and Cap saying you have doesn't make it so."

Holly looks up from her laptop screen and meets Bonnie's gaze. "But it isn't just Cap saying it—now it's fact."

"No, no, no." Bonnie shakes her head firmly, not a single red hair moving out of place as she does. "We have no idea what kind of positive outcome this show will have for the island. You're just stuck in the middle of it right now, and all you can see is Jake. Pull back—pull way, way back—and remember that we're going to be on *television*, sugar— and you got us there. We're going to become a household name no matter what happens with Officer Hotpants and this trollop."

Holly snorts. "Did you just call her a 'trollop'?"

"I did," Bonnie says matter-of-factly, sliding her pink-and-yellow reading glasses back onto her face. "But that's just my personal opinion of a young lady who sells herself by putting on a bikini and frolicking with men on a television show."

Holly taps the eraser of a freshly-sharpened pencil against her front teeth. "I don't know. Fiona still hasn't been able to find out anything about her. For all I know, she's a perfectly nice girl from a good family. And maybe she really likes Jake. Who am I to say this is wrong?"

"Honey, your gut says it's wrong, and that's good enough for me." Bonnie nods curtly, looking at the calendar on her screen again. "You don't need to know anything about this girl, just do what you think is best to help Jake, and the rest will sort itself out." The desk phone rings next to Bonnie's computer and she puts her hand on the receiver. "And remember: it don't rain *every* time the pig squeals."

Holly sets the pencil on her desk. "Meaning?"

The phone rings one more time before Bonnie answers it, and she levels her gaze at Holly across the top of their computer screens. "It means not everything that happens turns into a full-blown storm. But if you get ready for one every time you hear a pig squeal, you'll always be running for shelter."

* * *

The hum of the motor fills the air as the boat nears the dock. Holly is standing on her tiptoes in the sand, one hand shielding her eyes as she scans the ferry for River's face. The ferryman cuts the engine altogether as he slips into place, then Jerrod, the boat hand, jumps onto the dock with a length of rope in his strong hands. His muscles flex as he pulls the bow and stern lines tightly, wrapping them around the dock cleats in snug figure-eights.

With a racing heart, Holly stands, hands pressed together. The bi-weekly delivery of groceries is on this ferry, and Jerrod quickly unloads the bags and boxes, setting them in a growing pile on the dock.

"Hey, Holly," Jerrod says, giving her a sloppy salute. He's got tan lines on his thighs that Holly can see every time he bends over and his shorts ride up.

"What's the news from the mainland?" she asks casually, her eyes trained on the boat.

"College kids are out for winter break and Key West is a zoo," Jerrod says, flipping his hair with a toss of the head. "I hate it." He's only about five years out of college himself, but he already sounds like the crazy old guy in the neighborhood who doesn't like kids running across his lawn.

"Damn teenagers," Holly growls. She's joking, but he nods and gives her a thumbs-up as he steps back onto the boat.

"You've got two big boxes here," Jerrod shouts, jockeying as he tries to scoot two tall items to the lip of the ferry. "They've got FRAGILE stamped on the sides, and they're heavy as all get out."

"Let me help you." Holly steps up to the edge of the boat. She's momentarily forgotten that she's there for a much more important shipment than groceries and fragile boxes, and with some finagling, she and Jerrod get the two big boxes onto the dock next to the food delivery.

"What the heck are these?" Jerrod asks, wiping his brow.

"I think they're the chairs and shampoo bowls for our new salon." Holly tips her head about forty-five degrees to the left and reads the words written vertically in French on the side of the boxes. The phrase *shampooing chaise* are all she has to go on, but the rudimentary French she's still got knocking around in her head nearly a decade after college help her to decipher at least that much.

"Oh, and I've got your livestock here," Jerrod says, disappearing into the boat. A cold rush of fear washes over Holly as she wonders if she accidentally ordered live chickens or pigs with this order of food, but when he steps out again, Jerrod's got a taupe-colored donkey on a rope following him. The donkey has the big, dark eyes of a deer, and its nose and belly are white. It stands at the edge of the boat and stares at Holly like a nervous child being introduced to its new foster parents for the first time. Jerrod holds a clipboard in one hand, the end of the rope in the other. He consults the clipboard. "Says I was to bring you the grocery delivery, as usual, and one donkey." Jerrod gives a sharp laugh. "Says her name is Madonna."

"I forgot about Madonkey!" Holly cries with relief, bending at the waist as she approaches. "Hi there, sweet girl," she coos, holding out the top of her hand for the donkey to sniff. "Will she bite?" She pauses and looks up at Jerrod.

"No idea," Jerrod admits. "She seems pretty shy, so I doubt it."

"Come here, girl," Holly says, making kissing noises at the donkey.

"I wish you'd make this much of a fuss to get me off the boat," comes a voice from behind Jerrod. It's River, and he's holding a duffel bag over one shoulder, his wheat-colored hair tousled by the wind on the water, the grizzle of a gold five o'clock shadow on his smooth cheeks.

Holly had expected to shout, "GET OVER HERE!" or to say something incredibly witty when she saw River for the first time since August, but now that he's standing before her in a pair of jeans and a red sweatshirt, lips pulled into a sexy grin, all she can do is smile. He steps down from the boat and walks over to her, dropping his duffel bag on the ground and opening his arms.

As soon as she gets her wits about her, Holly takes the few steps that remain between them and vaults into his arms.

"Whoa!" River laughs, the force of Holly's full weight causing him to take a step back. She wraps her arms around his strong neck and winds her bare legs around his waist, locking them tightly. "Hi, yourself," he says into her hair, holding her close.

After what feels like a full minute, Holly loosens her grip on his neck and leans back so that she can look into his eyes. "Hi," she says. They stare at each other, re-learning the topography of one another's faces. "You look good."

"No, *you* look incredible." River smiles widely so all of his straight, white teeth are on display.

Jerrod clears his throat. "Not to interrupt here," he says, "but The Material Donkey is feeling a little left out."

River sets Holly on the ground reluctantly, but pulls her close by keeping one arm around her shoulders. "The Material Donkey?" he asks, amused.

"Her name is Madonna," Holly explains.

"Oh. Of course." River makes a face like, *duh, I should have known.*

"You need to take the delivery," Jerrod says, offering Holly the rope.

"Oh my stars in heaven! She's here! She's here! She's here!" They turn to see Ellen running toward them as Carrie-Anne watches from the front door of Mistletoe Morning Brew, smiling and waving.

"Hey, Ellen." Holly steps aside and pulls River with her. Ellen crouches in front of Madonkey, holding out a fistful of what looks like hay. The donkey sniffs it. "Where did you find hay?" Holly asks.

"It's barley straw," Ellen says, smiling happily as Madonkey nudges her outstretched palm and licks at the treat.

"Oh. Of course." It's Holly's turn to make the *I should have known* face.

"Anyway," Jerrod says, tapping his finger against his clipboard as he runs down the list of items, "we've delivered the food and supplies, two gigantic, house-sized boxes, our lone passenger, and a donkey named after the Queen of Pop. Guess it's time for us to shove off."

"Thanks, Jerrod," Holly says, waving as she wedges herself in more firmly under River's shoulder. "See you on Friday."

The ferryman gives a wave from behind the wheel, and within two minutes, Jerrod has them untied and ready to shove off.

"She's a beauty, isn't she?" Ellen asks them. She's kneeling in the sand, keeping herself at eye-level with Madonkey.

"Adorable," Holly says, placing a hand on River's chest as she moves in closer to him. "Did you get her all set up with a new place to live?"

"Yep, she's got a pen just a few feet away from the turkeys. We didn't want her to get lonely," Ellen explains, handing bits of barley straw to the donkey. "I'm so happy you're here," she says softly to the timid animal. Late afternoon sunlight plays off the gold rings on her fingers as she pets the donkey.

"Should we head back to my place?" Holly asks, looking up at River. His eyes spark in response to her question, and her body thrums with an electric current of desire. "We'll see you later, Ellen," Holly says, unable to tear her eyes from River's face. She lets go of him reluctantly so he can fetch the duffel bag he'd tossed aside carelessly. He slings it over his shoulder and offers Holly his hand as they stroll up Main Street together.

"Nice hat, Clark Griswold," River says casually, reaching up to tap the bill of the Mets cap he'd sent her after his summer visit. Their entwined hands swing between them, and Holly feels like they're walking down the halls of a high school in between classes. In fact, she feels almost as nervous as a high school girl now that he's finally back on Christmas Key.

"Thanks." Holly looks at him from beneath the brim of the hat. "Hey," she says as off-handedly as possible. "I was noticing…"

"Yeah?" River's footsteps are in sync with her own as they approach the B&B on their right.

"I was noticing that you hadn't exactly kissed me yet."

River stops walking. "I was a little distracted," he says, eyes dancing.

"By what?"

"By the giant boxes, the food, and the donkey I was sharing a ferry with. It felt like the 'Twelve Days of Christmas' come to life. I was waiting for the seven swans a-swimming and the six geese a-laying to crawl out of the life jacket boxes. Were you hiding any piping pipers below deck?" he teases, hooking a thumb over his shoulder in the direction of the dock.

"I forgot to tell you about the donkey," she says. "But then I forgot she was coming on the ferry today anyway. I was a little distracted myself."

"By what?" River asks, setting his duffel bag down on the sidewalk and putting his hands on Holly's waist as they stand in front of the fence that surrounds the pool deck of the B&B. The fence is almost as tall as River, and the Christmas lights hanging from the wooden slats are just inches from their shoulders.

"By the fact that the hottest ex-baseball player on the planet was coming to the island today," she says. The feeling of his hands on her hips is sending waves of heat through her body. She takes a step closer to him so that their chests are nearly touching.

"Wait, Derek Jeter is coming to Christmas Key?" River's face is incredulous. As he talks, his lips are getting closer and closer to Holly's. She's starting to feel dizzy again.

"I'm more of an A-Rod girl..." she jokes, taking off her baseball cap so it won't get in his way. "But you must have me confused with someone else, because I'm a diehard Mets fan."

River laughs throatily before putting his warm lips on hers, and Holly holds her hat behind her back, one foot lifting off of the ground as she melts into River's kiss.

* * *

The butter from the lobster is running down River's arm and dripping from his elbow as he tries to pull off the claws and separate the meat from the legs. Holly is amused watching him wrestle with the cooked crustacean.

"Need a bib?" She's holding her own lobster leg daintily between both hands as they sit on her lanai.

River is trying to eat the lobster without letting it slip from his greasy hands, so Holly sets her lobster down and hurries into the kitchen to find a dishtowel. When she returns, River is holding his oily fingers in the air triumphantly, the empty lobster leg discarded on his plate. Holly tucks the dishtowel into the neck of his shirt with a smile. Having him here again has already softened the rough edges of the stress she's been under.

After leaving the B&B that afternoon, Holly had run River back to her place so he could shower after the long cross-country trip. While he changed and unpacked, she'd driven over to the Jingle Bell Bistro to pick up the dinner she'd ordered from Iris and Jimmy, and now the table between them is covered with a mushroom risotto, biscuits, corn on the cob, lobster, and the bottle of Champagne Collet.

"That was delicious," River says after they've devoured the lobster. He wipes his hands on the dishtowel bib and reaches for his champagne flute. "I can't believe you ordered all of this for just the two of us."

Holly sinks back in her chair with a sigh of satisfaction. "I wanted it to be a memorable first meal."

"It will be—when we're awake all night with stomach pains." He sips his champagne. "And did you say there was dessert, too?"

"Just fresh passionfruit and guava—and we can eat that later."

"Later...hmmm. But what should we do in the meantime?" River looks at her over the candlelight that flickers from the hurricane lamps on the center of the table.

Holly tries to laugh, but it hurts too much. "Owww," she moans, holding her stomach with one hand.

"I guess that answers my question." River sets his champagne flute on the glass tabletop. "In the meantime we'll be digesting dinner."

River has changed into a navy blue pullover sweater and cargo pants, and his blonde hair is mussed after his shower. Holly got a whiff of his aftershave as she tucked the towel into his collar, and she's already imagined herself wearing his sweater to bed that night, River's scent wrapping around her comfortingly while she sleeps next to him. She's not sure if it's the champagne or just the fact that he looks incredibly good, but the desire to be in his arms is almost overwhelming.

"So, hey. I'm kind of stuck on something, and I need a little advice," she says, changing gears. Holly knows how the evening is going to end, but she'd rather linger over dinner for a few more minutes to avoid the very unsexy feeling of being overly full.

River rests his head against the chair as he looks at the shell wall behind Holly. "I didn't know you were going to drag me all the way across country to stuff me with lobster and talk shop, but okay, Mayor. Whaddya got?"

Holly puts her bare feet on the empty chair next to her. "Okay, so you know the situation with Jake, right?"

River inhales through his nose and exhales loudly before answering. "Yep. Game show. Hot chick. Love match. You don't approve."

"Reality show," Holly corrects. "And it's not that I don't approve of him making a love match. What I don't like is the way the producers are using him."

River stays silent.

"We had all sorts of ideas about how we could intervene and stop them from forcing Jake to propose—"

"'We' as in you and Fiona and Bonnie?" River lowers his chin and looks at her with a furrowed brow.

"Not just us—the whole island. We had an emergency village council meeting."

"Is this where you're asking me for advice?"

"Kind of."

"On Jake." He pauses. When she doesn't say anything, he sighs audibly. "Well, it seems to me that you invited the show here, and if you mess with their production now, then you might end up with a product you don't like later." River picks up the champagne bottle; he holds it up in question and Holly nods. "I think you have to trust the network," he says, pouring a few inches of the sparkling, bubbly liquid into both of their glasses, "and you have to trust that Jake has decent judgment. I mean, after all, he liked *you*." River sets the bottle down and leans back, glass in hand.

"But—"

"But nothing. You're a control freak when it comes to this island, but if you're really into this expansion thing for the long haul, then you have to pick and choose your battles. What's important to you here? What do you want to take away from this experience?"

The darkness beyond Holly's lanai rustles with unseen wildlife. Pucci is nestled under Holly's chair, and his head perks up at the sound of a possible animal close by.

"I think I ate too much to answer that," she says, dodging the conversation. "But I do have one other issue that I need help with."

River stares at her across the table for a long minute, the dance of the candles' flames touching both of their faces. His eyes shine. "I'm all ears," he says.

Holly absentmindedly taps the flat side of her knife against the stem of her champagne glass three times, and the chime rings out in the dusky night as she formulates her thoughts. "I found out something about Cap that I think could be helpful to me when it comes to shutting him down in the election."

"I can't imagine you'll really need to 'shut him down'—is anyone even taking him seriously?"

"I think more people are on his side than I'd like. It's because of *Wild Tropics*—they thought they were going to be on the show, and now they're mad at the way it's going. Some of them are kind of upset with me."

"But that's not your fault."

"Tell that to Mrs. Agnelli. She was ready to be a real-life Sophia Petrillo, and now apparently I've killed that dream."

"All right, let's talk politics. What kind of dirt do you have on Cap?"

"I don't know if it's really *dirt*, but Heddie told me something about his past and I'm trying to decide how to use it." Holly sets her knife on her plate and pushes the plate aside. It only takes her a few minutes to give him the rundown on what she knows about Cap and his alter ego, Caspar Braun.

River gives a low whistle. "Damn," he says. "I would have never guessed he was German."

"I *know*," Holly says, pounding her fist against the table for emphasis. "No accent…"

"Not particularly punctual or precise?" River ventures.

Holly shakes her head. "Nope. No lederhosen…No Heineken."

"Heineken is Dutch."

"Oh, right. I guess it would help if I were better acquainted with the beers of the world," she says. River laughs.

"The beers of the world aren't that exciting. Now, what do you have on Caspar Braun so far?"

"I looked, but I couldn't find anything online. I don't even know if I'm looking in the right places."

"Have you tried running any international background checks?" he asks.

"Based on what? He's not a criminal, and I don't think I have any German contacts to lean on."

"How about based on the fact that he's running for public office in a country where he may or may not even be a citizen," River says, leaning back in his chair triumphantly. "You might be able to disqualify him on that alone."

"Wow," Holly says quietly. She watches as a drip of candle wax makes its slow descent down the taper. "Clearly I couldn't come up with that myself because it was *too* obvious. So who do we call?"

River looks at his watch. "Well, it's nine o'clock here, which means it's about…three a.m. in Germany. We're going to have to give them a few hours before we start banging on their doors."

A sense of relief floods through Holly's veins—she finally has something. A possibility. A way to easily stop the freight train that's coming her way as she's tied to the tracks. These weeks of juggling the reality show, the mayoral race, the normal running of the B&B, and her mother have left her feeling like she's in the middle of the ocean on a beat-up raft, searching the horizon for a life boat.

"So what should do for the next six hours?" she asks innocently.

"I have a couple of ideas," River says. He stands up and offers her a hand.

"I bet you do." Holly blows out the candles.

Chapter Twenty-Three

Holly is up early the next morning. Because River is still on west coast time, her seven o'clock is his four a.m. She watches him for a minute or two in the dim morning light, admiring the way his blonde eyelashes brush the skin under his eyes as he sleeps. He's on his side, facing Holly, and she has to resist the strong urge to run her fingers through his sandy hair. Instead, she pulls the blanket over his bare shoulder and he rolls over as she slips from the bed.

Holly tiptoes through the cool darkness of the curtained house. In the small laundry room off the kitchen, she digs through the clean clothes in the dryer and finds a pair of sweat pants and a hoodie to throw on. The house has gone chilly overnight, and the early morning light spilling through the tiny window over the kitchen sink has a thin, weightless, winter feel. Holly rubs her hands together to warm herself, watching a cardinal as it sits inside the fan of a Florida Silver Palm outside her window. It preens in the muted sunlight.

The warmth of Buckhunter's bright kitchen beckons to her across the lawn between their bungalows. Holly can see him moving around in there, filling his coffee pot in the sink and rummaging through his re-frigerator. Before she can think of a good reason not to, she slips out into the cool morning wearing the flip-flops she always leaves by the front door.

"Hey, neighbor." Buckhunter opens his door with a surprised smile. "Come to borrow a cup of sugar?"

"Nah, I'm sweet enough already. But I *was* hoping I could steal a cup of coffee." Holly peers around him into the front room of his house. "Am I catching you at a bad time?" She searches for signs that Fiona might still be asleep or otherwise in the house.

"I'm alone. Come on in." Buckhunter steps aside. "I assume your fisherman is still passed out at this early hour?"

"Yeah, he's out cold," Holly admits. Buckhunter closes the door behind her and leads the way into his kitchen. Her grandparents had built the house on the same property where they'd built their own so they would have ample space for family to stay together on the island. When Holly's grandmother passed away, her grandpa had moved Buckhunter into the guest bungalow as a "renter"—something that had always annoyed Holly. She couldn't imagine why this stranger was allowed to share the land she'd inherited, and their salty relationship had further antagonized her, though she didn't like to admit that his ribbing and teasing sometimes stuck in her craw.

"Let me pour you a cuppa, milady," Buckhunter offers, pulling a chipped mug from his cupboard and setting it on the counter. He lifts his coffee pot and tips it over the mug, steam rising from the dark liquid as it fills her cup. Holly pulls out a dark-stained wood chair and sits down at the kitchen table.

Buckhunter has crafted nearly all of the furniture in the house from his own found wood, and she runs her hand over the sanded tabletop, thinking of the patient hours he'd spent on his front porch, working on each piece. It still seems strange to her that she's only known Buckhunter as her uncle for the past four or five months, and even stranger that she's been able to accept her beloved grandfather's indiscretions with Buckhunter's late mother as easily as she has. It seems like a miracle to her how quickly they've both come to terms with the situation and forged a new relationship in the shadow of their family secrets.

"I heard from Coco again," Holly says without preamble. Buckhunter hands over her mug of coffee.

"You want eggs?"

Holly nods. "She's got her lawyer after us, but I haven't responded yet." She holds the hot ceramic mug between both hands and blows on the coffee before sipping it.

"What does she want?" Buckhunter rolls up the unbuttoned sleeves of his thin flannel shirt, pushing them roughly over his elbow joints so that he can crack eggs into a bowl.

Holly stares at the back of her uncle's silver-blonde head before she answers. "Ten million dollars."

He tosses two halves of an eggshell into the stainless steel sink with a low whistle. "So she's saying this island is worth thirty mill?"

"I think she's factoring the infrastructure and any potential future earnings into the equation." Holly reaches for the carton of milk that sits —spout open—on the edge of the table. She pours some into her coffee and, for lack of a spoon, stirs it with her index finger.

"Ten million bucks ain't chump change. Where are we going to get that kind of money?" Buckhunter tips the bowl of raw eggs into the frying pan on his stove. It sizzles.

"I have no idea." And she really doesn't. At this point, the costs of keeping the island running every month are just barely met by the money the B&B pulls in and the rent she collects on the island's businesses, and they honestly do rely on pensions and retirement funds to keep the wheels of the local economy turning. It's been her hope that the small steps towards progress they've taken will lead to more prosperity and less stress about finances and the future. But this impasse they've come to with Coco has her seriously concerned.

"Let's not panic yet," Buckhunter advises, grabbing two pieces of thick-cut bread and sticking them into the slots of his toaster. "She can't force us to buy her out, but she can make our lives more difficult."

"How? She can't even outvote us on anything," Holly reminds him.

"By being a royal pain in our asses, that's how."

"Oh, right. I'm pretty used to that already."

Buckhunter butters the toast and sets it on a plate, expertly scooping a fluffy pile of eggs from the pan and dishing it up for Holly. "Breakfast is served, madam," he says, sliding it across the table. "Tabasco?"

"Just salt and pepper, please." She picks up the fork.

"Already in the eggs, but if you want more, it's in that cupboard," he says, pointing with a spatula.

Holly gets the salt and pepper and grabs the coffee pot as she walks by, setting it all on the table. Buckhunter joins her with his own breakfast, and they sit together amiably, forking eggs onto their respective pieces of toast and chewing in companionable silence.

"How are things going on the set?" Buckhunter asks, hunched over his plate like a lean, wiry lumberjack. He shovels the last bit of scrambled egg into his mouth with a fork.

Holly shrugs. "I've been kind of occupied with trying to keep my job as mayor lately."

"Huh," he says, not meeting her gaze as he eats the crust of his bread.

"Every time I go over there I feel…I don't know—I feel misled or something. It's not what I thought it would be."

"Well, when is anything the way we thought it would be?" He says this casually, like it's not a grand rhetorical question that encompasses all of life's disappointments and surprises in one smooth, compact nutshell. Holly lets the question sit there between them, its truth so solid that it's nearly tangible.

The sun sends a shaft of yellow light through the window, warming the scene and capturing it in Holly's mind like a butterfly trapped under resin. She smiles at this image of her weather-worn uncle, a man who is nearly as much of an enigma to her as he'd been before she knew they were related. It's nice being in his home, watching him do regular things. It's nice to be with someone who is family.

Holly reaches across the table for the pot of coffee and refills both of their cups. They drink it in the quiet of a peaceful winter morning.

* * *

Holly's call to the various offices she's dug up in Germany haven't yielded any results. She's left messages for and sent emails to half a dozen different mid-level officials, but by the end of River's first full day on the island, she's still turned up absolutely nothing on Caspar Braun. It's frustrating, but for the time being, she's shelved the issue in the back of her mind so she can focus on River.

When River awoke that morning at eleven, he and Holly had gone for a long walk on the beach, followed by lunch at Jack Frosty's. They'd barely been able to eat their grilled cheese sandwiches because everyone who'd seen them sitting at the bar dropped by to greet River and to welcome him back to Christmas Key. Holly had munched on her tangy dill pickle happily as River and Joe Sacamano caught up, and she'd finally dragged him out to her golf cart after Maria Agnelli stopped by to plant a loud kiss on his cheek. They'd laughed happily as Holly steered them through the woods in her bright pink cart, stopping with a click of the brake when she found the perfect Christmas tree to cut down and drag back to her bungalow.

"What do you think of this one?" he says now, holding up a battered wooden sleigh ornament made of popsicle sticks.

They've pillaged the storage room that Holly keeps at the B&B, dragging home a big plastic tub full of Frank and Jeanie Baxter's holiday decorations. Each ornament holds a special place in Holly's heart, and it takes real willpower to resist the urge she feels to cradle every one in her hands and to recount to River all the different memories that come flooding back to her.

There are the red and white pipe-cleaners that she and Emily used to twist into candy canes at her grandmother's kitchen table, and the strings of beads she made as a teenager, sitting on the floor and listening to the Psychedelic Furs in her bedroom. There's the collection of gold paper stars with glitter that her grandfather had taken with him on a trip and gotten laminated, and a small angel made of copper wires she remembers getting as a gift from Alfie Agnelli, Maria's late husband. There are so many memories in this box of ornaments that Holly doesn't even know where to begin, and so she doesn't begin at all—she keeps them tucked in close to her heart, smiling at each one as she takes it from the box.

"Do you always put your tree up this early?" River asks, fluffing out the stiff fabric of an angel's ivory-colored skirt.

"You think December thirteenth is early?"

"I just thought you might get tired of Christmas decorations at some point."

"Bite your tongue, man!" Holly shouts in mock-horror. "The smell of a pine tree in the house is one of my favorite things all year. I'd keep it up for three months if it didn't start dropping needles after the first two weeks."

"I do admire your commitment to the holidays," River says, walking over to the white-painted bookshelf where she keeps her family photos, books, and CDs. He takes a string of mini-lights and lays them gently across the tops of the books, winding them through knickknacks and picture frames.

"It's a lifestyle, that's for sure," Holly says distractedly, pulling her ringing phone from her back pocket. "Hello?" she says. "Yes, this is Holly Baxter." River keeps his back to her, plugging the mini-lights into an outlet on the wall so that the festive bulbs illuminate the bookshelf.

Holly takes her phone out to the lanai along with a pen and a pad of paper. The man on the other end of the line speaks in clipped English, his accent heavy as wet wool.

"You're sure?" she asks him.

"Quite. I've been researching this topic for many years."

"Huh." Holly holds the pen over the paper, ready to write something, though she isn't sure what it is she needs to note.

"If you give me an email address I will happily send you more information."

Holly gives him her email address and thanks him for his time.

Inside the house, River has finished wrapping her tree in gold tinsel. He's on his knees, double-checking the screws at the base of the tree that hold it in its stand. Holly drops the notepad on her coffee table with a loud slap.

"Important news?" River asks mildly, looking up at her.

"I'm not even sure what to think right now." Holly paces around the room. "I feel like I'm spinning plates, and I'm constantly turning my attention from one plate to another to make sure none of them fall and shatter."

"So which plate is this?"

"This is the Cap plate."

"As compared to the reality show plate and the Coco plate?"

"Right." Holly stops pacing and admires River's work. "That tree looks really good."

He stands and steps back to look at the tree. "I thought so. Now we just need some presents to put under it."

Presents are the last things on Holly's mind—she still has ten days to think about gifts. "Hey, would you mind if we changed our evening plans?" she asks suddenly, picking up a snow globe that has a Santa wearing swim trunks inside.

"You're so grateful for all of my decorating that you want to skip dinner and yet another viewing of *Christmas Vacation* and go right to dessert?" River asks with a smirk, putting his arms around Holly and pulling her in close. He jokingly tips her back like he's going to dip her.

"Actually," she says, placing both hands on his chest and pushing him away gently. "I need to go and talk to Heddie."

"Oh." River's face falls. "Sure—of course."

"I'm sorry. I won't be long—I promise. But she knows more about this Cap situation than I do…"

"No need to explain." River holds up a hand. "Do you want me to come, or should I stay here and take Pucci for another walk on the beach?"

"Pucci would *love* that," Holly says gratefully. As she's talking, she's already grabbing her striped canvas purse and slipping her feet into her tennis shoes without bothering to lace them up. "Where's my hat?" She spins around, looking at the couch and under the coffee table.

"Which one?"

"Mets, of course."

"You left it on the table in the other room," River says, his back to her as he surveys the tree. He's holding a red ornament in his hand, searching for a branch to hang it on. "I'll see you when you get back."

Holly stands on her tiptoes and places a kiss on River's cheek. "We'll eat dinner together later, okay?"

Holly is on the porch with her Mets hat on her head before River can even reply.

* * *

"Heddie!" Holly pounds on the window of Scissors & Ribbons with her fist. "Heddie!" The women in the salon turn their heads, curiosity on their lined faces. Heddie frowns. "I'm coming in!"

"Are you okay, sweetie?" Millie Bradford asks when she meets Holly at the doorway to the salon.

"I'm fine. Thanks, Millie." Holly is out of breath. "I just need to talk to Heddie."

"Well, come on in." Millie steps aside and waves her in. The smell of paint has diminished in the week since they painted the salon, and the two chairs and rinsing bowls that had come over on the boat with River and Madonkey are set up under a series of shelves that are stocked with shampoo bottles and folded towels. "We're unpacking the shampoos and conditioners right now, and I'm expecting my cash register and credit card machine to arrive on the next boat. As soon as I get it all set up we'll be ready to go."

Heddie is bent over a box of shampoo bottles; they're lined up and nestled inside the cardboard box like rows of white eggs. "It looks good, yes?" Heddie asks, standing up straight as she looks around the salon. She puts her thin hands on the small of her back. "Before we know it, we'll be an island of gorgeous women with perfect hair."

"We'll look like tourists instead of natives," Iris Cafferkey adds. She's sitting behind a table on one side of the salon, sorting bottles of bright nail polish and marking items off on a list with a sharp pencil.

"This is coming together really fast," Holly says with admiration. The overhead lights give everything a soft glow, and there are framed pictures lined up on the floor waiting to be hung.

"You should let me do a wash and blow-out on you, Holly!" Millie cries, clapping her hands together. The rings on her fingers clink as they make contact. "Your gentleman friend is here, and there's nothing like fresh hair to make a man want to run his hands through it." Mille walks over to one of the black leather shampoo chairs and pats it firmly. "Sit."

"That would be amazing, but I actually left my gentleman friend at home," Holly says, "and I promised him I'd be right back after I talked to Heddie."

"Are you sure?" Millie asks, disappointed. "I've got some coconut-lime detangler that I'm dying to try out on someone…"

"Can I make an appointment for the day you open? I'm pretty sure I need a trim anyway," Holly says, holding up the ends of her long, chestnut hair as proof.

"Of course." Millie walks behind the front counter, choosing a pencil from the black cup next to her computer. "I'll call you with a time as soon as I have the first day figured out," she says, pulling a small business card from a holder on the desk. "I'll just write you down for a cut and dry." She scribbles on the back of the card and hands it to Holly. "There you go."

"I can't wait. I feel more chic already." The business card is decorated with a pair of shiny scissors and a glittery red-and-white striped ribbon. Holly smiles at the Christmas theme.

"I assume you want to speak with me outside," Heddie says, material-izing next to Holly. "I've been bent over boxes here for a while, so I could use a walk anyway. Should we go down to the dock?"

"Let's," Holly says, holding up the business card to Millie. "I'm putting this on my calendar as soon as you call with a time, Millie."

Millie waves at them as they step out of the salon and into the lobby of Poinsettia Plaza.

It's nearly six o'clock, and the last rays of the pink-orange winter sun are reaching into the sky behind the trees to the west. Holly breathes in the salty air and looks up at the holiday garlands on Main Street as they pass beneath them. The faux evergreen boughs are a deep emerald green against the evening sky, and the holiday lights all up and down the street have already kicked on for the night. The lights are still on inside Mistletoe Morning Brew across the street, and as they pass Northstar Cigars, they can see Cap moving around behind the counter, stocking cigars and taking inventory.

"So, you've got something you wish to talk about?" Heddie asks, gazing ahead at the dock in the distance.

"I got a call back from the Department of War Research in Berlin."

"So then you've found Caspar Braun." Heddie looks at the street before stepping down off the sidewalk and into the sand that leads to the dock.

"I'm not sure what to do with this, Heddie."

"What do you think is the right thing to do?" Heddie asks, lifting her chin slightly as they step onto the dock. They walk side-by-side toward the infinity of the dark horizon.

Holly thinks about what she now knows, turning this new fact over in her mind. "I don't know," she finally admits.

"Then I advise you to do nothing yet. The information was merely to help you understand where Cap is coming from, not to help you destroy a man."

"Heddie," Holly gasps, stopping in her tracks. She puts a hand on Heddie's thin arm. "I would never destroy Cap—never. I hope you know that." It knocks the breath right out of her chest to think that someone who has known her as long as Heddie has would even have to caution her about how to handle this situation.

"I do. It just bears repeating. This is an incredibly delicate topic for Germans—and for Cap. It is not something to take lightly."

They stop at the edge of the long dock, listening to the water as it laps against the weathered pillars beneath their feet.

"I understand," Holly says in a near whisper.

"I knew you would. And I think you should know that your grandparents would be proud. This island wouldn't work the way it does without you."

"Thanks, Heddie. I needed to hear that."

They both look to the water as the brightest stars begin to appear in the still-dusky sky. Holly imagines her grandparents looking down at her from amongst the stars, winking their approval. And as long as she has their approval, she knows she can never go wrong.

Chapter Twenty-Four

The contestants have fallen away like dried leaves in autumn. When Holly pulls up to the sand dune off December Drive and parks her cart on Friday morning, she already knows from Leanna's early-morning text that they're down to the final three contestants. She's been summoned to visit so they can talk about plans for the final wrap show, and now she steels herself, shoving her phone into the back pocket of her white Levi's and kicking her Birkenstocks off before she hits the sand.

The mini tent camp has been pared down to just four tents. At this point, each contestant has his or her own sleeping quarters, with an extra tent available for the producers to use as a de facto on-site office. Holly is about to walk over to the camp fire when Leanna pops her head out of the office tent and motions for Holly to join her.

"Hey, stranger," Leanna says cheerfully, leading Holly over to the director's chairs in a dark corner of the tent. On a stool in front of the chairs sits an oversized laptop. Leanna hands Holly a pair of headphones to put over her ears. "Have a seat. I'm just watching the dailies from the last competition. You might like this." She slips her own set of headphones on and punches a series of buttons on the laptop's keyboard. "Right here," she says, sinking back in her director's chair and folding her arms.

Holly sits down, feeling uneasy. She folds her arms across her navy blue and white striped boat shirt. On the screen, Jake comes into view at a distance on the sand, his hands full of items that she can't quite decipher.

"It's our Christmas competition," Leanna says as an aside, not looking away from the screen. "The contestants are supposed to find a way to make gifts for one another from the things they find on the beach."

The cameras cut to Bridget kneeling inside her tent, a handful of items spread across the cot. There's a large piece of blue glass from the ocean, a collection of shells, and some small bits of wood. Bridget's tan is deep, and her skin shines in the light trickling through the tent flap. Her blonde hair is wavy with salt and sea air, soft tendrils curling at her temples. Holly can't tear her eyes away from the woman's natural beauty.

The third contestant is Violetta DuBois. The camera captures her sitting cross-legged at the edge of the trees, the tall palms rustling overhead as she weaves long, tough spikes of fallen palm fronds together into what looks like the start of a placemat. The only sound accompanying Violetta is the rush of the ocean air through a microphone, and the crash of the waves behind the cameraman.

"We'll add sound later," Leanna says too loudly. "But check this out." She points at the screen. Holly is already watching intently.

Jake has spread his finds across a huge driftwood log, and he's examining the shells, frayed rope, and husks of crownshaft that have died and peeled away from the trunks of the island's palm trees. He holds up a tide-worn shell, looking at the giant hole in the center. It's a small shell, its edges smooth and delicate, and he sets it aside. The rope has clearly been exposed to the elements, but Jake spreads it flat on the sand, kneeling before it as he tests its strings for breakage. Holly watches his strong muscles as he works—shirtless and tanned—entirely focused on his mission.

The cameras cut back to Bridget. She's holding a tube of glue in her hand, affixing shells to the four small branches of wood that she's laid out on her cot in the shape of a square, the ends touching to make a frame.

"How come she gets to use glue?" Holly asks, sitting forward in her chair.

"Doesn't matter," Leanna says, waving a hand to quiet her. But it matters to Holly; she didn't like watching the behind-the-scenes manipulations of resources during her first visit to the set, and she doesn't like it now. The cameras return to Violetta and her ever-growing blanket of woven palms. She stands, her supple, yoga-toned legs barely covered by a pair of battered khaki shorts that stop at the very tops of her thighs. Her tattooed biceps stretch as she spreads the blanket on the sand and stands back to admire its size and shape.

Holly sighs and shifts around in her chair. Watching the rough, unedited dailies is markedly less interesting for an untrained observer, and she decides that she definitely prefers the edited version of reality television. She's about to take off the headphones and hand them back to Leanna when the scene changes abruptly to show Bridget and Jake after dark. They're walking away from the roaring fire in the pit, hand-in-hand as they stroll to the water's edge. Just when it seems they'll be out of earshot, their microphones pick up the sound.

"Have you thought about what happens after it's all over?" Bridget asks. Her voice is smooth, her enunciation clear. Holly wants to roll her eyes at how obvious it is that Bridget is a trained actress, though Fiona still hasn't been able to dig up anything to support that notion.

"After the show is over?" Jake asks. His innocence is like a stake in Holly's heart, and she wants to reach through the screen to put her hand on his shoulder.

"Yeah, after all of this," Bridget says, their silhouettes cut out in the darkness as they sit down on the sand, shoulders touching.

"I'm not sure," Jake admits after a pause. "Before all of this started, I was already in a weird spot."

"Why?" she prods.

"I don't know—just in between things. I love my job, but I could use a change of scenery. I have friends, but no family where I live. I ended a relationship this year…I'm just in flux. How about you?"

"I'm always game for whatever comes my way," Bridget says suggestively, tossing her hair in the darkness. The light from the fire catches the sparks of her blonde hair as it lifts in the slight breeze.

"I can tell," Jake says, giving her a playful bump with his shoulder. Holly resists the urge to throw up in her own mouth. How can this feel even remotely okay to Leanna and Wayne? How can they prey on human emotions for amusement?

"Maybe there's something for us, you know, after this ends." Bridget turns her head to him, her small nose in profile as she faces him. Her lips are mere inches from the side of Jake's head, and even from a distance in the darkness, it's obvious she's waiting for him to turn his head and kiss her.

"I won't lie and say it hadn't occurred to me," Jake says, his voice raspy and vulnerable.

"Do you think about me in your tent at night? Because I think about you when I'm there in the dark, alone on my cot. I wonder if you're awake, what you'd say if I crawled into your tent while everyone else is asleep…"

Jake gives a hard, surprised laugh. His profile comes into view and their noses nearly touch. Holly knows what comes next, and she's about to look away from the screen when a loud voice interrupts their viewing.

"You ready for the presentations?" Wayne says, peering around the door to the tent. He raises a hand in greeting to Holly. "You here to watch this part as well?" His eyes cut to Leanna and silent words pass between them.

"Actually, I think it would be better for Holly if she watched the feed from here," Leanna says slowly, slipping her headphones off her head and holding them in both hands. "I can cue it up so she gets the unbroken feed from camera two."

Wayne nods, digesting the idea. "You're right. That's a better choice." He pats the canvas of the tent flap with one hand. "So Leanna will get you set up in here, and we're about to roll tape on the gift giving."

"So this was yesterday?" Holly asks, pointing at the laptop that's gone to black. "They were making these gifts yesterday, and now they're exchanging them today?"

"It all happened over the past two days, but on the show it'll end up looking like it happened in one day—that'll add an element of competitiveness to the whole thing. You know, having a time limit on how long they have to come up with gifts for each other makes it more interesting."

"Right," Holly says. "Yet another element of magic and trickery."

Wayne cocks his head, a funny look spreading across his face. "You say that like it's a bad thing."

There's an awkward silence between the three of them that leaves Holly feeling like she's made a major faux pas. Then—without warning —Wayne and Leanna start laughing. Holly joins in tentatively, even though she's not sure what's so funny.

"Anyhow," Leanna says, resting her headphones on the seat of her empty director's chair. "I'm going to go and get this scene started with Wayne. We'll loop you in on the laptop here in a few, and then you can watch."

Holly nods, pulling her headphones apart with her hands and setting them on her head again. She's alone in front of the blank laptop screen for about fifteen minutes, during which time she contemplates getting up and leaving no fewer than eight different times. Instead, she types River an apology text for leaving him on his own yet again, and as she sends it, the laptop screen before her flickers to life. The cameras are rolling on a scene that she didn't see when she walked up: a small tree is wrapped in lights and decorations, shiny glass bulbs dangling from its branches. The three contestants are being positioned around it by Leanna, and Wayne is standing off to the side, giving orders.

Holly's phone buzzes in her lap and she glances down: *I'm having lunch at the Jingle Bell Bistro. Fiona gave me a ride. Meet me here?* She makes a face. How can it be lunchtime already?

Let me finish up on the set...be there ASAP! Holly sends the text, and when she looks back at the screen, Bridget is presenting Jake with the picture frame she's made of driftwood and shells. Inside the frame is a hand-drawn charcoal picture of the two of them. It's beautiful.

Ryan comes up next to Holly and taps her on the shoulder. He has a habit of forgetting her name every time she comes to the set, and Holly always feels like they're meeting for the first time.

"Hey—Holly, right?" He tucks a long hunk of dark hair behind one ear.

She slides the headphones off, eyes still glued to the screen. "Yeah, it's Holly," she says, still distracted by what's happening on the laptop in front of her.

"You want something to drink?" he asks, digging through a cooler and coming up with a bottle of water.

"No, thanks." She's glued to the laptop screen.

"Nice drawing, huh?"

"She did that?" Holly tips her head at the drawing in the frame.

Ryan unscrews the bottle cap and takes a long swig. "Actually, I did it."

"*You* did?"

"Yeah, four years at art school and I can make a decent charcoal drawing. Go, me," he says dryly, making a *whoop-de-doo* motion with his index finger. "Too bad sketching alone won't earn me a living." He shrugs at her before heading back out to the beach.

On the screen, Violetta is presenting Jake and Bridget with a large blanket made of woven palm fronds. The blending of green, yellow, and slightly-browned leaves gives it an ombré look, but despite the creativity and effort that obviously went into making the blanket (if, in fact, she even made it at all—for all anyone knew, Ryan or someone else could have stepped in and done it the minute the cameras stopped rolling) it still looks stiff and uncomfortable.

Violetta is in the middle of giving a heartfelt speech about how the blanket is a co-gift that will help to keep Bridget and Jake warm as they go forward in competition and in life when Wayne steps into view of the camera and stops her.

"Can we try that scene again? See if you can work up some tears—this is a heartfelt moment," Wayne says to Violetta, hands on her shoulders. Holly rolls her eyes.

She suffers through three more takes of Violetta's blanket speech, then sits forward, elbows on knees, as Jake stands up and pulls the ring-sized shell from his pocket. He smiles earnestly at Bridget with shining eyes, and she puts both hands over her bow-shaped mouth.

Before he even speaks, Holly has her headphones off. She watches the scene unfold on the laptop without the benefit of sound. In her mind, she hears the swell of cinematic music, and she sees the panoramic sweep of the camera as it takes in the whole beach while Jake and Bridget hold each other lovingly at the shore line. She imagines them running into the surf, holding hands while the water laps at the ankles of Jake's pressed linen pants and soaks the hem of Bridget's antique lace wedding gown. She hears the music in her head soar once more and then the scene fades out on Bridget's bouquet of tropical flowers, discarded in the sand.

In reality, all she sees on the screen is Wayne interrupting once again to direct Jake, who listens intently. When Wayne steps out of the shot, Jake begins again, holding out the shell ring to Bridget the way he once held out a platinum ring to Holly. Her stomach lurches and she grabs her purse from the ground, dropping her phone into it heavily. She slips from the tent and back up the worn footpath to the dunes, flinging herself into her cart and putting it in gear. Without looking back, she tears away from the beach and onto December Drive, pushing the pedal to the floor as she loops around the beach.

Rather than cutting down Pine Cone Boulevard and running into Main Street, driving west until she can turn onto Holly Lane, then curving on the road past the chapel and ending up at the bistro, she takes the whole December Drive loop. It adds another fifteen minutes onto her trip, but Holly needs the time alone to process the image of Jake presenting Bridget with a ring.

The wind blows her loose hair around her shoulders, and the sun warms her hands and forearms as she drives. Holly feels calmer by the time she reaches the Jingle Bell Bistro. With River in town, it's almost possible to put everything else out of her mind when she's with him, and having lunch together on the deck that looks out onto the beach sounds perfect. In fact, she almost feels hungry, and the thought of Jimmy Cafferkey's clam chowder and Irish soda bread makes her stomach growl. Holly puts a happy smile on her face and runs her fingers through the ends of her wind-tangled hair. Lunch with River is exactly what she needs right now.

Except—as she stands in the center of the bistro's dining room, scanning the thin crowd of diners—she realizes that he's already gone.

Chapter Twenty-Five

The week before Christmas is always a rush of activity on Christmas Key, and the islanders gather to kick off the annual festivities on Sunday evening. People begin to arrive at the dock by cart and on foot around six o'clock, most wearing Santa hats and some combination of red and green. Ray Bradford is wearing a full Santa suit, and Millie is dressed in shiny red spandex pants and a belted red sweater.

Holly pulls a wagon full of Christmas decorations as River walks next to her with his hands in the pockets of his jeans. They're both in Santa hats and festive sweatshirts, and they've spent the afternoon together wandering around the island with Pucci at their heels. The wagon bumps down the sidewalk, making a loud, repetitive *thump* each time the one dented wheel rolls over again.

"Are you sure no one will care if I crash your party?" River asks, reaching for the handle of the wagon. "Here, let me pull that for you."

Holly hands it over to him. "Of course not. It's just a chance to get together with neighbors and kick off the holidays. Whoever is on the island is free to join us, guests included."

Things have felt sort of *off* between them all weekend—a little quiet and disconnected—and Holly isn't sure what's at the heart of their sudden awkwardness with one another. When she'd tracked River down on Friday after her visit to the set, he was wandering Main Street, chatting with people in front of Mistletoe Morning Brew. He hadn't seemed mad that she'd essentially abandoned him all morning, but there was an undeniable frost to his tone when he told her he'd made his own plans for Friday night to go over to Ellen and Carrie-Anne's and help them with their menagerie of animals. Rather than try to talk him out of it, she'd offered to let him use the B&B's golf cart, promising him that she had last minute election stuff she needed to work on anyway.

"So what's first tonight?" He looks down at her as they walk.

"Okay, it might sound strange, but we do this thing every year where we decorate the navigational sign like a Christmas tree." She points at the pile of tinsel and lights in the wagon.

"How do you keep the lights on?"

"We run an extension cord from the coffee shop and set the lights on a timer. It's a very sophisticated operation," she teases. "You can see the sign when you're out on the water at night and heading over to the island, which looks really cool. It's always been one of my favorite things that we do."

There's a good-sized crowd already gathered on the dock, most dressed in holiday gear. Someone has parked a golf cart nearby with speakers set up on the back seat, and 'Baby, It's Cold Outside' is playing loudly. Almost everyone has a white paper cup with 'Mistletoe Morning Brew' printed on the side.

"Hey, you two!" Carrie-Anne yells, waving exaggeratedly as they approach. "The door is open—stop in and grab coffee or hot cocoa for yourselves!" River pauses, pointing at the front door of the coffee shop with a questioning face. "Yeah, it's open, and it's free," Carrie-Anne confirms, cupping her mouth as she shouts.

"I'll grab some for us," River says, one hand still in his pocket. He gives her the handle of the wagon. "What do you want?"

"Coffee is good." Holly looks up at him. "Meet you over there?"

In answer, River places one hand on the small of her back, holding her gaze for a moment. It would be the right moment for him to bend down and kiss her, but he doesn't. Instead, Holly takes the wagon down to the dock, watching as River disappears into the brightly-lit coffee shop, its front window still covered with Ellen's version of a snowy nineteenth-century England.

"Hi, sugar," Bonnie says. She opens her arms wide to hug Holly. "Merry almost-Christmas!" Holly hands Iris Cafferkey the handle of the wagon and wraps her arms around Bonnie.

"Merry Christmas to you, too, Bon," Holly whispers in her ear.

A deep wave of sentimentality washes over her. Even with the constant presence of Christmas decorations, she's never numb to the nostalgic feelings that the real holiday evokes. Memories of her grandparents at the heart of this gathering by the dock fill her mind's eye. She remembers sitting in the back of a golf cart next to Emily Cafferkey every year, a blanket wrapped around them, cups of hot cocoa in their hands as they watched the adults laughing and decorating the navigational sign. They'd giggled together in their pajamas, talking about Santa Claus and whether his reindeer would really be able to find Christmas Key. Holly wipes at her eyes now, waving at Emily as she digs through the pile of holiday decorations and pulls out a long strand of tangled twinkle lights.

"One hot coffee," River says, holding out a cup with a paper sleeve around it.

"Thanks," she says, her eyes still prickling with the tears sparked by memories of Christmases past.

"Whiskey or Kahlúa, young people?" Joe Sacamano calls out, approaching with a bottle in each hand. "Whiskey'll give it a bit more of a kick, but Kahlúa will sweeten things right up," he says with a crooked grin, his snowy white curls peeking out from under his lopsided Santa hat. Rather than a Christmas-themed sweater or a red and green shirt, Joe's got on his famous holiday Hawaiian shirt.

"I'll go with whiskey," River says, holding out his coffee cup and popping the lid off. "And I like your shirt, man."

Joe tops off River's coffee with a splash of whiskey and glances down at his own shirt. It's covered with white-bearded Santas in swim trunks and youthful-looking Mrs. Clauses in red bikinis. "This shirt is as much of a tradition as this little gathering you see here," Joe says, holding the whiskey bottle out to indicate the knot of villagers mingling on the dock. "We've been doing this since these girls were knee-high to an elf. They'd come out here every year and fall asleep long before the festivities ended." He nods at Holly and looks over in Emily's direction.

"We never fell asleep, Joe!" Holly argues, taking the lid off her coffee so he can add a swig of Kahlúa.

"All right, sugarplum. You never fell asleep trying to spot Rudolph's nose in the sky while he took a test run around the planet before Christmas Eve." Joe splashes some liquid into her coffee with a wink. "I've got my story straight now."

"You have a lot of history here," River says, watching as Joe moves on to the next group and offers to top off their coffees. "I guess I forget sometimes just how entrenched you are in this place. It's really who you are," he says wistfully.

"And Oregon isn't like that for you?" Holly blows on her coffee before she puts the lid back on.

"Oregon is home, but it's not *who I am*," he clarifies. "I love it there, but I don't think it's shaped me the way this place has shaped you."

Holly is about to answer when she sees Emily waving her over to get things started. "Will you hold this?" She hands River her coffee. He takes it, clutching both cups in his hands as he watches her blend into the crowd with ease.

"Okay," Holly says with a laugh, holding her hands out to quiet everyone down. "Welcome to our annual decorating of the sign." A happy cheer and a smattering of applause break out around the dock. "You all know how much my grandparents loved this part of our holiday festivities, and most of us have seen the sign lit up from the water," she says, looking around at her neighbors.

"It's a thing of beauty," Cap calls out. Holly makes a mental note that (for the first time in recent memory) he has no drink in his hand. "It makes this island look like a real port in a storm."

"That it does," Holly confirms. "There's something about plugging in the lights on this sign that signals Christmas for a lot of us, and I'm pleased to kick off the festivities for this year. You all know how this works: grab some tinsel or an ornament and a rubber band, and when it's your turn, just make sure whatever you put on the sign is secured. We don't want any of this blowing off into the water and hurting our wildlife—"

"Here, here!" Ellen shouts, holding her coffee cup in the air like she's seconding a motion.

"So, without further ado, let's decorate this sign!" There is a full round of applause this time as people step up to the pile of decorations and start sifting through the ornaments and lights.

"You want to put something up?" Holly asks River when she walks back over to him and takes her drink.

"No, I'm good—you do your part." He taps his paper coffee cup against her own in a toast. "The mayor has official duties here, and I am but a humble servant to this whole operation." His tone is joking, but there's an edge to his words that nags at Holly. She sips her coffee quietly, thinking.

"You sounded like Jake when you said that." She watches her neighbors wrapping the wooden sign in tinsel and lights like a Christmas tree in a village square. Cap drags the cord from the lights across the sand and shoves its prongs into the outlet of the power cord; the navigational sign glows with red, green, pink, yellow, and blue lights, and everyone cheers. Everyone except Holly and River.

"Yeah, well, I'm starting to see what he was up against." River drinks his whiskey and coffee, watching as Bonnie ties an ornament firmly around the westward-pointing wooden slat that says "Santa Barbara, CA —2,352 miles." Wyatt Bender is standing behind Bonnie with an orna-ment in one hand and his coffee drink in the other, taking in the view of her curvaceous backside.

"Meaning?"

River is about to say something but stops. His strong jaw clenches and unclenches a few times. "Meaning...nothing." He looks at her directly. "Never mind. It's Christmas, and I'm being dumb—ignore me."

Holly gives him a long look before she speaks. "I'm sorry—for every-thing." She sips her coffee. "This ended up being a hard time for you to come down here. It's not how I wanted it to be. I've been preoccupied, and that's not fair to you."

River shakes his head. "You have your life. It wouldn't be fair to you if I showed up here and expected you to drop everything for me."

"Well, *that* wasn't very Jake-like," Holly says. Spontaneously, she lifts her heels off the ground and holds onto him, kissing the side of his jaw.

"Whoa, whoa—hold up there." River takes the coffee from her hand and sets both of their cups on the ground next to his feet. "We can do better than that."

Holly laughs in surprise as River grabs her around the waist and lifts her off the ground. She puts one hand on her Santa hat, holding River around the neck with her other arm as her feet dangle several inches above the sand.

"Nice work, slugger!" Bonnie shouts, giving a little whoop. Wyatt, who is standing next to Bonnie with their shoulders touching, gives a forward tip of his cowboy hat in Holly's direction.

The momentary snag in River's visit is all but forgotten by the time he finishes kissing her and sets her down on the ground again, a happy smile on his handsome face.

* * *

Monday morning is about as welcome as a visit from Coco. Holly wakes early to the sound of Pucci nosing around the bedroom, whimpering quietly to let his mistress know he needs to go out.

"Come on, boy," she whispers, yanking on the jeans she'd tossed over the chair in her room the night before. River is still buried under the duvet, his head lost in a sea of pillows.

In the front room, Pucci is running in circles, his tail wagging in anticipation. "I know, I know," she says, not bothering to clip a leash on him. "Let's take a drive, okay?" Without further coaxing, Pucci runs onto the patch of grass in front of Holly's bungalow and does his business, then bounds across the lawn and onto the front seat of the golf cart. "You ready?" She waits while he finds a comfortable spot, his back wedged firmly against the seat, paws dangling over the edge.

Holly puts the cart in reverse, and with her fur-lined slipper-boot, she punches the gas pedal and pulls out of her driveway.

Things are still quiet on Main Street when she gets to Mistletoe Morning Brew, and Pucci follows her when she leaves her cart by the curb. There's no point in avoiding Cap anymore; they're forty-eight hours away from the election (give or take) and Holly is resigned to the outcome—no matter which way it goes. But she casually peeks through the painted front window and does a quick scan of the coffee shop anyway. "Stay here, Pooch," she says to her dog, pointing at a spot under the table by the front door. He sniffs around, turns in a circle, and sits under the table obediently.

The speakers inside the coffee shop are blaring a rousing, gospel-tinged version of 'Joy to the World' as Holly approaches the counter.

"Mayor," booms a gruff voice from the far corner of the shop. She turns to see Cap. "Hoping you wouldn't run into anyone this early?" He gives her an amused look over the top of his newspaper, taking in her messy hair and slipper-boots.

She was hoping wouldn't run into *him*, of course, but instead of saying so, she smiles politely. "I'm just out on a coffee run before I get ready for work," she says, holding up her wallet as if to prove her mission.

Cap nods. His rough hands grip the sides of last Thursday's *Miami Herald*. Most of the islanders are accustomed to reading their papers a few days late, given the delivery schedule, and those who prefer their news in real time watch the evening news or, less frequently, catch up online. But Cap is always a holdout, preferring to wait on his news until the real paper arrives.

"Grab a cup and come sit for a minute," he says, shaking out his paper and looking at the page in front of him like he couldn't care less whether she sits down with him or not. But it isn't an invitation—it's an order. Holly considers refusing before she realizes that this chance to sit down with Cap might not be a bad idea. She orders a Rose Maylie Mocha and carries it gingerly over to the table in the corner. They're still the only customers in the shop, and Carrie-Anne disappears into the back room again once she's sure they have what they need.

"I've been wanting to talk to you," Holly starts nervously. She can't make herself look into his eyes. "I shouldn't have left it until this late, but…I wasn't sure how to bring this up."

Cap lays the newspaper flat on the table and folds it in half, then in half again. He pushes it away with one large hand. There must be something in the way Holly's voice wavers, or in the slight shaking of her hands as she sets her mocha on the table, but Cap waits patiently, lacing his fingers together on top of the table. He says nothing.

"I know you've been a very vocal opponent of the things I've been doing lately, and I hate that you're unhappy—"

"Listen, honey," he says, reaching a hand across the table and clamping it over her own. "It's not you I'm opposing; this isn't personal."

"Well, it feels personal," Holly says, examining his hairy knuckles as his hand covers hers.

"But it isn't." Cap draws his hand away. "I'm going to be honest with you: part of what got me fired up was the drink. You know I've been on the wagon for several years now, but a couple of months back…I don't know. I fell off the damn wagon like a ton of bricks."

Holly nods. This is not news—to her or to anyone else on Christmas Key.

"When I drink, I'm not myself. But," he waves a hand around like he's erasing an old-fashioned chalkboard in front of his face, "that's not even my point, it's just what pushed me to be such a loudmouth about this whole thing."

Holly reaches for her mocha.

"It's true. But the real bone I want to pick with you is about the invasion of privacy here. You never really *asked* us how we felt about having this reality show come to our island, you *told* us that it was coming and expected us to fall in line."

It's easy to get her haunches up and to feel defensive about this harsh assessment, but deep down, Holly knows he isn't wrong. She gives a slight nod, hoping he'll go on.

"In the end, they're not really in our business too much, and I can see that you've even had second thoughts about them being here, given this whole arranged marriage thing they're planning for Jake."

"I don't know if I want to say that I've had second thoughts, but I have wished I'd found out more about reality shows before inviting them here and letting them kidnap one of our own."

Cap's smile is nearly beatific. "I guess that's enough of a mea culpa for the time being," he says. "So what is it that you wanted to talk to me about?"

Holly narrows her eyes. "Are you still going through with the election on Wednesday, or are you withdrawing from the race?"

Cap turns his palms to the ceiling and shrugs. "I'm a little curious about how many votes I'll get. I probably won't win—in fact, I'm sure I won't—but I've enjoyed campaigning and raising some hell around this place."

"I think you should bow out gracefully," Holly says firmly. The voice of reason in the back of her mind is telling her to get up now and leave the coffee shop, but she ignores it. "If you aren't going to win anyway, then it would be the gentlemanly thing to do."

"I'm all for being a gentleman, Mayor, but we're talking about an election here, not a debutante ball."

Holly tucks her wallet under one arm and picks up her to-go cup from the table. "Fine," she says, standing. "If that's what you want. Maybe I can stop Bonnie before she prints the ballots this morning so I can make the necessary changes."

Cap's white eyebrows are pulled together and a deep, vertical line forms between them. "What changes?"

Holly takes two steps toward the door and then stops. "Given the circumstances, I think the ballot should give voters the choice of voting for Holly Baxter," she pauses, swallowing her nerves, "or Caspar Braun."

Chapter Twenty-Six

"There is no way on God's green Earth that man will win," Bonnie says with fiery conviction, though her words come out mumbled. She's standing behind Holly in the B&B's office on the morning of the December village council meeting, two bobby pins held between her lips as she pulls a brush through Holly's long, tangled hair. She spits the hairpins into her palm. "And why aren't you over at Scissors & Ribbons having Millie do this for you, child?"

"Ouch," Holly says under her breath as Bonnie's brush catches a snarl. "Because I'm here now, and I don't want to leave until this is all over." Even though Bonnie is several inches shorter than she is, Holly stands and faces the window while her assistant smooths her hair into a low ponytail. She's wearing a stretchy, peach-colored shirt with long sleeves, and a pair of low-waisted black pants. When she arrived at the B&B, Bonnie had tsk-tsked over her flip-flops until she'd agreed to drive home and trade them for the black sandals she's now wearing.

"Silly girl," Bonnie says, using one of the bobby pins to anchor the twist of hair she's making at the nape of Holly's neck. "Sounds like you and Cap already had your pre-election run-in, so I doubt he'd confront you even if you ran smack into him on the sidewalk."

"I know. But I'm still afraid of what's going to happen today." Bonnie jabs the other pin into Holly's hair, scraping the skin of her scalp as she does. "Owwwww," Holly complains. She puts a hand to her head protectively.

"Well I never did have a daughter, sugar. None of my boys had much use for hair-brushing and bun-making, so I did the best I could here." She licks both palms unceremoniously and runs them along the sides of Holly's head so the stray hairs will lay flat. "You look pretty as a September peach."

"Thanks, Bon." Holly sits at her desk and places one hand on her lower back.

"You okay?" Bonnie opens the office's mini-fridge. She pulls out a bottle of water and hands it to Holly.

"I slept wrong, I think. River takes up most of the bed, so I keep waking up hanging off the side. My back hurts today." Holly cracks the seal on the water bottle and drinks. "Thanks for this." She lifts the water in the air.

"Drink up. I don't want you getting all dehydrated and fainting dead away in the middle of this meeting. That just won't do. 'Course, in my humble opinion, I think Cap either needs to fish or cut bait with this whole mess, but Lord only knows what motivates that man. Truly." Bonnie holds her hands to the sky like she's sending an *amen* up to the Big Guy.

"I can't even imagine how this is going to go today," Holly admits.

"Then let's not." Bonnie pats the desk firmly with both hands. "We've got an hour to kill until the meeting starts, and there's still work to be done."

Holly puts her hands around her neck and makes a gagging face. "Why can't we just close down for the whole week of Christmas and not work at all?"

"Because we aren't teachers, doll, and we don't get to send the kids home for the holidays."

"Ain't that the truth. Hey, are any of your boys coming down this year?" Holly takes off her sandals and pulls her feet under her on the chair, moving around until she's sitting comfortably.

"No, not this year. Davey wanted to bring his girls down, but his ex-wife gets them until six o'clock on Christmas Eve, so…maybe next year." Bonnie's eyes go soft and Holly instantly regrets asking.

"Hey, let's do Christmas Day at my house!" Holly says, reaching into the candy dish on the desk between her and Bonnie. She pulls out a mini candy cane and takes off the cellophane wrapper.

In an instant, Bonnie's sadness is gone, replaced with the spark that Holly is used to seeing. "That would be wonderful, sugar! What can I bring?"

"Just yourself," Holly assures her, sucking on the straight end of the candy cane and holding the hook between her fingers.

"A pumpkin pie? Scalloped potatoes? I'll think of something, don't you worry," Bonnie promises.

They both go quiet, and the hum of the mini fridge fills the small office.

"We still have about fifty-three minutes until the meeting," Holly points out.

"We could talk about Coco?" Bonnie offers, tapping her pencil against a thick notepad.

Holly levels a gaze at her from across the desk. "I'd rather shave my legs with a machete and rubbing alcohol."

"So then that's a no, right?"

"How about the show's finale—we should probably be talking about what the network wants us to do." Holly studies the cuticles on her right hand.

"About that…" Bonnie coughs delicately.

"What?"

"That Leanna creature stopped in on her way out of the B&B this morning—it was while you were running home to put on a decent pair of shoes—anyway, she left you this." Bonnie pulls a sheet of paper from under her laptop and slides it across the desk.

"What is it?" Holly frowns, reaching for it.

"Looks like details on the party to me," Bonnie says innocently.

"Why weren't you going to give it to me?" Holly asks, scanning the page.

"Because you have enough on your plate this morning."

"So it looks like they're wrapping up this week, huh? They want to do the party on Friday the twenty-third—oh my God, that's the day after tomorrow!" Holly flings the paper onto her keyboard.

"I already called Joe to get the Ho Ho set up, just like they asked us to," Bonnie says in a soothing tone. "And I invited all of the family members they wanted to have on hand."

Bonnie reaches across the giant desk that Holly's created by pushing together two smaller white wicker desks and plucks the piece of paper off the keyboard. "Says here they need a few holiday items, and they want some tropical foliage on hand…listen, sugar." Bonnie sets the paper on the edge of the desk gently. "I'll deal with the things they want, you just deal with this election stuff, okay?"

Holly nods. Her stomach kinks up as she consults her tank watch. "I've also got River stuff to deal with."

"Bad stuff?"

"I'm not sure," Holly says, pulling her feet out from under her and putting her sandals back on. "It's been an awkward visit because I've had so much going on. He feels kind of…distant."

"Not to sound rude, sugar, but I think it's you."

Holly laughs, taken aback. "You think it's me?"

"I mean," Bonnie says, rolling her eyes when she realizes what she's just said. "I mean I think it's all in your head. You've got a lot on your mind, and I'm sure you're just imagining that things are different between you two."

"I hope you're right."

"Honey, I know I'm right. I saw that boy the other night at the decorating of the sign, and I tell you, mmm, mmm, mmm." Bonnie looks out the window dreamily. "He is one smitten kitten."

"Maybe. I don't know." Holly pushes away from her desk and stands up. "But do I look okay? I want to at least be presentable when I have to hand over my gavel and all my dignity."

"Come on, girl, you'll be fine out there," Bonnie reassures her. "Now go get 'em, sugar."

* * *

"Thank you all for coming," Holly says. "I'd like to call the village council meeting for December twenty-first to order now."

The crystal chandelier hanging in the B&B's dining room has been polished, and the light from the windows catches the bits of glass, sending dancing sparks onto the four walls of the large room. The carpet is freshly vacuumed, and a small table with platters of barely touched pastries sits near the entrance. Every seat is filled, and the crowd hangs visibly on Holly's words.

"After more than a month of campaigning, it's finally time to make our contribution to democracy by casting our votes." Holly puts her weight on the podium, lifting her leg behind her and dangling her black sandal from her left foot nervously. She looks out at the room full of familiar faces and a sense of calm falls over her. She puts her foot back on the ground.

She'd told Bonnie a bit of a white lie when she said her back hurt because of River hogging the bed. She'd never even put her head on the pillow the night before, instead pacing her bungalow, her heart heavy with conflict and confusion.

"You know us both as candidates, friends, and neighbors," Holly says to the crowd. "You know what we stand for, and now you get to choose who you'd like to have as mayor of our fair island."

Heddie sits to the right of the podium, wearing a French twist, a lemon yellow cable-knit sweater, and a pearl necklace at her throat. Cap sits to the left, his usual khaki cargo shorts and loose, unbuttoned shirt replaced by long pants and a fully-buttoned dress shirt. From their posture and their unwillingness to look at one another, it's obvious that Cap knows who told Holly about Caspar Braun, and that Heddie fears what Holly has done or will do with that information.

And she's certainly given some thought—some deep, soul-searching thought—as to how she should proceed with Cap. But in the end, after much contemplation, she's decided that it's best to simply do nothing. The man who'd called her from Berlin had done as promised, forwarding several scanned documents by email and answering all of Holly's follow-up questions. There's enough there to do any amount of damage to Cap's shroud of secrecy if she wants to, but Holly has pondered, prayed, and consulted her grandfather's carefully typed notes about island life, and in doing so, she's come to the conclusion that outing Cap isn't her place, nor is it in the spirit of kinship that the island was built on.

"The ballots you picked up on your way in are marked with two names: Holly Baxter and Cap Duncan, and I'll ask you to—"

"Wait," Cap says loudly, standing up. "Before we vote," he turns to Holly, "may I speak?"

They stare at one another for a long moment before Holly moves aside. She folds her hands in front of her, standing straight as she watches Cap step up to the podium. His white hair is combed neatly into a low ponytail, and he's removed his gold hoop earring for the meeting. There's something almost heartbreaking about watching him simultaneously disguise himself in the uniform worthy of a mayor, and reveal himself with what she knows he's about to say.

"Take your pens and pencils," Cap says, holding his index finger in the air. "And cross off the name 'Cap Duncan' on your ballots, please."

Next to Holly, Heddie has stopped taking meeting minutes, so stunned is she by the anticipation. Holly can only imagine what she must be feeling.

"Instead, you may write 'Caspar Braun' in its place. That's B-R-A-U-N." The crowd whispers feverishly, people elbowing one another and asking whether or not they're hearing Cap correctly. "That's me: Caspar Braun. However, you cannot vote for me at all, because I'm not an American citizen." At this, mayhem breaks out in the dining room. No one even pretends to whisper as they grab onto one another and openly discuss this revelation.

But there's only so much to say about the fact that Cap isn't an American citizen, and once this has been established and confirmed by the islanders with better hearing, everyone turns their attention back to him.

"I was born in 1944 to Ilse Braun, an unmarried woman who was an amateur ballroom dancing champion in Europe."

Holly glances over at Heddie, who is listening, chin raised proudly. In her eyes is the unmistakable glint of support. And maybe love, though Holly isn't sure whether it's love for the Cap who's up at the podium now, or love for the man Heddie had once talked books with, dancing the evenings away in his strong arms.

"According to the history books, Ilse died without ever having children. But this is wrong," Cap says, eyeing them all carefully. "I was born to Ilse and Franz Müller, a member of the Wehrmacht—the Nazi armed forces. The year after I was born," he says, and then stops. He puts his index finger to his lips, as if to hold his secret in just a moment longer. Holly is tempted to stand beside him as he speaks—not to touch him or to offer physical support, but merely to be present—but he goes on. "The year after I was born, Ilse's sister, Ava Braun, married Adolf Hitler."

Maria Agnelli stands up and starts fanning her wrinkled face with her ballot. She's gone white and is moaning quietly, hand clutching her chest like she might faint.

This time the crowd doesn't break into chatter, it forms a collective gasp, mouths dropping open all across the room. There are hands placed instinctively over time-weakened hearts, brows furrowed and folded in consternation, and looks of dismay from the front of the room to the back, from one side to the other.

"I've spent my life running from my past, and now I stand before you, ready to own up to something that isn't even my fault."

The crowd is still. On their faces are lifetimes of experience, decades of prejudices and understandings borne of the firsthand knowledge of what war means. Some of the older islanders remember a time when Hitler's dark reign colored the world, and others can easily recall the sentiments of friends and family who lived through WWII. Several of the Jewish islanders sit, arms folded, faces guarded. It is a moment of uncertainty amongst a group of people who have always moved forward with absolute certainty, and Holly knows she will never forget it.

Heddie stands up, pushing her chair back slowly and quietly across the carpeted dining room floor. She pulls herself to her full height, hands at her sides. Without a word from her lips, her body language says it all: she stands with Cap as a fellow countrywoman and as a friend. Holly feels her own shoulders straighten. Out in the sea of faces, she spots River—he's near the back, looking uneasy, but he gives Holly a small nod.

"I was raised by a kind couple when the war ended," Cap continues. "My mother didn't wish to have a child with a Nazi soldier, and she gave me up. I never saw her again." Cap's voice is ragged, the story of his life spoken aloud for the first time in years. "But no matter how completely my past was erased from my daily life, I could never get over the fact of who I was—who I *really* was—and so I left. I packed my bags at eighteen and found my way to the water."

People are still listening curiously, a wash of emotions on their faces like a wave that's crashed for some and is still cresting for others. Some look stunned to hear that Cap isn't just a surly, cigar-hawking former pirate—as they'd always assumed—and others are clearly not sure what to make of a man with ties so close to Nazi Germany.

"I traveled the world until I wasn't Caspar Braun anymore. I sailed and lived by the tides until I was no one but Cap Duncan—not a German, not an American, not anything but a man who loved the water. And then I came here."

Holly looks at Heddie; there are tears in the older woman's eyes. The majority of the people sitting in this B&B—living on a tiny island in the Gulf of Mexico completely by choice—are there because life and circumstance have deposited them there. Recognition ripples through the crowd as people begin to see themselves in Cap's story. Heddie left behind a star-studded career as a German film actress to live alone on an American island, and no one really knows who or what pushed her to move to paradise; Iris and Jimmy Cafferkey had abandoned busy lives as attorneys in Dublin to raise their young daughter with Down Syndrome there; Fiona fled a terrible relationship in Chicago by accepting a two-year appointment to the tiny island via a government program to place doctors in underserved areas. Holly's eyes roam across all these familiar faces as she thinks of their individual stories.

"And I think we know that secrets can drive a man to take extreme measures. Not one of us relishes the idea of having that which we find abhorrent about ourselves flapping around in the breeze like a flag for all to see." Cap looks at Buckhunter and then tips his head at Holly, reminding the crowd without words of that summer's revelation about Frank Baxter's marital indiscretions. Frank's desire to keep his little family safe and protected from his own secrets had driven him to purchase Christmas Key in the first place.

"So, if you will, I would ask you to please remember that I am still Cap Duncan, man of the world." Cap places one hand on his heart; his face is sincere. "I am not perfect. I drink too much. I say the wrong things, and I'm a crotchety, confirmed bachelor. But I am not, nor have I ever been, a fan or friend of the Nazis. And while I am German—this is true—I am every bit as much of an islander as the rest of you." Cap looks down at the podium, the pause between his words stretching to the point that Holly nearly steps forward to take over. Cap looks up again. "Finally, I would ask you to forgive my drinking and rabble-rousing when it comes to this election. Holly is—and always has been—this island's true mayor."

Without hesitation, the room erupts in applause. Holly can't hold back her tears as her fellow islanders rise to their feet. Some move quickly, others slowly on aging hips or with the help of canes, but after a minute or so, everyone is standing, their eyes shining as they look at Cap with the neighborly affection that Holly has come to expect from her friends. Maria Agnelli still looks shaken, but she reaches forward with a thin, liver-spotted hand, taking the steps from the front row up to where Cap stands, her hand outstretched the whole way. When she reaches him, she wraps her arm around his waist, and he tucks her petite, fragile frame under his arm gently, a grin spreading across his face.

Several more people come forward to shake Cap's hand. Firm nods of understanding are exchanged, and there are very few dry eyes in the room. Holly waits until everyone else has had their moment with Cap before she steps forward, unsure about what she should say.

"Hey, kid," he says, putting out one arm. Holly hugs him, her cheek pressed against his crisp button-up shirt. Rather than the usual sweet scent of cigars, Cap smells like soap and a light, musky cologne. "I clean up all right, don't I?"

Holly nods, her arms still wrapped around him. "I'm proud of you, Cap," she says. There's an apology on her lips, but something stops her. Maybe it's the knowledge that things have ended well for both of them, or (and she's much less inclined to entertain this thought) maybe she really isn't that sorry after all. Cap's been an admitted adversary for her these past months, and the competitive part of her knows that she did what she had to do in order to keep their collective train from jumping the tracks. So she hugs him more tightly, but she doesn't apologize.

"Congratulations, Mayor," he says, releasing her. Holly stands behind the podium in the nearly empty room, her eyes scanning the chairs for River. She finds him near the door, back against the wall as he waits.

"Want to grab a drink?" Cap asks shyly, his back to Holly as he faces Heddie. "I'll be drinking lemonade, but I wouldn't mind some company." His hands are clasped behind his back like a schoolboy speaking to a prim and proper nun.

"I would enjoy that—yes," Heddie says after a brief internal deliberation. She picks up her notebook from the table and slips her purse over the crook of her elbow. "It's been a long time since we talked books." Heddie shoots him a dubious look, then walks down the aisle without waiting to see if he'll follow.

Cap grins. "Yes, yes it has," he says, almost to himself. Hands still clasped behind his back, he follows Heddie's long, lean figure down the aisle and out the door.

"Typical village council meeting?" River asks from his spot by the door. The dining room has emptied out, and Holly sighs, looking at the rows of chairs left behind. People had stopped to pick through the pastries on their way out (she'd noticed Maria Agnelli slipping a few into her handbag) and now she needs to clean up the room.

"Pretty much." Holly switches off the microphone on the podium. "Just another day in the life around here."

"Want some help with all of this?" River's eyes sweep the room.

Holly makes a split-second decision. "Nah, let's go to the beach. I've got a hankering for a picnic and a make-out session on a blanket with my favorite baseball player." She walks over to the bank of lights to hit the switches on their way out.

"So Jeter finally showed up?"

"It was A-Rod," Holly reminds him. "And no, he never showed." She shoots him a saucy look. "But I guess you'll do in a pinch."

Holly pulls the French doors to the dining room closed gently as they leave the darkened room. Having the election and the strife between her and Cap behind her is a relief, and she feels a lightness in her heart as she takes River's hand and leads him through the B&B's lobby and out to the beach.

Their retreating figures are reflected in the glass panes of the doors as they go.

Chapter Twenty-Seven

The reality show's wrap party feels like a bookend to the whole production. It's the day before Christmas Eve, and a dedicated group of islanders have gathered at the Ho Ho early in the morning to decorate the open bar the way that Leanna and Wayne have requested. People have turned up in jeans and work clothes to pitch in, cups of Mistletoe Morning Brew coffee in hand, and Maria Agnelli is there with a tray of homemade cinnamon rolls that everyone is pretending to eat. There's a rumor going around that she's used powdered curry instead of cinnamon, and Bonnie has carefully relocated the tray of breakfast rolls to the table closest to the open doorway.

As Holly steps over the strings of Edison bulbs that she and Joe Sacamano have spread across the open floor of the Ho Ho Hideaway, she thinks back to the hot, sultry Halloween night the islanders spent in this same bar with the crew of the show. This is the very spot where Jake had signed up to compete on *Wild Tropics*. Without knowing it, Halloween had been the night he'd sold his soul for a little bit of fame.

Holly is lost in thought for a minute as she stares out at the ocean, the gray sky hanging low over the navy blue waves that roll angrily toward shore. A small storm is brewing out in the Gulf, and it suits Holly's mood. It won't turn into a wind-whipper of tropical storm proportions, but it should put a bit of a damper on the party anyway, and this pleases her.

Bonnie and Millie are walking around with six-foot lengths of gold tinsel draped around their necks the way tailors wear their measuring tape. Bonnie points at the next pillar that she wants to wrap in tinsel.

"Grab the tacks, Millie!" she calls out. Millie searches through a fishing tackle box that's filled with string, glue, nails, small tools, and—ostensibly—thumb tacks. She comes up empty-handed.

"Hey," Fiona says, coming up behind Holly and pinching her on the waist. Holly pulls her arm back sharply. "Whoa, girl," Fiona says. She takes a step back.

"Sorry," Holly says, averting her gaze. "You surprised me. I'm just jumpy today."

"I can see that." Fiona's eyes narrow with concern. "Anything I can do?"

"Occupy River," she says under her breath, assessing the knot in the string of lights that she's planning on hanging from one corner of the bar to the other. If all goes as planned, she'll have strings of lights hanging from every corner of the room and meeting in the center, illuminating the dance floor in a soft haze.

"You want me to take your man off your hands?" Fiona chuckles.

"I'm kidding. Kind of. I think we've gone off script, Fee," Holly says, looking around and lowering her voice. "Everything will be good one minute—like it was when he was here in the summer—and the next minute one of us is getting touchy about something stupid."

Fiona chews on the inside of her cheek, thinking. "Well, you have been under a lot of stress lately."

"Right. The Cap stuff was stressful, having the reality show here has been more work than I expected, and Coco is always under my skin, but I don't think I have any real reason to be so out of sorts," Holly says earnestly, tugging on one end of the lights.

"Hmm." Fiona purses her lips. "Okay."

Holly stops what she's doing. "What's that supposed to mean?"

"I just think there's more to it than that."

"Bonnie?" Holly calls. "Did you bring that bag of candy canes I bought? Joe wants them crushed so he can rim the martini glasses with peppermint."

"I'm on it, boss!" Bonnie gives her a salute from the top step of a short ladder. She's holding the gold tinsel on the post as Millie jabs tacks into the wooden pillar to hold it in place.

"Look, we don't have to talk about it now—or ever," Fiona says, following Holly even though she's turned her back and refocused her attention on the lights. "But it might not hurt to talk about the Jake situation."

"There is no Jake situation," Holly says flatly, walking over to the bar with Fiona on her heels.

"Holly, you broke into his house *twice*, and you called an emergency village council meeting to save him from the treacherous jaws of a buxom bikini babe," Fiona points out. Her voice is strained as she finally says the things she's been holding in. "Everyone can see what's going on, but no one wants to point it out."

Holly spins around, hands on both hips. "Everyone can see *what*?" she asks with blatant exasperation. She's wearing a gray Mickey Mouse sweatshirt and a pair of jeans with holes in both knees. With her Converse and Yankees cap, she has the look of a petulant teen.

Fiona puts her lips next to Holly's ear. "That you're not over him," she says plainly. And there it is again: the truth. The kernel of unpleasant truth that sends Holly's stomach into a tailspin.

The scene in the bar fades out in her field of vision, and the salty air from the sea—normally one of Holly's favorite smells—makes her nauseous. Suddenly everything is wrong: the decorations look cheap and gaudy, the weather feels oppressive and cloying. Even Holly's jeans feel too tight.

"I think—" she starts, finger ready to point, retort ready to roll off her tongue. "I think…"

Fiona stands there, eyebrows raised, waiting to hear what Holly thinks.

"I think I'm going to go home and change," Holly finally says. "I'll be back in a while."

* * *

Holly left Bonnie and Millie to oversee the Ho Ho's set up for the party, and now, after changing into a pair of red satin overalls and a thin, black cashmere sweater, she's back at the B&B to make sure everything looks good for the cast and crew's arrival.

Since Fiona called her out that morning, all she's done is replay her actions and behaviors in her head to see whether the truth has been there all along, hiding just out of her view. She suspects that it has, and the thought that everyone sees it but doesn't want to point it out fills her with mortification.

"Wyatt to Holly," comes a scratchy voice over the walkie-talkie Holly has shoved into her back pocket. "I've got River here at the spot where the crew will be approaching Main Street. Do you copy?"

Holly pulls the walkie-talkie from her pocket and presses the button. "I copy, Wyatt." She takes her phone out of her other pocket and checks it. "ETA for the cast and crew is ten minutes from now. Do you copy?"

"We copy." Wyatt clicks off. He'd stopped by the B&B about an hour before, looking for a pair of pliers to fix a wayward Christmas wreath on the front of North Star Cigars, and had enlisted River as his sidekick. Holly is secretly relieved to be left alone with her thoughts, and she can't stop thinking about Fiona's accusation. Her concern for Jake is purely platonic, and she knows that any friend would have another friend's back the way that she has his.

The lights are off in the lobby of the B&B and she has a cozy desk lamp turned on instead. From outside on the street, passersby can only see the dim lamp and the swags of mistletoe and ivy that she's draped across the front windows. She drove the street several times herself to see what the cameras might pick up as they follow the contestants up Main Street, and she's satisfied that all of the buildings look appropriately inviting. Wayne and Leanna are still planning to surprise the last two contestants standing (well, technically it'll only be a surprise to Bridget) with the fact that they've been on a Christmas-themed island all along, and it's Holly's job to make sure that the wow factor is there—not just for Bridget, but for the cameras as well.

She sinks into the chair behind the front counter, reveling in the peace and quiet of the moment. Jimmy Buffet's 'I'll Be Home for Christmas' is coming from the small speakers tucked away in the corners of the lobby, and the potted palm tree next to the front desk is wrapped in its very own string of multi-colored blinking mini-lights.

Holly puts her elbows on the desk and rests her chin in her hands. Has this all been for Jake, or has this been for her? She runs through the thoughts she's had about Jake and his well-being since Halloween, and then her heart compares it all to the way she feels about River. Shouldn't his being here trump everything else? Shouldn't the fact that a man traveled across country to spend the holidays by her side be enough to banish Jake from her mind entirely? She puts her hands over her face, her elbows sliding out on the desk until her forehead touches the cool bamboo. She needs to see Jake back in his natural habitat so that her mind can reconcile (once again) the fact that she's over him. Completely and totally over him. Moved on. Happy in the arms of someone else.

"Wyatt to Holly. Wyatt to Holly. The eagle is soaring toward Main Street, ready to make a landing. Do y'all copy?"

Holly lifts her head from the desk. She copies, all right. She most definitely copies.

* * *

Just as Leanna and Wayne had hoped, Bridget's reaction is priceless. Holly loses count of how many times she hears "Oh my *word!*" and "How is this *possible?*" from the hoodwinked girl, and she rolls her eyes inconspicuously as Jake plays along from his seat beside Bridget in the golf cart.

Wayne is standing in the middle of a crowd of islanders on the sidewalk in front of the B&B as the golf cart pulls up. The street is fully decked-out in Christmas cheer, and Holly has even approved one bag of biodegradable rainbow confetti for each person to throw, with the understanding that the crew members will clean it up as best they can, and that the next rain that comes along will take care of the rest. Everyone is cheering and clapping, enjoying their big moment on camera and hoping they won't end up on the cutting room floor.

"Welcome to Christmas Key!" Maria Agnelli shouts frantically, waving an American flag on a stick in Bridget's face. Bridget curls into Jake's side, looking a little shell-shocked. Maria is wearing a sequined Santa hat and an oversized denim jacket covered in patches procured from various Elk clubs around the country. Everyone on the island has grown more than accustomed to Mrs. Agnelli's eccentricities, but it's hard to tell how her quirkiness will play out on national television, and it's abundantly clear that Bridget isn't sure what to make of her.

The triplets are lined up on the other side of Wayne, laughing and waving at Jake and Bridget like they've never seen either of them. Jimmy

Cafferkey offers a hand to help Bridget from the cart, pulling her lithe body out of her seat like she's made of cotton candy and dandelion spores. Jake slides out on the curb side of the cart, holding up one hand in a static wave and not meeting anyone's eye. He puts his other hand on Bridget's lower back as he guides her through the crowd of fake paparazzi. She's like a Barbie in her tattered, weather-beaten jungle threads, but even with the layer of dirt that coats her tanned skin, she is young and gorgeous and wide-eyed.

Holly can see it on the faces of everyone around her and in the looks they exchange with one another: Jake is thin and gaunt, and they all watch as his narrowed shoulders and arms disappear through the front door of the B&B. Holly bites her lower lip, remembering his formerly broad, muscular torso. And even though she doesn't like to cook nearly as much as she likes to eat, there's a part of her that wants to tie on an apron and start cooking whatever she can think of that might fatten him up again.

Once the crew is inside with Jake and Bridget, Holly searches the crowd for Bonnie; she's standing several feet away, listening to something that Ray Bradford is saying. Fiona and Buckhunter are farther down the sidewalk in front of Jack Frosty's, but Holly has successfully avoided Fiona since leaving the Ho Ho earlier that day, and she isn't ready to talk to her just yet. Holly slips her hand into the pocket of her satin overalls and fingers the item she's been carrying around all afternoon. This calms her, knowing that she's about to make one last concerted effort to set the things right that she's turned upside down by bringing the show to the island.

Wyatt Bender's golf cart winds through the crowd as he drives down the center of Main Street with River in the passenger seat. They've completed their duties as lookouts, and—like everyone else—they're ready to move on to Phase II of the evening, which is the party at the Ho Ho.

"Hop on?" River asks as they slow to a stop. "We'll give you a lift."

Holly hesitates. "I need to do a couple of things here first," she says, letting her ankle roll nervously as she moves her foot around on the pavement. "I've got my cart here—meet you at the Ho Ho?"

Wyatt shrugs noncommittally and presses the gas before River can say anything, but he doesn't have to, because Holly can see the knowing look in his eyes as they pull away from the curb.

* * *

"Tell us again about the shark!" Maria Agnelli is standing at Jake's left elbow, her head just barely clearing that particular joint on his arm. "And how you saved this nincompoop from getting eaten alive," she adds, tipping her totally gray head in Bridget's direction. Holly smothers a smile by turning to River.

"Are you hungry?" she asks him with laughter in her throat. "I'm dying to try that roast beef that Jimmy and Iris made."

"Sure. Let's eat." He takes her hand in his and leads her across the bar, turning his shoulders as they move between the other bodies in the room.

"Hey, how do you feel about going to church with me tomorrow?" Holly picks up a white plate from the pile of dishes at the end of the buffet table.

"Sure. We can do that." River dumps a pile of mashed potatoes onto his plate.

"Are you just going to say 'sure' to everything?"

"Would you be mad if I said 'sure'?" His face breaks into the first real smile she's seen from him all day. "Sorry, I'm just kind of overwhelmed."

"By what?" Holly pours a ladle full of gravy over her meat and potatoes.

River looks around the room, gesturing at the wall-to-wall people, the tropical Christmas guitar music, the over the top decorations, and—not least of all—the cameras filming the whole scene. "By *this*," he says, eyes wide. "I don't think I've ever had Christmas dinner in a bar with a hundred other people and a camera crew."

Holly looks at him skeptically. "What about the wild team dinners while you were on the road with the Mets?"

"Nothing like this," he says, grabbing silverware for both of them from the containers at the end of the table. "I would ask if you wanted to eat on the beach, but…" River peers outside, looking at the sky. He holds his plate in one hand. "It looks like it's still coming down out there."

By the time the crew of *Wild Tropics* arrived at the Ho Ho with Jake and Bridget, the palm fronds next to the bar were dripping with water and the pelting rain was leaving tiny divots in the sand.

"It's okay. It's getting dark out there anyway. We should probably grab a spot at one of the tables." Holly leads the way to the tall bistro tables next to the opposite wall.

"Drink?" River sets his plate down and motions at the bar.

"Sure." Holly jokingly copies the noncommittal attitude he'd given her earlier. "Whatever." She's hoping that teasing him will lighten his mood, but he doesn't take the bait.

"I'll get us red wine," River says decisively, leaving her there. She watches him cut through the crowd, admiring his lanky frame. River's ears are already pink from the time he's spent on the island, and the back of his neck has taken on a golden hue that will be a tell-tale sign of a tropical vacation when he returns to Oregon.

With her fork and knife, Holly cuts off a piece of her meat, her eyes still on River. In spite of their uneven moods and her various distractions, she knows that River's gotten a look at the real Holly during this visit, not some sanitized, ready-for-tourists version of who she actually is. She's hated leaving him out of things and being so busy, but in the end she knows it was probably good to let him see what the mayor and part-owner of a growing island has to juggle in order to keep things moving forward. If he's ever going to be with her, he's going to have to understand what he's really in for.

Joe is chatting River up at the bar, pouring a bottle of red slowly into two goblets, and Holly's eyes drift to Jake and Bridget. She desperately wishes Fiona had been able to dig up something on Bridget that would have forced Jake to discount her on his own, but absent any really damning information, all she can do is try one last time to gently remind him of the values he holds closest to his heart.

She's still watching them together, their heads bent close under the hundreds of dangling lights, when River sets her wine on the table. Holly snaps to attention. "Thanks," she says with a watered-down smile, intentionally adding a cheerful note to her voice to make up for the slight downturn in her mood.

River sits down across from her and picks up his silverware. The tables are the right size for two people, but the Ho Ho isn't generally the place for a full holiday dinner. If anything, the tall bistro tables are just the right size to hold bowls of pretzels or nuts to nibble over drinks.

"I like your overalls there." River turns his fork over and bites off the hunk of meat he's speared with the tines. "They look like pajamas."

"I'm not sure that's what a lady really wants to hear about an expensive ensemble." Holly looks down at the red satin.

"Kidding—only kidding," River says. "They look nice. Hey, where do you buy clothes around here?" She can tell by the look on his face that this thought has just occurred to him. "Amazon?"

She pushes the mashed potatoes and peas around on her plate. "Sometimes. But I usually shop when I go to the mainland. I got these in Miami." She tugs on one of her overall straps.

"You look cute," he says. "Like a really sexy farmer." This makes Holly laugh and she covers her mouth with the back of her hand, trying not to choke on the bite she's just taken.

"Can we have your attention, please?" Wayne says into the microphone on the small stage where Joe usually plays his guitar. He taps the mic. "Is this thing on?"

Everyone stops what they're doing and looks at the stage. Some of the islanders are standing in the middle of the room holding plates and glasses, some are still at the buffet table, and others are finishing up their dinners at the tables along the walls. Joe cuts the music so Wayne is only competing with the roar of the ocean for their attention.

"I'd like to thank you all," Wayne says, holding onto the microphone and turning from side to side with a jovial smile like he's hosting the Oscars. "You've been most welcoming to us as we've filmed our little reality show on your lovely island, and we've had a wonderful stay at the B&B, as well as amazing meals at your fine establishments." A round of polite applause breaks out amongst those whose hands aren't full with plates and drinks. "Now, as you know," Wayne continues, the overhead lights glinting off his white teeth as he talks, "we've wrapped up our production for the time being. At this point, we're ready to reveal to you who the winner of our show is, with the understanding—of course—that you will not divulge *any* information about the outcome of the competition before the show airs in the spring."

For some reason, Holly can't blink. She hasn't had the chance to talk to Jake quietly, and she's afraid that he's about to make a huge mistake.

"After a physically and emotionally draining round of competitions, and with an intense display of sportsmanship, a winner has emerged. So, without further ado, I'd like to introduce our runner up, Miss Bridget Lindt!"

Bridget accepts a side hug and a peck on the crown of her head from Jake while the crowd claps tamely. As she passes through the sea of locals on her way to the stage, she lowers her head nervously, looking up through her eyelashes. "Hi," she says into the microphone, looking out at all the faces. "Thank you—this has been a completely insane experience."

"And," Wayne says, taking over the microphone again. "As you may have deduced, the winner of season one of *Wild Tropics* is…Mr. Jake Zavaroni!" The entire bar breaks out into wild applause and loud cheers. Cap puts two fingers in his mouth and whistles loudly like he's at a ball game, and the triplets jump up and down. Jake approaches the stage.

"I'm sure Bridget is wondering why no one cared that much about her," Holly says to River, covering her mouth with her hand as she whispers loudly.

"Hey, thanks," Jake says, accepting the giant conch shell that Wayne hands to him. He looks down at his parents in the front row of the crowd and smiles at them. Holly hasn't had the nerve to go over and greet them all evening, and she watches now as Jake winks at his mom. "This is quite a prize for first place." He holds the conch shell up high, hoisting it like a heavy trophy. "And Bridget," he says into the microphone, holding out his hand to her. "I know today has been full of crazy surprises, but I have something else I need to add."

Bridget steps forward hesitantly, hands clasped in front of her. She's had time to shower at the B&B and put on fresh clothes, and she looks stunning in her clingy white dress and gladiator sandals, her blonde hair pulled up in a clean pile of curls on top of her head. She looks at Jake expectantly.

"So, in addition to the fact that we've been living on an island for the past six weeks alongside more than a hundred locals," he says, his eyes trained on her, "there's also been hot water, indoor plumbing, and more food than you can imagine within arms' reach." The crowd chuckles. By now, Bridget has both hands over her mouth, and she's clearly waiting for the other shoe to drop. "But aside from all that, I have to tell you the truth: I'm no stranger to Christmas Key. In fact, I've been living here for a few years, and I'm actually the island's only police officer."

Bridget blinks, stunned.

"I have to give her credit," Holly says, leaning across the table to River. "She's either a great actress, or she's really that dumb and naïve. It makes her seem younger than she probably is."

River makes a face, but Holly's already turned back to the stage so that she doesn't miss whatever is coming next.

"You might be thinking that my living here gave me an unfair advantage," Jake says to Bridget. "But I know for a fact that the production crew made me climb uphill both ways to ensure I didn't win simply because I know the lay of the land." Bridget smirks at him. "Anyhow, with that out of the way, I need to say that—as most of us know—to the victor goes the spoils."

Holly sucks in a sharp breath, holding onto the edge of the round bistro table with both hands so tightly that her knuckles go white.

"Bridget, you and I have had some really…special times," he says quietly, his eyes warm as he looks down into hers. Bridget moves in closer to him. "And I hate to think those times are over. So, to that end, I have something I want to ask you."

For what seems like an eternity, all Holly hears is the drizzling rain and the sound of the waves as they blend together like static in her ears. She looks around the room and sees faces that are joyfully surprised. Jake's parents look on expectantly. Wayne and Leanna are watching from beside the small stage, obviously pleased, and the look on Wayne's face tells Holly that he thinks he's about to get exactly what he wants. Holly projects forward in her mind, imagining a televised wedding on the beach with a reception in the B&B's dining room. She puts her fork down and reaches for her wineglass.

On stage, Bridget's cheeks are flushed and she looks giddy.

"I was wondering," Jake looks around at his neighbors and then back at Bridget, his face a mixture of nerves and unabashed joy. "Bridget Lindt, do you think you might want to—"

"No," Holly says firmly and audibly, shaking her head. "No," she whispers again, this time to herself.

"—stay here on the island with me for a while? I'm not ready to let you go yet."

"Nice work, Jakey my boy!" Jimmy Cafferkey whoops. As always, Iris whacks him on the arm to quiet him down.

Bridget has her hands over her mouth again, and her eyes are shining. She smiles hesitantly at first, and then more decisively. "Yes, I want to stay," she says loudly enough for the microphone to pick up. "This is all insane, but I *really* want to stay."

In an instant, Jake sweeps her up in his arms right there on stage. The crowd claps and cheers, happy to see young love in full bloom. Without thinking, Holly joins in, clapping along with everyone else, though no part of her feels excited. Across the table, River is clapping more enthusiastically than she is, a smile on his face like he's watching a buddy shoot the ball from half-court in a contest to win a million bucks. Holly looks for Fiona over by the bar and their eyes meet for a split second. She knows that everything she feels is written on her face, and that she needs to get out of there as soon as possible.

"Will you excuse me for a second? I need to do one little thing and then we can go," Holly says to River, not waiting for an answer.

As their neighbors shake hands and introduce themselves to Bridget in the middle of the bar, Holly makes her way toward Jake. She's got her hand in the pocket of her overalls, her fingers worrying the item she's been holding there all afternoon.

"Jake," she says throatily. "Talk to you for a second?" It comes out awkwardly, like she's trying to speak and swallow at the same time. He follows her through the bar and down the steps, and just like that, they're alone on the beach at night again, exactly as they'd been that summer. Only this time, there's no chance that Jake will ask her to dance at the water's edge while Joe Sacamano plays Beach Boys songs from inside the bar, and there's no way he'll ask to take her home for the night.

"Pretty good ending, huh?" Jake stares out at the darkened sky hanging over the water. Holly notices that he's keeping his physical distance from her.

"Yeah, about that," Holly says, not able to meet his eyes. The rain has finally stopped, but the air is misty around them. There are no visible stars in the sky, no moon to illuminate their faces. "I feel responsible for this."

"For me winning?"

"No, for—" Holly wiggles her fingers, unable to find the words. "For…you know—getting you mixed up with a reality show. And they didn't feed you, and you're so—" She reaches out and puts her hand around his bare arm, the feel of his skin on hers both familiar and strange. She pulls her hand back.

"Okayyyy," he says, his brow knit in confusion. "I mean, you don't need to apologize, Hol. This has been a crazy experience, and I can eat all I want now that I'll be back at home." He stands there, waiting for her to make a point that's worth hearing.

"I'm not doing this right." Holly looks down at her feet. "I just wanted to say that I missed you—we all missed you around here. And more importantly, we don't want you to turn into Mr. Hollywood or anything."

He laughs. "I won't. I'm sure you'll all keep my head from getting too big."

"But what I mean is," she swallows hard, "what I mean is that you have values and a strong character, and I don't want the promise of fame or whatever to change you." Holly rakes a hand through her hair. From her pocket she pulls the timeworn wedding ring that Jake keeps in the box on top of his dresser. She holds it up between her thumb and forefinger, the gold glinting in the light that comes from the Ho Ho. "You always said you wanted what your grandparents had, and that you wouldn't settle for anything less, so…I just didn't want you to forget that."

Jake says nothing—he doesn't even reach out a hand to take the ring from her.

"Here. Take it." She reaches for his hand and turns it over so that his palm faces up. He's still making a fist, so she unfurls his fingers with her own. Looking into his eyes, she places the ring in his hand. "*It was ever thus*," she says softly, echoing the engraving on the inside of the ring. They stare at one another for a long moment before Holly walks back up the steps to the bar, leaving Jake alone on the beach.

On the dance floor of the Ho Ho, Holly cuts through the crowd, ignoring the drinking and merrymaking. She blocks out the Christmas music that's playing once again, and finds River near the bar.

They drive back to her house in silence.

Chapter Twenty-Eight

The rain is gone when Holly wakes on Christmas Eve morning. In the kitchen, River stands before the window over the sink, holding a cup of coffee and staring out at the yard.

"Hey," Holly says sleepily. She's wearing boxer shorts and the Depeche Mode concert t-shirt she's had since college. River doesn't respond as she slips her arms around his waist and rests her cheek against his hard back. "Merry Christmas."

They stand that way for a good minute, with River not moving or speaking. Finally, he turns around to face her. With a reluctance that Holly can feel all the way into her bones, he puts his arms around her shoulders and rests his chin on top of her head. She'd woken up hoping for gingerbread pancakes at the Jingle Bell Bistro, followed by a Christmas Eve walk on the beach with Pucci and River. In a perfect world, the day would end with an evening at the chapel with the other islanders, but in her heart she knows that there's been a shift between them these past couple of weeks that's going to change all of her hopes and plans on her favorite day of the year.

"We need to talk about last night," River says, his chin still resting on her head. He sways slightly as he speaks, and in his voice Holly hears his reluctance to let go of her and face the issue at hand.

In response, she holds him tighter. "Can I get coffee first?" she asks.

"Go sit on the couch. I'll get you a cup."

Holly pads out to the living room and curls up on the couch. She grabs the fleece blanket from the arm of the chair next to her, laying it over her bare legs. If there's any way to have a last-minute Christmas wish granted, she prays for it now, hoping above all else that this discussion will be a simple step back, maybe a chance to look at how different things are from their heated summer romance without throwing the baby out with the bathwater. She hates that term—has hated it ever since a college professor wrote it across the top of her first essay in an English course where she'd denounced all British literature as "dull" and "drafty"—but it definitely applies here. If River can just remember the fun they've had together, then maybe he can look at this uneven visit as a bump in the road rather than a roadblock they can't work around.

River's hair is still wet from a shower that she slept right through, his cheeks smooth from a recent shave. He hands her a steaming mug and sits in the chair next to the couch. This seating arrangement isn't a good sign, but rather than let her concern show, Holly looks down into the swirl of cream that's spreading through her coffee, watching as it pools and blends.

"So." He holds his own cup of coffee in both hands and watches her intently. "What do you think?"

Rather than answer, Holly takes a sip of her hot coffee and lets the caffeine work its way into her system. She isn't awake enough to be having this discussion.

"Maybe we should start with what *I* think," he says, more plaintive than sarcastic. "I think there are too many miles between us."

"But you knew I never wanted to leave this island," Holly says, jumping to her own defense.

"I don't mean physical miles, though that isn't helping." River stares at her. "I mean we're in completely different places."

"We're both single, no kids, busy lives, and we like each other. Those things don't seem all that different to me." Holly sets her coffee on the low table in front of the couch and pulls the blanket tighter around her legs.

"I like to have fun," River counters. "I'm quippy and spontaneous, and those are the things I liked about you when we met last summer."

"Quippy?"

"It's a word," he promises.

"If you say so," she says, stopping herself from going off on a tangent. "But now? Now I'm not those things anymore? And I'm not quippy?"

River stands up and sets his coffee mug on the table next to Holly's. He ambles over to the Christmas tree; the lights are already on, and he stands there for a moment, watching them flicker. "I don't know. You're so busy running around, trying to make everyone own up to who they are, but you won't even own up to who *you* are."

Holly's eyes narrow. "And who do you think I am?"

River faces her, hands open like he's expecting the answer to fall from the sky. He lets out a huge breath before he answers. "I think you're a girl who can only pledge her allegiance to one thing: this island."

"I can pledge my allegiance to other things," Holly croaks, her defensiveness melting into tears.

"Really? You can?" River's eyes have a dark gleam to them that she's never seen before. "Okay, Yankees or Mets?"

"That's not fair—"

"Progress or total control?"

"Both," Holly says decisively, her chin jutting out. The hot tears she'd felt brewing just a minute ago have subsided.

"Jake or me?" They both go silent. This, of course, is at the heart of everything. All of the running around she's done since Halloween, all of the fretting and worrying. Jake's well-being. Jake's happiness. Jake's love life. And, more importantly, the fact that Holly can't accept his current romantic entanglement. Fiona had been right, of course—everyone has been able to watch her wage an inner battle over two men and she hasn't even seen how obvious it's been.

"Yeah," River says simply, sadly. They don't really have to say anything else, because they both know that River can't be across country without wondering whether she's switched teams again, and she can't promise that it won't happen.

"Buckhunter said he'd run me over to the dock so I can catch the ferry that's taking the television crew to Key West. I've got a lot of travel ahead of me, but if I leave now and don't hit any flight delays, I can make it home for Christmas Eve dinner."

There isn't much to say now. Holly begging him to stay won't fix the fact that her indecisiveness has ruined this visit—not to mention Christmas. And him staying wouldn't give either of them the space they need to think.

"If that's what you want," Holly finally says, her voice small.

River nods, eyes fixed on the floor of her living room. "It is."

She stays on the couch under the blanket, watching the lights on the tree as he leaves to gather his things. The mini-lights wink and twinkle, flashing different colors on the only package under the tree. Holly's heart sinks as she realizes that it's from River, and that she hasn't even had time to think of what to get for him. In an instant, she knows that he's right to go.

"I'm not the kind of guy who can wait around, just hoping you'll pick me," River says from the doorway between the kitchen and the living room. He's standing there, duffel bag next to his feet, shoes laced up, windbreaker zipped over his sweatshirt. In his hand is the Mets hat he'd sent to Holly. "Let me know if you ever decide to be loyal to one team," he says calmly, walking over to her. He puts his warm lips on hers, lingering just a few seconds too long before he breaks away. "Merry Christmas, Holly." His eyes are sad—not angry—as he backs away, setting the Mets cap on his blonde head and pulling the brim down low.

"Merry Christmas," she whispers back as he heads through the house and out the front door. He closes it so softly that Pucci doesn't even lift his head from the floor.

Holly pulls the fleece blanket over her head and starts to cry.

* * *

The chapel is draped in icicle lights, and the palm trees outside its doors are wrapped in strings of white fairy lights to match. Inside, flickering candles sit in the windows, sending a warm luminescence out into the darkness. The sun has been gone for hours, and the clear night is the perfect backdrop to the tiny, glowing chapel on the beach. There hasn't been an official minister or preacher on the island since Alfie Agnelli's passing, but each year—regardless of religious orientation—the islanders gather on Christmas Eve to sing carols and hymns together, and this year is no different.

As he has for the past decade, Cap oversees the holiday proceedings.

"Come one, come all!" he says merrily, standing on the steps of the chapel. He's left his white hair loose, and the gold hoop is back in place on his earlobe. Holly approaches the chapel from the sandy road, her small purse clutched tightly in her right hand. As she always does on Christmas Eve, she's traded in her Converse and baseball hat and dressed in her finest—this year a floor-length forest green ball gown that she'd found on clearance after the previous year's holiday season. She'd spotted it in a window display at the mall in Tampa, and after begging the sales- girl to pull the last size six off the mannequin for her, she'd taken it home.

The high-necked bodice of the dress is made of a rich, green velvet, and the skirt flares out at the waist with layer upon layer of glitter-flecked green tulle. It hits the ground around her, so technically she *could* get away with wearing her beloved flip-flops or Converse beneath it, but the occasion calls for something much nicer, so she's wearing the silver flats that she bought with the dress.

"Sugar!" Bonnie calls. "Aren't you a Christmas vision!"

Holly stops at the bottom of the stairs to wait for Bonnie. The triplets and their respective husbands pass by, greeting Holly with hugs and pats on the shoulder, and Carrie-Anne and Ellen approach the chapel in matching black velvet pants and holiday sweaters. As Ellen hugs her, Holly gets a whiff of her vanilla-scented perfume.

"I'm coming, I'm coming," Bonnie says, hurrying to the chapel from the spot on Holly Lane where she's parked behind the other golf carts. She's always fully done up when it comes to hair and make-up, but tonight she's traded her usual pants-and-blouse combo for a short, red lacy cocktail dress, nylons, and high heels. It's a look Holly knows is partially for the holiday, but mostly for Wyatt Bender.

"Is old Slugger already in there saving us a pew?" Bonnie asks, putting her hands on both sides of Holly's face and forcing her to bend forward for a red-lipped kiss on the cheek.

Holly says nothing and Bonnie lets her go. The smile falls away from Bonnie's smooth, round face as she looks deeply into her young friend's eyes. "Oh," Bonnie says quietly. "Oh, honey."

"It's okay," Holly says in a rush. "It's for the best—at least for now. Everyone should be happy on Christmas, and if I wasn't making him happy here, then I want him to be at home with his family."

"Of course you do," Bonnie clucks.

"I'm fine, Bon. I promise." She tries to look convincing. "Should we go in?"

Holly is about to offer Bonnie a hand up the stairs in her high heels, but from nowhere, Wyatt swoops in and sticks out the crook of his elbow. "Milady?" he says in a faux British accent. "Take you to your seat?" Bonnie stops and stares at the proffered arm. "I have another arm for the mayor," he says, putting out his other elbow for Holly to take.

With a laugh, the women accept Wyatt's genteel offer of assistance. The three of them ascend the steps to the chapel's open front door, stopping to greet Cap.

"Good to see you," Cap nods to Wyatt. "Evening, Bonnie," he says, taking Bonnie's hand gently in his. "And Mayor," he says, pausing as Holly stops in front of him. "Merry Christmas to you." In his eyes is a softened peacefulness that she hasn't seen from him in years—if ever.

"And to you, Cap," she says, standing on her toes and holding his forearm for balance. Holly can feel him smile as she plants a kiss high on his cheek, but she follows Bonnie and Wyatt up the aisle to their pew before she sees the blush that colors Cap's face.

In short order, the pews are filled with rustling gowns and men in sport coats, and the air is thick with perfume and whispered holiday greetings. Fiona waves at her from across the aisle, and Holly waves back, a sad, apologetic smile on her face. "I'm sorry," Fiona mouths at her from her spot next to Buckhunter. She forgot that Buckhunter had driven River to the dock, and so he'd certainly have told Fiona what was going on. "It's okay," Holly mouths back. She was never mad at Fiona anyway, only at herself for acting like an idiot and avoiding the truth. Still, it feels good to know that everything is solid between them.

Cap walks down the aisle to stand at the rustic-looking pulpit. Joe Sacamano is next to him on a stool, his favorite guitar resting on one knee, the sleeves of his black shirt pushed up to his elbows. Cap's linen jacket and pants look like they've never met an iron, but he is sober and clear-eyed, just as he'd been for years before his recent battle with the bottle.

"Villagers, friends, loved ones," he begins, looking out at all of them. "We are fortunate enough to enjoy the frills of Christmas year-round, and to never tire of the glitz and baubles and tinsel. But today is the culmination of all of those trimmings, combined with the real spirit of the holiday. Today we put aside our differences, our widely varying religious beliefs, our longings for people who live far away and for those long gone." Cap pauses, letting everyone have a moment to reflect on the people they love and miss. Eyes around the chapel mist over with memory and melancholy, and several people reach for the hands of those sitting closest to them.

"It's today that we get to dress up in honor of this important holiday and in honor of one another. And if I didn't get the chance to say it to each of you as you passed me in the doorway, you all look fabulous." Laughter ripples across the pews, and Joe chuckles on the stool next to Cap, his eyes crinkling happily as his hands move silently up and down the neck of the guitar, searching for the chords he'll play. "We've had a bang-up year around here, and I know the year ahead is going to bring new...*surprises*," Cap says, a wry smile on his face. "And hopefully new rewards. Now, we've got one new neighbor among us tonight, so let's all welcome Bridget into the fold." Cap gestures at the back of the church. Holly tries to glance casually over her shoulder to catch a glimpse of the newcomer, but as everyone else twists around to see Bridget, she realizes that she doesn't need to see her now—not tonight.

"So let's start our celebration with a song, shall we?" Cap picks up a leather-bound hymn book from the pulpit, opening to the spot he's got marked with a blue velvet ribbon.

Joe begins to strum his guitar, the notes of 'Silent Night' drifting up to the high-pitched ceiling of the airy chapel. The door is still propped open, and the voices of everyone on the island knit together to fill the church with an almost unspeakable beauty. There is nothing more than this to the pared-down holiday service, but there is plenty of laughter, lots of singing, several tears, and an abundance of gratitude for another year spent together.

When it's all over, everyone trickles out into the night, calling out warm good-byes on the sandy lane as they climb back into carts and wish one another a Merry Christmas. Plans are made to meet for meals the following day while Holly and Bonnie stay behind to blow out the candles and put the song books away.

"Are we still on for tomorrow, or would you rather just stay in bed and eat chocolate frosting out of the container?" Bonnie asks sympathetically, using a long candlelighter to extinguish the flame of a candle that sits up high on a shelf and out of her reach.

"Oh, please. If I wanted to stay in bed and eat my misery away, I'd need the frosting, a hunk of cheese, a baguette, two pizzas, an order of chicken fried rice, and some sweet potato fries," Holly says, gathering her skirts in one arm as she bends forward to stick a book into the pocket of the pew in front of her. "I need you to come over and make sure that doesn't happen. In fact, it's now part of your job description at the B&B: 'keep Holly from pigging out when she's upset.' Can you do that?"

"I used to help my daddy bring in the horses and cows during lightning storms, but I don't know that I'm brave enough to come between you and a pizza, doll," Bonnie says, setting the candlelighter in its holder by the pulpit.

"Fraidy cat," Holly teases, one fist on her hip like a kid taunting a friend on the playground. "But are you okay with a nontraditional Christmas dinner? I'm thinking tacos."

"Sugar, I'm okay with a bowl of popcorn and box of Milk Duds if that's all you want to eat."

Holly laughs. "I think we can do better than that. But we just had a big holiday dinner last night at the Ho Ho, and I'm hungry for tacos."

"And margaritas!" Bonnie says excitedly. "Tacos and Christmas margaritas on the lanai."

"Wow, you're easy." Holly turns off the lights, leaving them in the doorway to the darkened chapel.

"Maybe a little," Bonnie says, popping a hip saucily. "But don't tell Wyatt, you hear? A true lady never wants a man to know she's easy."

"My lips are sealed."

They unplug the extension cord that connects to the lights on the palm trees, and Holly clicks off the switch that feeds the dangling icicle lights on the church, leaving them with only the light of the moon and stars to guide them.

"Where's your cart, Holly Jean?" Bonnie asks, holding Holly's arm as she slips her feet out of her high heels and steps onto the sand. "I've got to take these things off."

"I walked," Holly says, breathing in the night air.

"From the B&B?" Bonnie holds her heels in one hand, the other hand still gripping Holly's arm as they walk over to her cart, which is the only one left on the road after everyone else has gone home for the night.

"No, from home."

"Well, hop in. I'll drive you back, sugar." Bonnie climbs in behind the steering wheel and pats her passenger seat. Holly briefly contemplates getting a ride home, but then looks up at the night sky, pointing at an airplane's red light as it blinks amongst the stars.

"Look, it's Rudolph!" she says, remembering how many times she and Emily had said that same thing on Christmas Eve after singing songs together in the chapel.

"There's no doubt in my mind," Bonnie says, following Holly's gaze as they look up into the heavens together.

"You know what? I think I'll walk home, but thanks anyway, Bon."

"Are you sure?" Bonnie asks, tipping her head as she looks up at her friend.

"I am. And don't worry," Holly says. "I promise I'm fine, and I'll call you as soon as I get home. But wait—do I run straight or in a zigzag to get away from a gator?" She's smiling, but her eyes are serious.

Bonnie looks at her but doesn't say anything. When Holly finally nods to let her know she's really okay, Bonnie puts her cart in gear. She crunches over sand and shells as she pulls away, rounding the bend that leads back to Main Street.

Instead of following her, Holly turns the other direction and cuts through the sand dunes to get to Snowflake Banks. It's a long walk that'll take her over the boardwalk of Pinecone Path and, eventually, all the way up to her house. But the night is bright and her heart is somehow both full and empty, and she knows that walking is exactly what she needs.

When she gets to the beach, she takes off her silver flats, the cool sand firm beneath her feet. The light of the full moon catches the glitter in the layers of her tulle skirt. She can still hear Joe Sacamano's acoustic rendition of 'I'll Be Home for Christmas' in her mind, and she pictures him, swaying slightly on his stool as the flames of the candles danced in time to the music. It had been the moment—the one moment she always waits for during the Christmas Eve service—that filled her with the unmistakable feeling of *auld lange syne* as only the holidays can.

With no one around to hear her now, the words to the song bubble up from within, and soon she's singing aloud, her eyes filling with tears. Of all the Christmas songs, this one most reminds Holly of her grandparents, of the happiness and safety of family and childhood. Singing it now, she starts to run, her shoes still in one hand, the skirts of her dress bunched up in her arms.

She runs and runs—all the way to the boardwalk, the words coming not from her throat, but from her heart as they choke her with tears.

She runs and runs—away from the confusion and the answers about life and love that she doesn't have.

She runs and runs—the light of the moon snagging on the tiny flecks of glitter like her dress is made of malachite and glass and diamonds. And as she runs, she shoots off a million sparks of radiant light.

* * *

I hope you enjoyed this book! The next book in the series is a novella called *Jake's Story*, and it's now available on Amazon. Grab your copy here:

https://www.amazon.com/Jakes-Story-Christmas-Key-Novella-ebook/dp/B01M26GVNZ/

Or search Amazon for "Jake's Story."

Want to know when I release new books in the series? Here are some ways to stay updated:

- Join my mailing list at: https://redbirdsandrabbits.com/subscribe/
- Follow me on Facebook: https://www.facebook.com/redbirdsrabbits
- Follow me on Twitter: https://twitter.com/redbirdsrabbits

Made in the USA
Middletown, DE
09 March 2021